SHADOW MENAGERIE

MICHAEL AYOOB

Grimgata LLC • Pittsburgh, PA

This is a work of fiction. All of the characters, organizations, and events portrayed in this novel are either products of the author's imagination or are used fictitiously.

Grimgata LLC • Pittsburgh, PA

www.grimgata.com

ISBN 978-0-9962791-0-9

First Edition: October 2015

ACKNOWLEDGMENTS

Allan Becer for his research papers about the Allegheny Arsenal explosion of 1862. His writings were an inspiration and valuable resource for this novel, as was *Andrew Carnegie and the Rise of Big Business* by Harold C. Livesay.

My parents and sister Rachel for their encouragement and support.

Liza Sherburne for being there during the toughest times.

Jane Bernstein, Seth Burdick, Brad Crutchfield, Joe Guzzo, Sarah Labarge, Brian Maloney, Brendan McLaughlin, William Moner, Patrick Mullen, Blake Petty, Brad Powell, Mike Rent, and Bob Scott for being themselves and helping one way or another.

In loving memory of Amber Pack

TABLE OF CONTENTS

SHADOW MENAGERIE

I. 1980

Maura paced the small bedroom in her grandmother's house. The alarm clock ticked toward ten. She had to choose between staying in and sneaking out. She had already fixed her hair and put on her jacket and makeup, but she just couldn't leave.

She had been staying in that room for three months, and it never felt like home. Gram's age reflected everywhere in the decor. The lace curtains and doilies, faded wallpaper, and crucifix over the bed all told Maura she didn't belong there. Her own stubbornness didn't help, either; she refused to unpack, letting stacked boxes stifle the already-tight space.

Worse yet, the bedroom was a constant reminder of her mother. It had belonged to Mom, once upon a time, when she was Maura's age. Mom had been painting even then, and she'd left two pictures on the walls: a fruit basket and a ballerina in mid-leap. Maura had stashed them under the bed, unable to look at them. Nailheads still jutted out, though, and the wallpaper's coloration traced where the frames had touched.

Staying in felt like a punishment; sneaking out felt dangerous. A boy had invited her to a beer party that night, a Thursday no less. She'd never done such a thing before, never would have considered it if Mom were alive. Maura was an A student with soccer and track trophies stored in those boxes and a dozen scholarship applications on the dresser. But she found herself in a new school, new town, new rules, new pressure to join a new crowd. All that newness had a way of turning noes to maybes, making bad ideas look like opportunities.

The floorboards creaked in the hallway, and a timid knock followed. Her little brother Oscar then opened her door. He was ten years old to her seventeen, red-haired to her black, pale to her Mediterranean skin. While she wasn't one to back down or wilt, he was undersized and easy pickings on the playground. "Runt" was the kindest name his classmates called him.

"I can't sleep, sis. It's Tony Kroague and those kids. I tried ignoring them like you said, but it just makes it worse." Oscar showed himself in, noticed how she was dressed. "Where to?"

Maura looked at the clock. "Out. With some people from school. And don't you even think about telling on me."

He sat on her bed, consumed with his own problem. She sat beside him, guessing he wouldn't leave without reassurance. How to finesse this, send him off without blowing him off?

"Why don't you hit him? Next time Tony Kroague bothers you, say, 'Fuck you, shut up.' If he doesn't, walk up to him and throw your best punch right in his face."

"I can't do that! He's twice as big as me. He'll kill me."

"We've been over this a hundred times. If they're not sick of picking on you, and you won't go to the principal, I don't know what else to tell you. You want me to go to the principal? You want me to call his mom?"

"I'd fight them for you if I could. I'd love to knock Tony Kroague on his ass, but that wouldn't be fair, either, would it? Sooner or later, Oscar, you're gonna have to defend yourself. If he beats you down, at least you took a stand. You'll feel better, and everyone will respect you more. Hit him hard enough, he might even leave you alone."

Oscar rolled his eyes to the floor, said nothing for a minute.

"I hate this place, sis. I hate everything about it."

"I'm not crazy about it myself, but we're stuck here. You know that. We have to get through this year, and we will."

2

"Take me with you tonight. There's no way I'm gonna sleep. Gram snores so loud, and –"

"I'll take you to the arcade on Saturday. You can play *Asteroids* for an hour again if you want."

Oscar sulked it over and mumbled an okay. Maura kissed him and listened to his retreat, his door closing. She turned to the mirror, saw herself in her new blue satin jacket, embroidered rainbow over the left hip. She saw a girl who wouldn't settle for staying in, confined to a room that brewed self-pity.

Gram had lived in Burdock Downs since the 1940s. The Downs was booming back then, Gram said, crammed with families drawn to the MacAdder Works. Maura found such prosperity hard to imagine. The mill was laying off people as long as she could remember, and all she saw on Gram's street were signs of decline. The next-door neighbor's roof was rotted through, windows boarded up. Five doors down, the husk of a VW bus rested on cinder blocks. She passed more rundown houses with buckling porches, lots jungled with waist-high weeds. Bottle shards crunched under the soles of her red Cheetah sneakers.

Maura couldn't fault Oscar for being miserable here. Losing Mom was hard enough for both of them, and the Downs was a few degrees rougher than their old neighborhood. Even so, she lost patience with her brother. When he came to her with something like this Tony Kroague crisis, hell if she knew what to tell him. She never expected to raise him, but the job had become hers overnight and without directions.

Maybe she screwed up. If Oscar did get the crap kicked out of him, then what? Her advice worked for her, but Oscar wasn't like her. He was a brittle kid, high-strung and moody. Then again, maybe a fight would toughen him up, make him less of a wuss. She walked and thought about it and came no closer to answers.

Sheridan Street led up to a railroad crossing. A procession of coal cars was rumbling past, left to right, stopping Maura in her path. She watched the metal roll through the darkness, catching glints from the streetlights. She felt the sidewalk vibrate beneath her, the thunder rattle her knees.

Maura took the moment to look down over the hill she'd climbed. Gram lived in the Slopes section, which overlooked Broadway. Dots of red and white light crawled along that main drag, the only hint of nightlife in town. Beyond Broadway lay the Flats, and beyond the Flats flowed the Monongahela river hidden in the night. Tiny flares marked the Works and its stacks far off to her left. The Downs has its own kind of beauty, she thought, if you could forget what it does to your lungs.

Mom hadn't talked about growing up here. Nor had she told stories about high school or sneaking out at night. Maura wondered if Mom had ever felt homesick for the Downs after she'd left.

Too bad you'll never know. Too bad and too late. You never knew her, and now you never will. You're alone. You can curl up under the covers of her old bed, but out here you're alone.

"Stop it," she whispered to herself, to those thoughts always lurking, needling her since her mother's death.

The last car trailed off and took the rumble with it. The train horn blared, its sound echoing through the valley. Somewhere a dog howled in response.

On Foster Street the gaps between houses widened and filled with woods. Tree branches swayed about the streetlights, which dappled the leaves silver. The sidewalk gave way to dirt, and twigs crackled with Maura's every step. Listening closer, she thought she heard the same sound behind her, too. She stopped, and the sound followed suit. She turned around to see trees, parked cars, houses with blue TV glows in the windows, but no one else outside. You're being paranoid, she thought, trying to scare yourself.

She kept walking and listening, and damn it if the sound didn't resume. Someone else's footsteps, someone following. She stopped again;

4

the sound followed suit again. Maura spun around and saw no one again. No sneaking creep, nothing moving but the branches. She stared into the woods, distrusting them and their shadows, but no one emerged.

Maura stepped out onto to the street, walked down the middle of the pavement. She made herself conspicuous, and if she had a stalker, she dared him to do the same. Still no one appeared, and she heard no footsteps but her own.

Look at you, in the street, asking to get run down after what happened. Mom did everything right, don't forget, crossing when the signal told her to. He was drunk, coked-up, and speeding through a red light, going sixty-five when the signs said twenty-five. If she saw him, she had no chance to react. So where are you going now? To drink. Walking the double yellow line on your way to drink. How proud you must be.

"Shut up," she said, and looked back once more. The same trees and parked cars. Blue-black clouds drifting over a sliver of moon. No one was watching her; no one was following her. She walked and told herself to lighten up, for God's sake, quit being such a coward.

At least she didn't have far to go. Maura soon reached Suncrest Kindergarten stranded at the dead end of Foster. The school had closed years ago, leaving a big white-brick canvas for every graffiti artist in the Downs. They answered the call with pot leaves, spurting penises, and portraits of KISS. "Class of 77" collided with "Class of 79." "No Nukes" overlapped "Nuke Iran." Someone had attempted Led Zeppelin's angel-god logo but botched it up, settling for a deformed falcon.

Flickering light and boys' voices guided Maura to the back of the building. The fire drew her eyes first, flames contained by a ring of rocks. Sight adjusted, she discerned a playground in the darkness. Swings, monkey bars, and a slide stood nearby. A pavilion and picnic table were farther off, edged against the woods.

Two boys were leaning against the swings. Vic Valducci had a horseshoe mustache, curly hair poking out around his maroon baseball cap. He drank a beer and listened to Grady Kagan talk about a fight. Grady

5

played nose tackle for the Burdock Downs Spartans. He was bull-thick with muscle and glad to slam it around off the field, too. Maura had seen him trip up a kid and kick him for no reason this past week. If she'd known that he was going to be at Suncrest, she might not have come.

A third boy, lanky with glasses, was sitting on the slide. Maura recognized him as Andy Dorovich, a shy kid in her advanced European History class. Almost a month into the school year, and he hadn't spoken a single word. She never would have placed him at a beer party, especially with someone like Grady. He was the first to notice her arrival, but he looked away before she could say hi.

Colton Hauser and Alison Todd were perched atop the monkey bars, beers in hand. Alison and Maura had gym and study hall together, and Alison had been kind enough to invite Maura to her lunch table. Colton had stopped by that table, Alison introduced him, and then he came by every day. Then he'd made a point to visit Maura at her locker between classes. Yesterday he'd told her about the party, said she should come.

Maura knew she shouldn't and knew she would. Colton was the Downs' star quarterback. He'd led the Spartans to a regional title last year and was set to repeat this year. A lot of girls would've clawed each other's eyes out for him. His looks matched his status, too, Maura had to admit. He was tall with broad shoulders, muscular without being bulky like Grady. He had blue eyes, black hair, a face handsome enough to make straight men stare. Maura didn't trust him – he complimented her too much to not want something – but she couldn't help liking him. His charm was easy, his smile contagious. Their eyes met across that fire-lit playground, and for a moment no one else was there.

"Hey, you made it!" he said, and jumped down off the bars.

Alison and Maura exchanged a look while Colton went to the cooler.

"I didn't know you were coming," Alison said, sounding surprised but not pleased.

"Sorry. Maybe I should've said something at lunch. I didn't –"

"Don't apologize. I never thought you'd show up," Colton said, and handed her a bottle of Iron City.

Maura felt everyone watching her as she took a gulp. It tasted nasty, but she couldn't let them see that. Couldn't let them think she was a princess.

"Maura Dougal. That's your name, right?" Grady said. "What's your story? I heard you're rich, super-smart, on your way to Harvard."

"I'm not rich, but yeah, I do okay in class. Like your friend Andy over there. Hi, Andy. How'd a nice, studious boy like you end up here?"

Andy started to speak, but Grady said, "I heard you're stuck-up, too, that you walk around with your nose in the air."

"Leave her alone. She's cool," Alison said. "God, you're such an asshole sometimes."

Maura took another gulp and stepped up close to Grady. Looking him in the eye with a smile, she said, "You know what I heard? That you got manhandled in that game against Jefferson last week, blown off the line on every down. Their center squashed you like a windshield smacking a bug. Any truth to those rumors?"

That brought a round of oohs and laughs from the group.

Maura held out her hand for a shake. "Nice to meet you, too."

Grady's face burned a deeper red. He ignored Maura's offer and turned to Vic. "Anyway, if you really think *Highway to Hell*'s better, you're a moron."

"I ain't saying *Back In Black* ain't good. I'm saying Bon Scott was better. That new singer they got, he's too screechy. It gets on my nerves."

"'Screechy'? What are you, an old woman?"

Vic appealed to Andy. "What do you think? You with me on this?"

"Nobody cares what he thinks," Grady said before Andy could open his mouth.

The boys continued their AC/DC debate while Maura followed Alison and Colton to the pavilion. The girls sat on opposite sides of its picnic table. Colton sat beside Maura.

"You guys come here all the time? You've never been caught?" she asked.

Colton and Alison looked at each other and laughed.

"Don't you know that Colt's dad's the mayor and Grady's dad's the police chief?" Alison said. "Getting caught's not their problem. Acting like decent human beings is."

"Oh, really?" Maura said to Colton. "It's not enough to be the football hero. You had to be the crown prince of Burdock Downs, too. Must be nice."

"We can't pick and choose our parents," Colton said. "And I never said I was a hero. I just know what I want. I go for it, and I get it. Nothing wrong with that."

"Depends on what you want," Maura said.

"To win. At everything every time, no regrets."

"To be the cock of the walk is more like it," Alison said.

Colton dismissed that with a smirk.

"And what happens when you don't win?" Maura said.

"I don't know. It's never happened."

"Well, champ, there's a first time for everything."

"What would you know about first times?" Colton said, smirk intact.

Maura felt herself smiling, heart quickening as they locked stares.

Alison looked from one to the other, down to her wristwatch.

The second beer hadn't tasted so nasty, and Maura opened a third. She was beyond buzzed and didn't care. Tomorrow no longer mattered, not when she felt joy for the first time in months. She finally discovered why kids like to drink and wished she hadn't deprived herself before. The Maura who was afraid to sneak out already seemed so lame, so naive.

So long to her. Let her go, let her die like the mother who raised her.

Colton was talking about the time he and the boys pranked Coach by filling his car with water and goldfish. At some point in the story, he laid his hand on Maura's thigh. She didn't push it off.

Grady let out a resounding belch over by the fire. Vic giggled and answered with a fart, which prompted Grady to crumple a beer can and throw it at him. Andy lay on the slide, stargazing and oblivious to his friends.

"It's getting late, Colt. See you later," Alison said, and touched Maura's arm as she started away. "Come with me for a second? I gotta tell you something."

Maura followed her past the fire and the boys. They stopped alongside the school, in a pocket of darkness between the brick wall and woods.

"You should leave with me," Alison said.

"I was gonna stay a while. You worried about walking home alone?"

"I'm worried about you. You're drinking too fast. And I wasn't kidding about them being decent. They're not always nice boys. And the more they drink, the worse they get."

"No offense, but why are you here, then?"

"I've known them since first grade. They don't even see me as a girl. When they do, I can handle them. But you? Look, I didn't know Colt invited you here. If I did, I would've told you this before."

She's not lying. She's trying to help you.

"Thanks, but don't worry about me. I'm fine."

"If you knew how they talked about you –"

"Even Andy?" Maura said with a laugh. "I'm fine, really. After the shit I've been though lately, I think I'm due for some fun."

"Last time I'll ask. Come on, let's go."

"See you tomorrow."

Alison looked Maura up and down and walked away shaking her head.

Grady was standing on a swing and squeaking its chains when Maura returned. "Hey, where'd Alison go? Don't we get a lezzie show?"

"It already smells less fishy 'round here. You ever notice that, how Alison smells like carp?" Vic said.

"No. Walleye all the way," Grady said, and Vic laughed.

Andy was standing by the fire, staring into the woods. Maura stopped beside him, waited for him to acknowledge her. After a silent minute, she waved her hand before his face.

"Hey, you don't have to be so shy. I'm not gonna bite," she said.

Andy blinked out of his trance and glanced at her. "I was looking at that spot over there. I think I saw somebody."

"Oh, yeah?" Maura scanned the trees, saw nothing but rustling shadows. That someone could be hiding in them reminded her of something, something recent, but her mind struggled to specify it.

Because you're drunk. You've made yourself stupid. Are you happy yet?

Her walk along Foster, of course. The feeling of being followed. It took her a few seconds to remember, but she did and chose not to mention it.

"Nobody's there. Quit being a pussy," Grady said. "Ever since we saw *Friday the 13th*, you been seeing killers in the woods."

"No, man. Me and you watched it; he sat there like this," Vic said, and shielded his eyes with his hands.

Maura looked at Andy as his friends laughed at him, to the pavilion where Colton was waiting. "I hate horror movies, too," she said, and left Andy with a pat on the shoulder.

Colton was drinking Maura's beer when she sat with him. He offered the bottle. She declined, and they shared a lull.

"You know, I think Alison's jealous of you," he said.

"She has no reason to be."

"Sure she does. You're the prettiest girl in school."

"Colton, you're so full of it."

"I mean it. Anyway, I think it's gotta be tough to be you. The new girl, moving here after... what happened."

"Let's not talk about that, okay? Once I start talking about it, or thinking about it, it drags me down. Like sinking in quicksand."

Go on, tell him. Tell him about the visit from the police, the funeral. Tell him how you spent July in bed, crippled with depression. How God only knows where you and your brother would've ended up if Gram weren't around. How your father didn't bother to send a card.

"Yeah, let's stop talking," Colton said, and moved in for a kiss.

She let him, on her lips. She kissed him back, sliding her tongue over his. She felt his strength as he held her, as he pressed against her.

Colton unzipped her jacket, reached up under her t-shirt. He pulled down her bra straps, undid its hooks. He rubbed her nipples with his fingertips, coaxing them to firm.

"Hold on," she whispered. "Not so fast."

Colton didn't listen. He lifted her shirt and licked her breasts. Maura didn't want him to stop, not yet, just to slow down. She'd become hot and lightheaded and didn't know if it was the beer or how he was touching her. She let it happen, his teeth biting and stretching her nipples, let it happen until he backed her down onto the bench.

Straddling her, he unbuttoned and unzipped her jeans.

"Colton," she said, and pushed his hand away from her crotch. "Colton!"

Didn't listen. He slipped his fingers past her panties and into her. Maura jerked upright, shoved her palm to his face.

"What?! What's your problem?" he said.

"Not here. Not like this."

"Calm down. You're gonna like it."

"I want to go home."

"You're too drunk to know what you want," Colton said, and leaned in to kiss her again.

11

Maura tilted her head aside and said, "Stop, I'm telling you."

"Or what? You'll scream?" Grady said with a laugh. "For who? My dad?"

Maura turned around to see him and Vic standing close to the pavilion. They had quietly migrated over from the swings. Andy stayed by the fire, its light reflecting off his glasses. He was watching her, too, but then pretended to see something in the woods. An excuse to look away.

You're in it now, aren't you? What'll you do to get out of this? You know what you'll do. And you know you deserve it. What did you think would happen when you came here? What did you think he wanted? What did Alison tell you?

Maura turned back to Colton. He had the same handsome face but without the charm. Anger festered in his eyes. His jaw tightened with the petulance of a spoiled child.

"It'll be fun. You'll like it," he said, trying to sound playful.

Submit. You know you will. You won't fight them off. They're too big, and you're too weak. You'll take it, however they give it to you, because that's just how empty you are.

Maura no longer had the will to argue with herself. She could blame beer, fatigue, or fear. A lapse in common sense, a lack of character, even a death wish. All, any, or none of those might have led her to that moment. In the end, what mattered was the breakdown within her as she laid upon the table.

Rape me, debase me, make me bleed, she thought. You can't hurt me any worse, take any more than I've already lost. Out here I'm alone and exposed and letting everything go.

2. 2005

In the same town of Burdock Downs, Shelton Gundy poured sugar and cream into his coffee. He stirred the mixture to blond and dropped the spoon in the sink. Leaning his ample rump against the counter, he drank and surveyed the kitchen. Footprints crisscrossed the linoleum floor, some leading to the red wagon parked in the corner. Dog hair and dust clumped under the fridge. Cruddy dishes filled the sink.

Shelton told himself he'd clean after work, but he knew he wouldn't. Lately he'd been lumbering through life in a stupor. He was always tired on workdays, did little on the weekends but watch TV. Forty-three wasn't that old, he thought, not old enough to feel so leaden so often. He wondered if this was depression, which seemed to afflict at least half the American populace anymore.

No, he decided, depression's an easy excuse for laziness. And that's all he was: just another lazy white man, fat and sagging in the face of middle age. There was nothing special or tortured about him. To even think about himself so much felt distasteful.

A thud sounded from Reggie's bedroom, and Shelton quickly put on his Dad mask. He stood straighter, tried to look untroubled as his daughter appeared.

Reggie was ten years old, adopted as a baby. She was pale, bone-thin, and non-talkative. She had gray eyes and a way of staring through people, holding her gaze long enough to make anyone uncomfortable. Her abundant black hair reached her waist even as two ponytails stuck atop her head like the antennae of a cartoon Martian. Between her demeanor and hair, Shelton often joked (to himself, never aloud) that her birth parents must have been space aliens.

Reggie's dog, Bullet, followed her into the kitchen. Shelton had adopted the beagle just before he'd adopted Reggie, and the years showed. Bullet had become bloated and decrepit with age, and lately it pained Shelton to see him waddle around the apartment.

"You sleep okay?" Shelton asked.

Reggie answered with a one-shoulder shrug, watching Bullet slop and snort through his food. Once he finished, she rolled the wagon out of its corner and lifted him onto it. She then wheeled him out to the hallway and proceeded to hitch the wagon to her homemade invention, the Bullevator.

Last year, when Bullet could no longer climb the steps, Shelton considered putting him to sleep. He tried to raise the topic with Reggie, who refused to hear it.

"No. He's not done yet. Give me a week to come up with something," she said.

Throughout that week, Shelton found her drawings discarded around the apartment: sketches measuring the steps, diagrams of wheels and rails, doodles of stick figures operating a rope-and-pulley device. He thought the drawings were sadly cute until Reggie approached him and said, "Okay. I got the stuff. I just need you to install it."

She led him down to the basement, where she had stockpiled rain gutters, a bicycle wheel with no tire, a roll of nylon rope.

"Where did you get this junk?! You've been messing around that dump again. What did I tell you about that?"

"I didn't steal any of it. And it's not junk. It's stuff people gave up on," she said, and handed him her final drawing.

Reggie planned to fasten two gutters to the steps. Parallel and braced with supports, they would serve as rails for her wagon. To solve the problem of lifting and lowering the wagon, she figured on a pulley fixed to the hallway floor. The rope would run from the wagon's handle, around the pulley (bicycle wheel), to the gloved hands of the operator. It was a simple combination of two simple machines, she said. Pulley and inclined plane.

Shelton looked at her, the junk she'd collected, the drawing. Well, what the hell. He had to respect the effort.

Of course building the thing involved much more work than drawing it. Shelton had never been handy, and it took him two weekends to finish the project. Bent awkwardly over the steps, he sawed, hammered, and screwed. Sweat poured down his brow, his back ached, his arms twitched with spasms. Meanwhile, Reggie lay on the living room sofa, reading a *Sailor Moon* comic book, unfazed by his occasional curse-filled outbursts.

When Shelton tested the device, however, it worked perfectly. He tried it with the added weight of a few phone books, then with Bullet. The wagon glided up and down the steps so smoothly, the dog didn't seem to mind the ride.

"You gotta be kidding! It works! I can't believe it works!" Shelton said, blundering into the living room.

"Why wouldn't it?" Reggie said, and stared at him as he stood there dripping with sweat.

Amazing what you get used to, Shelton thought, watching her lower the wagon. He marveled over how they'd been using the Bullevator for a whole year, how it had become a fixture of their home. How she was already ten, this weirdly beautiful little human, his one good reason to keep trudging through the daily blahs.

He followed her out to the front porch, where beer cans crunkled under their feet. Such was life in a duplex with frat-boy neighbors. At least he and Reggie didn't have to step around vomit this time.

"Don't forget breakfast. You need to eat. I can see your skeleton when you stand in the sun."

Reggie stared at his gut and said, "Okay, Dad."

"I'm not kidding. I don't want to hear from your principal again," he said, and kissed her cheek.

Reggie lifted Bullet off the wagon, walked him around to the rear of the duplex.

Shelton went to his '92 Cavalier parked on its allotted bit of Pike Street. Every night the train passed on the other side of Pike, trailing a mist of filth. Every morning he found his car coated with coal dust and turned into a message board. "Scrap me" somebody had finger-written on its back window overnight, along with "I suck dick."

He drove, taking Pike past grimy row homes like his own. A stretch of woods blurred by, then a gravel lot with puddled craters and a sad assemblage of storage units. An underpass cast a brief graffitied darkness that gave way to more woods. Trees screened the river lurking off to the left. The rails flanked Pike to the right until they veered off, opening a stretch of asphalt between the street and tracks. A locomotive sat in that gap, detached and stranded and cankered with rust.

A ramp branched off Pike for the highway. Shelton turned onto it and sped away from the Downs. For miles he bore down on anyone who drove too slowly and cursed anyone who did the same to him. He sought open road, breathable air, a place less dead.

He settled for Gladbury Parke.

It had begun as a typical office complex in the early '90s, a maze of winding roads lined with bland corporate buildings. As businesses fled Pittsburgh for the lower taxes of Locust County, Gladbury sprawled like mad. It grew to include housing plans with names like Londontowne and Willowbrooke. It clear-cut a hundred acres for a pampered golf course, added a manmade lake sludged with algae. Lately it squeezed a hotel between a sports bar and ice rink.

Shelton navigated the curves of Technology Way, a hilly side road studded with glass boxes. Tinted different colors, branded with different logos, all the same box, he thought. His happened to be black with red lettering that read "Concilicom."

Concilicom received complaints regarding municipal services in Locust County. It did nothing to resolve those complaints, but it recorded and forwarded them to the appropriate offices, which ignored them. If anything, Concilicom was a buffer between the public and the bureaucracies it subsidized and despised.

Municipalities liked the deal because it saved money. By hiring Concilicom, a municipality could stop hiring clerks and receptionists, boast about cutting costs, and stash the freed chunks of its budget for kickbacks. For its part, Concilicom pretended to fill the service void with three shifts of underpaid grunts like Shelton, who received scant benefits and no union protection.

It was a great arrangement as long as you didn't need anything from your local government.

But say you live in the borough of Hazlett for example. On a January morning, you wake to find your street buried under a foot of snow. You reluctantly call your job and tell your boss you'll be late. Hours pass, but the snowplows don't arrive. You wait, and you wait. Still no plows. You hesitate to call Hazlett's Public Works because you're not the whiny type. So you continue to wait, hours continue to pass, and you finally burn a personal day.

At dinnertime you do call Public Works (not to complain, you're not one to complain) just to see what's going on. An automated answering service redirects you to Concilicom, and its representative promises to forward your concern to Public Works. This extra step seems odd, but you're willing to trust the process.

Day becomes night, still no plows in sight. You go to bed thinking someone will do something about this by morning. You wake up to the same foot of snow untouched by the road crew *you're* paying for, damn it, with the taxes gouged from *your* paycheck. You deserve better. You dread having to call off work again, and why should you lose another personal day? That's *your* time. So you try Public Works again, and its answering system redirects you to Concilicom again. Now you're pissed and stressed and entitled to vent – all the more so if you have kids – and you're who Shelton talked to all day. It was his job.

"Morning," said Myrt the receptionist, not looking away from her monitor.

"Morning," Shelton echoed, not stopping on his way to the Service Hub.

Dozens of workstations filled the room, arranged around a large cylinder in the center. The cylinder had a mirrored surface of one-way glass and contained a perch from which the supervisors observed the floor without being observed in return. All the workstations faced away from the cylinder, lending it the power of constant over-your-shoulder surveillance.

A performance board hovered above every workstation. Mounted on poles and visible to all, the boards tracked each employee's call volume and customer satisfaction. Total calls registered on the left in white digits, satisfied callers on the right in red. According to the Concilicom handbook, this public display of productivity fostered healthy competition among the staff.

Shelton noted his neighbors' boards as he reached his workstation. Jeff's showed 012 calls, 010 satisfieds. Cindy's white 007 ding-donged to 008, her red 004 beep-beeped to 005.

Fine, he thought. The game was on. He rolled up his sleeves and donned his headset. His computer whirred awake. Text flashed across its monitor.

> Caller: Arnold Sauter
> Location: Conklin, PA 15178
> Subject: Refuse Collection
> Hostility Index: Low

Shelton hit the Enter key and said, "Concilicom. Shelton Gundy speaking. How can I help you?"

"Christ! I been on hold for an hour! What kind of bullshit is this?!" Mr. Sauter said.

"How can I help you, sir?"

18

"My garbage ain't been picked up for three weeks. I got rats runnin' round my property, spreadin' the fuckin' plague for all I know. I saw one of your garbage men sleepin' in his truck last month. I got a picture of it. They gettin' paid to sleep on the job?"

"Okay, sir, I —"

"No, it ain't okay. Whatcha gonna *do* about it?"

"I'll file your complaint for the official record and forward it to the Conklin Public Works department, who should act upon it. I can't tell you when, or how, or if they will, but they should."

"I called them already, and they bounced me to you! Are you a front for them? What *do* you do?"

"I've explained what I can do, sir. Is there anything else I can help you with today?"

"So you're fuckin' useless! You bastards. You goddamn bastards! I won't take this, you hear me? You hear me?! I'm calling the news!"

"Yes, sir. Now, if you're satisfied with our assistance, please dial 1 before hanging up. Thank you, and have —"

Mr. Sauter hung up. Shelton rubbed the back of his tense neck and took a few deep breaths.

His performance board ding-donged, the white 000 becoming 001. Then it buzzed, the red 000 blinking but remaining 000. Ever conscious of being watched, he wiped his oily brow and took the next call.

Two hours later, he'd notched 018 calls and 005 satisfieds when the Service Hub's intercom sounded its two-note tone. Myrt announced, "Shelton Gundy, you have a call on 101. Shelton Gundy, 101."

He picked up the nearest phone. "This is Shelton."

"Mr. Gundy? It's Sadie Klemko. Sorry to bother you, but we're having a problem."

Klemko was Reggie's principal. Shelton heard sirens and screaming kids in the background. Klemko muffled the mouthpiece and told someone, "Shut them up! I'm on the phone with the father!" Then unmuffled, "Mr. Gundy? Are you still there?"

"What's the problem?"

"Please don't panic. Regina climbed onto the roof and won't come down. She's not threatening to jump, exactly, but it might help if you could get here. It might help a lot. Could you get here?"

3. Fish Tank

Shelton swerved into the MacAdder Elementary lot, screeching his tires. He ran toward the front doors, where a crowd of kids had gathered. They were screaming and laughing and ignoring the pleas of their teacher, Miss Lillian, to calmly go back inside. Some were chanting, "Jump! Jump! Jump!" A cop stood nearby, doing nothing but eyeing Miss Lillian's behind. Klemko was talking to volunteer firefighters when she noticed Shelton.

"Mr. Gundy! She went to the restroom and never came back to class. We searched the school, and the janitor found the roof hatch open. We don't know how she got up there, and she won't respond to anybody."

The cop strolled over. He had curly dark hair and a horseshoe mustache. "V. Valducci" was engraved on his name tag. "You're the dad? We been waiting for you to see this yourself so when she falls you can't say we caused it and go suing us."

Shelton looked at the firefighters, who looked like teenagers intimidated by the cop. He called up to the roof, "Reggie! Reggie, it's me!"

The ponytails peeked up over the edge, then her entire head. "Hi, Dad," she said.

"Reggie, what's wrong?"

"Duh! She's crazy!" a kid said, and others laughed. Some resumed chanting, "Jump! Jump! Jump!"

"Stop it, children! Stop it! Go back inside! Single file, single file!" Miss Lillian cried.

"Don't you move! I'm coming up there!" Shelton screamed over the noise.

"Yo, tubs, that's too many steps! You'll never make it!" another kid said, and others laughed again, drowning out Miss Lillian.

Shelton jogged up the stairs, cursing the little shit for being right. He was sweating and sucking wind by the third floor, where the janitor awaited with a stepladder. The old man wore coveralls and a mesh baseball cap that read "USMC" in gold letters. He regarded Shelton with bewildered pity.

"Take it easy, big man. I don't do CPR."

"How'd she get up there?"

"Beats me. She won't say. I only found her 'cause she left the hatch open. See those rungs in the shaft? God knows how she got to 'em without a ladder. This here's the only one in the building. I brought it here myself *after* she got up there."

The janitor steadied the ladder while Shelton climbed. Up through the shaft he went, out onto the roof. Reggie was still there, still near the edge. She glanced back when she heard his footsteps on the gravel but turned away like she hadn't seen him.

Shelton stopped about ten feet from her, as if coming any closer could push her over. The kids were still screaming, but she didn't seem to hear them. She just stood there, hands in the pockets of her kelly green jacket, gazing at the landscape.

"Reggie, this isn't funny. Come here."

"Look at all the stuff you can see. There's Broadway. There's Pike and the Little League field. You can see our house."

"I'm telling you to come here. I'm not asking."

"There's the Flats and the river. You see that big cube? You know what that place is, Dad?"

Shelton crept toward her, the wind lashing his face. He didn't like heights. They weakened his knees, made his whole body wobbly. As he closed in on Reggie, he scanned her view. Hills, trees, highway. Houses, the river. Okay, got it. No need to linger on it or look down over the edge.

Something out there transfixed her, though. She didn't acknowledge Shelton standing beside her, didn't react when he held out his hand.

"Don't move," he whispered, reaching, touching, and finally gripping her arm. "Don't move. I got you. It's okay."

Reggie didn't flinch or resist as Shelton pulled her back from the edge. He grabbed her up, carried her toward the hatch, and planted her down. Holding her by the shoulders, he shook her hard enough to sway her ponytails.

"What's wrong with you?! You could've died, you know that?!"

Reggie blinked and looked around. At once she became confused, like she didn't know how she'd ended up on the roof or why he was so upset with her. The change startled Shelton enough to shut him up. Answers could wait. He bear-hugged and kissed her, squeezed her against him, cradled her head.

While Reggie stayed in the hallway, monitored by the cop, Shelton sat in the principal's office. Klemko had settled behind her desk, frowning, probing him with toad-like eyes. A manilla folder lay open before her, damning pages awaiting.

Dr. Wohler, the school psychologist, was sitting to her left. He was a bald man with a goatee and glasses that magnified his eyes to twice their normal size. Shelton had met him before and wasn't thrilled to see him again. Wohler seemed like a creep who enjoyed listening to people voice their fears, who secretly got off on cataloging their flaws.

"Mr. Gundy, I called Dr. Wohler here to discuss our options going forward. As you know, this isn't our first incident with Regina," Klemko said, and skimmed the top page. "Two years ago, she constructed a miniature guillotine for art class with Popsicle sticks, string, and a weighted blade. To test its effectiveness, she decapitated a classmate's Barbie doll."

"Come on, I explained that before," Shelton said. "An old black-and-white movie of *Tale of Two Cities* was on TV. Reggie saw the guillotine and got curious about it. I mean, if you can't let your kids watch the classics..."

Klemko turned the page. "A month later, she constructed a miniature iron maiden with a coconut shell, door hinge, and nails."

"That was extra credit for science class. The assignment was to build something that could juice an orange. And you know what? It worked."

"Yes, but it's a good thing her miniature electric chair didn't!"

"Okay, so she had a thing for capital punishment. It was a phase."

"She has a morbid imagination! Need I remind you what she said last April?" Klemko flipped through more pages, found one she wanted. "During an assembly guest-taught by a visiting sex-educator, Regina asked if applying cocaine to the clitoris really causes, and I quote, 'volcanic orgasms.'"

"Look, a bunch of frat-boy Neanderthals live in the downstairs apartment. They drink, and they talk loud. In the summer, your windows are open, your kid's gonna hear things she shouldn't. Does that make me a bad parent? Does that make her a bad kid?"

"No one's saying that Regina is bad, but she's clearly troubled," Klemko said, and consulted yet another page. "She exhibits strong antisocial tendencies. She has no friends and doesn't seem to want any. She makes no effort to talk to anyone, sometimes going weeks without speaking. When her teachers call on her, she typically responds with a yawn and a blank stare."

"And she still aces her classes, doesn't she? So she's bored," Shelton said.

Wohler cleared his throat and said, "Mr. Gundy, I understand your need to protect your daughter. But, as Ms. Klemko so accurately noted, Regina is troubled. Rationalizing the problem will only make it worse. Her behavior aside, Regina appears to be undernourished and sleep-deprived.

Altogether she exhibits common symptoms of depression. Do you think she might be depressed?"

"I don't know. Maybe."

"It doesn't bother you if she is?"

"Who isn't these days? She watches TV, she picks up on things. She remembers 9/11. She knows we're at war. She saw Katrina hit New Orleans, the tsunami wipe out South Asia. Hell, every time she walks out our front door, she sees filth, garbage, and the scum of humanity. Maybe she should be depressed. The world's a depressing place."

Wohler looked at Klemko, who closed the folder.

"This isn't about your worldview," she said. "Your daughter climbed onto the roof of this building and wouldn't come down. She easily could have fallen and killed herself. How would I explain *that* to all the other parents who send their children here, Mr. Gundy? Do you think they would understand how *special* Regina is?

"I'm suspending her for two weeks. During that time, I strongly urge you to find help for her, whether it be therapy, medication, or both. Now, Dr. Wohler here can recommend several –"

"Of course. Here we go with the shrinks and the meds. Who's gonna pay for this help? My insurance won't, I'll tell you that. And who's gonna watch Reggie while I'm at work?"

Klemko threw up her hands. "I don't know! Our budget's been gutted this year, too. Dr. Wohler came here today for free. We can barely supply lunches, let alone extensive counseling. I wish we could solve every problem for every child, too, but we can't. I'm sorry, but I don't know what else to tell you."

Shelton returned to the hallway and found Reggie on the bench where he'd left her. He reached for her hand, but she was cuffed to the armrest. Officer Valducci stood nearby, talking to another, much bulkier cop who'd arrived while Shelton was in the office. The second cop wore a white shirt, his thick neck straining its collar. His skin was red, eyes beady and angry.

"Come on, man. Is this necessary?" Shelton said, meaning the cuffs.

"She's a freak show, and you can't control her," Valducci said.

"She's ten. You never climbed a tree when you were a kid?"

"You're gonna argue now?" the second cop said, and barreled toward Shelton. "I'm Chief Kagan. You got a problem?"

"I wouldn't be here if I didn't."

"You getting smart with me, fat boy? You got a problem?"

"No. I just don't see why –"

"You got a problem?! You want a problem?! Do you?!"

Shelton shrank back, cowed in the face of pointless rage.

"Vic, uncuff the brat," Kagan said.

Valducci followed the order, making a point to look at Shelton and say, "You're a fuckin' pussy. You know that?"

Reggie stared at the officers as they walked away laughing.

Father and daughter took their seats in the car, alone for a quiet moment. Only a few hours had passed since they'd parted ways on the duplex porch, but that felt like weeks ago to Shelton. He sat there stressed and exhausted, too drained to turn the key. Reggie passed the time picking at her cuticles, as inscrutable as usual.

"I guess I'm in trouble," she said.

"Two-week suspension."

"That's supposed to be a punishment?"

"Not funny, Regina Marie Gundy. Not funny at all. Tell me what you were doing up there."

She blinked, looked outside. She had something to say but clenched her jaw and kept it in. He gave her another minute; she gave him the stonewall.

"Okay, listen. You win. You stumped everybody. Nobody can figure out how you got up to that shaft. Obviously you can't jump that high. So tell me what you did."

That made her smile. She wiggled her fingers at him and said, "Magic powers. Whoo-ooh! Whoo-ooh!"

Shelton started the engine and revved it hard. He jerked the car into reverse and ground the gears to go forward. Otherwise, it was a silent drive home.

He popped open a Yuengling and slouched in his recliner. The six o'clock news cut to the weather for the fifth time (unseasonably warm for early October, the reporter enthused) before more commercials. Nothing on that screen registered, not with the problem on his mind. He had to do something, but what?

Spanking her was out. Shelton wouldn't hit a kid, even a rotten one, and Reggie was hardly rotten. She'd always obeyed him without much fuss, was never loud, obnoxious, or violent. Until that morning, she'd never even caused a scene.

He saw no point in grounding her. Reggie already spent all day in her room and didn't eat enough. She did like her manga comics, and to draw, and to cobble together the occasional project. If he were to restrict all that, what was she supposed to do, stare at the wall like a mental patient?

She hadn't injured anybody, stolen anything, or damaged property. Yes, it was wrong to sneak up onto the roof and to lie about how she did it, but it wasn't like she'd brought a gun to school. She'd always been a weird kid. Since when was that a crime?

Stop kidding yourself, he thought. You are rationalizing it, like Wohler said. Don't forget, she was so spaced out that you had to shake her back to reality. That happened, and you can't deny it.

Worse yet, this mess forced him to revisit a topic he preferred to avoid. For all his private jokes about Reggie's birth parents being space aliens, he really knew nothing about them. Nothing, except the way they abandoned her.

Ten years ago, a different group of guys had been living downstairs. They were gearheads in their twenties, a rougher, dirtier version of his current neighbors. Shelton tried to talk to them once, a simple hello when he first saw them on the porch. One belched, the other three laughed, and that was that.

They were running an unlicensed car-repair outfit. Random people would drop off vehicles at all hours, and the guys would leave greasy parts scattered about the porch. Shelton often overheard arguments between the guys and their customers, usually over money, sometimes escalating to death threats. Such blow-ups became routine background noise along with blaring heavy metal and girlfriends' orgasmic screams.

Shelton had grown so used to the guys, he didn't even notice they'd disappeared until the cops came asking about them. If he knew their whereabouts. If he'd talked to them before they left. If he'd seen a guy whose head was bandaged "like it got rammed through a windshield."

No, sir. Never really knew those guys.

Months passed, and the downstairs apartment stayed vacant. No man with a mummified head ever showed up. Aside from the hoses, battery, muffler, and bumper they'd left on the porch, Shelton had no reason to remember his neighbors. In fact, he was happy to forget them.

When he came home from work on June 23, 1995, however, he noticed a new object among the junk. Someone had left a twenty-gallon fish tank, water emptied but glass still wet, bedded with blue pebbles and plastic seaweed. Something pink squirmed upon the pebbles. Some kind of overgrown hairless rodent, Shelton thought. Then he froze, realizing. It grabbed for the fake plants with little fingers. Eyes closed, mouth open, it coughed like its throat hurt, like it couldn't breathe. It was a she.

He stood there stunned. So many questions collided in his head, it took him a moment to see the note taped to the glass. He swiped it off, eager for clarity, but it gave him just four words.

take it its yours

Shelton knew even then, as he ran to phone, that he would adopt her whatever the bureaucracy or cost. He would love her, protect her, show her that life had worth. He would provide, take care, give her every chance. Those were absolutes he'd never questioned, not once in ten years.

But what if Reggie had a mental illness or genetic defect that ruptured that morning? Or what if her birth parents had been junkies who'd harmed her fetal brain? How serious was this, what did she need, and what if he couldn't afford it?

"This... is... *Jeopardy!*" announced a voice on the TV, and the game show's theme song played to studio-audience applause.

"No shit," Shelton grunted, and lumbered to the fridge for another beer.

4. Town Hall Meeting

As Shelton drank and pondered, a town hall meeting was about to begin. People filed into the Burdock Downs council chambers, a small but stately forum. Oak panels lined the walls. Brass chandeliers glowed overhead. The council members seated themselves at a long table, facing rows of benches for the public. The U.S., Pennsylvania, and Locust County flags hung in the corner to council's left. A glass case to the right displayed a scale model of the MacAdder Works steel mill.

The regulars had arrived on the public side: Tom Sligo the librarian; Mrs. Bidwell the old civil-rights marcher; the Goleski sisters, whose father had been killed in the Strike of '39; Jerry Kropke the hunchbacked stalwart of the *Burdock Downs Dispatch*. About twenty others had shown up, too, a larger-than-usual turnout for any council meeting.

Kropke's reporting had stirred some of this interest. Last month, the mayor had proposed a sweeping redevelopment plan for Broadway, which would gut and reconstruct the core of the Downs. The council president, who'd always hated the mayor, naturally opposed the plan. They sparred through the *Dispatch*, calling each other "crooked," "incompetent," "delusional," "asinine," "cowardly," and so forth. For many in attendance, the meeting was a chance to see them throw down in person.

The chamber doors opened, and the mayor entered.

Colton Hauser still carried himself with confidence at forty-two. His face had aged but remained handsome, and he'd stayed in shape. The old-timers would always see him as the kid who'd quarterbacked the Spartans to regional titles in '79 and '80, a living reminder of better days for the Downs. Colton was aware of this and tried to pride himself on it.

Although his father had served as mayor, Colton refused to coast on the Hauser name after high school. He earned a business administration degree from Duquesne University and returned home to marry Lorna Duncan, the prettiest girl in the Downs. Then he won a council seat followed by two mayoral terms. He faced no opposition for a third because everyone knew he would win that, too, if he wanted it.

Chief Kagan and Officer Valducci accompanied Colton, as they often did for his public appearances. While the officers stood by the doors and stared down the attendees, Colton's staffers prepared his presentation. One set up a podium, laptop, and digital projector. Another placed a portable screen before the flags. Colton scanned the seven council members, knowing he owned three.

Libby Chandler, who spent the meetings knitting sweaters? Bought. (Medicare only covered so many of her husband's orthopedic bills.) Craig Womack, the thirty-year-old who still lived with his mother, always prattling about social justice? Bought. (Student loans.) Burt Brushki, the illiterate welder with a missing finger? Bought. (That last DUI would've meant jail time if the chief hadn't withdrawn the charge, but he could still refile it).

That left three undecideds on the mayor's plan, plus Gus Bixler, the council president who wanted to kill it. Incorruptible contrarian pain in the ass Gus Bixler. Mr. Old-Timey Civic Duty, sworn enemy of the Hausers, still pissed about losing elections to Colton's father, still doddering around wearing a bow tie and suspenders like a rejected extra from *Our Town*. Dead skin patched his bald head and flaked onto his collar. Little white hairs grew from the tip of his nose. His putrid breath wheezed forth from worm-colored lips.

Colton acknowledged Bixler with a sarcastic smile and began, "My fellow citizens, esteemed council, I thank you all for coming tonight. I assume you know what's on the table and what it means to our borough. If you don't, let me be clear. Burdock Downs is economically crippled and limping toward bankruptcy.

"I don't blame anyone for this problem. Our predecessors couldn't have anticipated the collapse of the steel industry in the '70s. Unfortunately, we've been struggling with the aftermath ever since. It's no secret that we've lost half our population since the Works shut down in '82. Few communities could survive such devastation, and frankly, it's a miracle that we've hung on this long.

"As bleak as all that sounds, I am not here to mourn. No, my friends, quite the opposite. Tonight I'm here to announce a new day for the Downs, one that will bring jobs and the three Rs: rebirth, regrowth, recovery. We are going to resurrect Broadway, restore it to the thriving commercial district it once was. Allow me to show you what I mean."

A staffer dimmed the lights. Colton typed a few keystrokes on the laptop, and the projector beamed onto the screen.

A grainy black-and-white photo appeared, showing a block of Broadway as it was. No people on the sidewalk, only an overturned garbage can. Zelda's Gift Cards stood vacant, its painted sign weathered away to Z da s Gi ar s. Morton Hardware languished next door, front window cracked and x'd with duct tape. A padlocked lattice curtained off the empty shell of Sugar Polly's Bakery. Slappy's Tavern decomposed on the corner, a wooden smiley face screwed to its facade. Eyes sleepy and mouth slack, the smiley looked tanked enough to vomit a gutful of acid cheer.

The photo disappeared for a colorful sketch of the future Broadway. Trees lined a clean street. Faceless pedestrians strolled past an art gallery, a clothing boutique, a frozen yogurt shop. Other figures gathered at sidewalk cafe tables, drinking coffee and eating pastries. A yoga studio replaced Slappy's, and two slender women in tights exited the place, twin visions of health and well-toned youth.

Another black-and-white photo, another slab of failed retail. The Sunny Dawn grocery had shut down three years ago, attracting squatters no matter how often the police drove them out. The picture showed the building on a winter day. Swaths of plaster had fallen from the broadside wall to expose the brickwork beneath. Two men in heavy coats leaned against those bricks, drinking, while a third sat on milk crates, huddled against the cold. Fire burned in a nearby drum placed just a few feet from the lot's ever-growing tire pile.

Keystroke, and no more homeless. A combination green space-farmer's market replaced the rundown building and lot. Parents crowded around booths stocked with fresh produce, their children ran free in the grass. A girl blew bubbles, two boys chased a soccer ball. In the background, more children were flying kites, red and yellow diamonds aloft in vast, cloudless blue.

The next black-and-white photo showed Burdock Downs Hospital. Unity Pittsburgh Medical, the healthcare giant that owned every hospital in western Pennsylvania, had deemed BDH hopelessly unprofitable. UPM shut down BDH over the summer even though BDH was the Downs' leading employer. That UPM had made such a cut while posing as a nonprofit (for tax purposes) added to the Downs' bitterness. The sight of the hospital drew boos from the audience, as Colton had anticipated.

"I know, I know," he said, playing to the room. "But please bear with me."

He tapped a key, and the hospital vanished for a glass box like those of Gladbury Parke. It spanned the same blocks as BDH but shimmered with gold skin. A large red cross in a circle was the building's only signage, implying that it, too, would be a medical facility.

An appreciative murmur arose from the audience, which triggered Bixler to push himself to his feet.

"Enough! Enough of this nonsense! Turn on the lights!" he said.

Colton nodded to his staffer to go ahead, turn them on.

"You sure know how to push buttons and pull strings, don't you, Colton? Don't be fooled, people! Don't buy this Candy Land fantasy!" Bixler grabbed pages from the table and waved them. "This plan is a betrayal! He's selling us out to a fly-by-night contractor! What is this Condor Development Corps? Why can't we find any information on it, any public record? We've yet to see a single representative of this company, and here you are, asking us to kowtow to it."

Colton took a breath and said, "I respect your candor, Mr. President, but it doesn't change the fact that we're broke. There, I said it. We're broke. This is a crisis, and it demands action, not obstructionism."

"Spoken like a true Hauser," Bixler said, and pursed his lips. He hooked his thumbs around his suspenders and continued, "Smells funny to me. Have *you* met anyone from this company? If so, why haven't you brought them here before council and the public? Or is Condor just a new name for your daddy's buddies? Who's getting the kickback, Colton? Which member of the old boys' club?"

"That's out of line! I'll remind you, I have the floor!" Colton said.

"You have nothing! *I* have the power. *I'm* the president, and I demand transparency!"

"I have the floor, you pompous, crusty-skulled..." Colton felt a hand clamp down on his shoulder and turned to see who touched him.

At first Colton mistook the person for a teenage girl. He stood a foot shorter than the mayor with long reddish-brown hair and wore a navy blue t-shirt two sizes too big. "CONDOR" read the white text across his chest, rainbow colors swirling within the Os. A backpack weighed upon his slight frame. While his stature and fashion suggested youth, his wan and drawn face hinted at someone older and diminished by experience. His eyes were sunken and dark-circled and unblinking.

"Thanks, champ. I'll take it from here," he said, his voice especially soft after all the shouting.

"Excuse me, it's not time for public comment yet," Colton said.

"I'm not the public. I'm Lonnie Waters, founder and CEO of Condor Development Corps."

Colton froze, as did Chief Kagan, who'd started toward the podium. The audience buzzed with oohs, whoas, huhs, and whats. Even Jerry Kropke stopped jotting, eyebrows raised.

"Yes, yes. Shock and awe," Waters said. "You've done enough. Go join your friends."

Colton hesitated, red-faced and lost, and wandered over toward the police.

Bixler chuckled and said, "What kind of a joke is this? You're supposed to be a CEO? You're just a runt. You're not big enough for your own clothes, and you want to redevelop this town? Oh, please, boy! Please, keep humoring us. Tell us why you're here tonight. Why grace us with your presence now after so much secrecy?"

"There's no secrecy, Mr. President. I've been sitting here watching these proceedings for months. You just didn't notice me, and that's okay. People only show their true selves when they don't think anyone's watching. Right, champ?" Waters said, and looked at Colton.

"Um, yeah, sure," Colton said, not sounding very sure.

Waters took off his backpack, unzipped one of its pockets, and pulled out a compact disc.

"Some context for what you're about to see, people. The year was 1937. Clarence Grace was a chicken farmer who owned nothing but his coop, a shack, and a tiny plot in Lawrence County, Ohio. On an August morning, Mr. Grace found a hole in the coop, his chickens gone. He went searching for his birds, tracking them to the farm of one Orville Bixler. Mr. Bixler's wife, Clarissa, happened to be nursing her baby by the farmhouse window when Mr. Grace arrived on the property. They made eye contact, which offended Mrs. Bixler. She accused Mr. Grace of peeping, and because she was white and he was black, well, you may see where this is going."

Waters slipped the disc into the laptop and looked at Colton, who signaled one of his staffers to dim the lights.

A sepia-tinted image lit the screen, showing ten white men posing with the dead Clarence Grace. He hung from the rafters of a sawmill, naked from the waist down. Bullet holes gaped in his torso. Blood ran down his legs and dangling feet. One of his killers held a rifle, others smoked celebratory cigars, a few more smiled at the camera. A boy stood among the men, pointing at the corpse and laughing.

Waters hit a key on the laptop. An animated red line circled the laughing boy's face.

"And that would be Orville Bixler's oldest son, Gus, at age twelve, shortly before he moved to the Downs," Waters said.

Gasps blended with whispers of "Oh, my God!" "Oh, dear!" "Oh, my!" Mrs. Bidwell, who was black, cried, "Good Lord!" Kropke scribbled, his eyes darting from the audience to the screen to Bixler.

"Hold it now!" Bixler shouted. "I can explain! I was young! I was an ignorant child! We've all made mistakes!"

"Yes, but for someone who demands transparency, you tried to hide this mistake, didn't you?" Waters said. "I found the records of this incident in the archives of the Racial Reconciliation Society in Washington, DC. And here I have a copy of the letter you personally wrote to the Society, just five years ago, requesting they either 'expunge' those records or entrust them to your office."

Scattered boos sounded as Waters pulled copies of Bixler's letter from the backpack and passed them around. He reached into the bag again and took out a stack of glossy 8x10 copies of the lynch-mob photo, along with packs of markers, and passed those around, too.

"Attention, everyone, I've also brought glossies and Sharpies. If you'd like Mr. President to autograph this photo for you, I'm sure he'll oblige after the meeting," Waters said.

An aghast Bixler could only watch as Kropke, Colton, and others grabbed up copies of the photo.

Tom the librarian said, "Oh, no, you don't! You're not gonna swiftboat this man! Gus isn't on trial here. He might've made mistakes as a kid, but he's been a fine public servant in this town ever since! For you to come here and assassinate his character, it's abhorrent!"

Waters went back to the laptop as if he hadn't heard Tom. He projected another photo, this one showing a young black woman in a motel room. Her striped dress and little hat dated the picture to the late '50s. She held a bouquet, and several more lay at her feet. There was a trace of embarrassment in her smile.

"Remember her, Mr. President? Why don't you tell everyone who she was?" Waters said.

Bixler flinched at the image. His worm-colored lips twitched. His palms oiled the table with sweat.

"Cynthia Winslow, your favorite mistress," Waters said. "The woman you referred to as 'Fudge Muffin.' Things were great for a few years, weren't they, until she became pregnant. Did you know she kept a diary, Mr. President? According to her family, you did, and you tried like hell to obtain it from them over the years. Turns out I was a bit more persuasive than you."

Waters reached into the backpack, pulled out a book bound with brown leather. He held it up for all to see and opened it to a marked page.

"On Thursday, February 23, 1961, Ms. Winslow wrote, 'I feel I have to do this, that I have no choice. Gus' career depends on it, and I do love him even now. His own wife would never do such a thing for him. Please, God, forgive me. This goes against everything I believe, everything I am. Please, God, understand.'"

Waters clapped the book shut, looked at the audience. "Mrs. Winslow died the following night at the hands of a back-alley abortionist hired by your council president Gus Bixler. I'll spare you the bloody details, people. Just know that Gus overcame his racism, at least in the bedroom. That counts for something."

He tossed the book to Tom. "You're the librarian. Go shelve that."

Negative audience noise filled the room: curses, groans, vows to throw these crooks out of office. "To hell with you, Gus! You lying bastard!" Mrs. Bidwell screamed on her way to the doors, sparking a round of applause.

"Order! Order!" Bixler whimpered, and fumbled for his gavel, which fell to the floor.

Waters let the noise subside and said, "Are you begging, Mr. President? That won't stop it. We're going harder, we're going deeper, we're going all night, and I don't think you can take it. You frail types never can."

With a gleam in his eyes, Waters looked to the laptop once again. "People, in 1971 your council president Gus Bixler vacationed in Cancun. While his wife slept in the resort, he ventured out to the streets and met – what was his name, Mr. President? That fifteen-year-old boy you took to the spa for your little journey of self-discovery? Maybe I should pull up a photo of him, which I happen to have."

"No! Stop!" Bixler said, "I order you to stop!"

"Ramon Marquez. That was his name. What's wrong? Don't like little boys anymore? Let's revisit Ramon when he was so *pretty* to you."

Bixler rocked like he'd been decked. Councilman Brushki leapt up to steady him. "Jesus, Gus!" Brushki said, and recoiled from the old man.

Waters walked over to the lights and rebrightened them himself. Everyone in the room saw what he wanted them to see. Bixler hadn't just lost control of the meeting, he'd also lost control of his bladder. Wetness spread from his crotch and down his pant leg. The urine smell traveled from council's table to the front rows of public seating.

"He pissed himself!" "Look at that!" "He did! He did!" Nervous laughter mixed with spiteful laughter. Someone clapped and someone else whistled, provoking more laughter. Camera phones flashed. Most of the audience, however, were too shocked to move or make a sound.

The degraded president hobbled from the table to the exit, a liquid trail marking his retreat. He passed the mayor and Waters with downcast eyes. The door closed behind him, and the room quieted.

"Anyone still undecided?" Waters said, and looked at council. Each member looked away and said nothing. He zipped up his backpack, slipped it on, and surveyed the crowd.

"I'm not your friend, people, nor will I pretend to be. I respect your intelligence too much for cheap theatrics, and I won't try to sell you on Condor. If you want to know anything about it, go to its website. If you can't access the website, then you don't matter. Not in this decade.

"Here's all you need to know. I'll deliver everything the mayor promised and one thing he didn't. I will personally beautify Broadway with a sculpture garden of my own design. It will open a new world within the new world shown on that screen tonight. It will contain wondrous animals you've only seen in your dreams. It will give you Truth in a form you can touch. Who wouldn't want that?"

Waters met every stare, from Tom to Kropke to the Goleski sisters and every citizen in between, to the police officers, and finally to the mayor. "Looking forward to working with you, champ. The floor's still yours," he said, and headed for the exit.

Colton then felt the room's eyes returning to him.

5. Smash Heap

Regina watched Dad slurp down his coffee and drop the cup in the sink. He checked his shirt for stains, swiped his car keys off the table, stopped on his way to the door.

"What's the plan again?" he said.

"I call to check in at noon. If I don't, I'm in bigger trouble."

"What else?"

"I can take Bullet out to poop, but I have to come right back. You might call to check on me anytime. If I don't answer, even bigger trouble."

Dad stooped to kiss her cheek. "And just because you're not in school doesn't mean you won't have work to do. Think about what you did yesterday and write a three-page report on it."

"Three pages by the time you come home?"

"If that seems like a lot, use your magic powers," he said, and closed the door as he left.

Regina looked to Bullet for support, but he was busy lapping up his water.

She stepped out onto the porch and into a sunny morning. Across Pike Street and past the railroad tracks, the wooded hill showed off its first reds, oranges, and golds. The wind rustled those leaves, floating the smell of fall.

Regina lifted Bullet off the wagon, walked him into the gap between the duplex and its neighbor. They went downhill to Cherry Way, a side street that led to the Little League field. No one else was there, which was fine by her. Every so often she'd run into mean kids who called her names or threw things at Bullet. Over the summer they even tried to bean him in the head with a baseball. Those kids confirmed her belief that it was best to avoid people. Some, like Dad, seemed to be okay, but most were not to be trusted.

Regina unleashed Bullet on the grass, freeing him to waddle about on his stubby legs. His go-fetch days were gone, but he seemed excited to be outside. She watched him and wondered if his floppy dog-ears could hear the phantom song that caused her such trouble.

It had begun in class last week. While Miss Lillian was talking, Regina heard a simple melody. A chord played twice, notes flowed downward, back to the chords. Chords, descending notes, and chords, all played on what sounded like a synthesized violin. Each note echoed, lingering a few seconds before fading. Regina didn't mind the music itself, which she felt was sadly lovely.

The problem was that nobody else heard it. Miss Lillian and the other kids carried on like it wasn't playing. Regina even nudged Kiley, her nearest classmate, and said, "Do you hear that music?" Kiley looked at her like she was nuts.

Regina excused herself and followed the song into the hallway, where it sounded louder. She went upstairs to the third floor, where it played louder yet. It stopped when she came to the hatch in the ceiling. At that point Regina made a double pact with herself: she wouldn't tell anyone what happened, and she would find a way to reach that hatch.

Bullet pooped, and Regina picked up his turds with a plastic bag. He followed her to the garbage can by the dugout, the spot where she usually released him and headed back home. But not today and not just yet, she decided. The weather was too pretty, and a boring chore awaited her. She might as well enjoy this bit of freedom and visit the Smash Heap.

She took Cherry Way away from the field and toward the surrounding woods. The street shed its houses, then sidewalks, then pavement, narrowing down to a dirt road. Regina walked the central hump between its furrows. Bullet wove around the trunks, plowing through leaves. He found his favorite tree and circled it, looking up and squealing. No squirrels this time. They teased him to a frenzy when they were home, shaking their tails at him, even dropping twigs on him, and yet he always came back for more.

A steep hill rose to the right, and a creek tinkled in the groove between Cherry and the base of the slope. The creek ran a ruddy color like tomato soup, and even Bullet knew not to drink from it. To the left, a clearing opened for Regina's secret playground.

A shack once stood there long before she was born. At some point someone had wrecked a Plymouth Horizon into it, buckling the walls and dropping the roof. Nobody ever removed the car or cleaned up the debris. Instead, people used the site for a dump, burying the shack with stuff they didn't want. Castoffs were piled as high as the shack's brick chimney, and from there the jumble expanded into the clearing.

Dad had banned Regina from the Smash Heap a hundred times. "Rats, tetanus, derelicts. End of discussion," he said the last time she asked for a reason. Regina kept sneaking trips anyway. The Heap felt safe to her. She had never encountered anyone there, including rats or derelicts. She loved the randomness of the mess, how objects were thrown together in ways that made no sense. Sometimes she even discovered something valuable, like the four bungee cords she'd fastened together to make the grappling line for the hatch. How mad would Dad get if he found out about that? Best not to dwell on it, she thought.

With Bullet at her feet, Regina skirted the perimeter of the Heap. She passed the ripped-up sofa and bathtub full of broken records. She stepped up onto the TV with a cracked screen, jumped off onto the rusty box spring. No bounce, as always, but that never stopped her from trying. She opened the fridge to find the same dirty magazines as last time, growing fuzzy with mold. She kicked a salad bowl, watched it clunk against an air conditioner.

Regina moved inward toward the main pile, and everything looked the same as last time. She picked up a stick and whacked a filing cabinet just to hear the hollow clang. The stick spun like a helicopter blade when she chucked it, and it thunked into the open mouth of a clothes dryer. "Gooooal!" she said to Bullet, who was sniffing a toaster oven.

She was looking for another stick when the chord played twice. The notes followed, and the chords repeated. Then it looped all over again, and again, the echoing song. Regina scanned the premises, saw no one. She ran to Bullet and crouched to lift his chin.

"Can you hear that? Listen. Do you hear it?"

Bullet licked her fingers and showed no sign of hearing anything.

The sound seemed to come from above again, from somewhere on the hilltop over Cherry Way. Regina crossed the dirt road and paused at the creek, craned her neck back to look up. This rise before her wasn't a mountain, but it was still forbidding enough. She had never climbed it before, never had a reason to try. Falling from it probably wouldn't kill you, she thought, but you'd still get jacked up.

Regina didn't care. She jumped across the creek, landed at the foot of the hill. Bullet stayed behind, watching her from the roadside.

Locusts and oaks grew near the bottom, gripping the earth with thick webs of roots. She scrambled upward, slipping a little with every step. Touching the trunks for balance, careful not to twist an ankle, she heard the song all the while.

The slope tilted against Regina, but she kept up her pace. She climbed over fallen trunks, dislodging discs of fungi, and pushed through tangles of chapped vines. The ground hardened, and fall leaves gave way to evergreen needles that grazed her face.

Regina was sweating, her breaths were shortening, and her heart was thumping double-time. Yet she never looked back to see how high she'd climbed, never even slowed. Chord, chord, notes flowing downward, chord, chord. She couldn't stop, not until she reached the top, not until she saw the source of the song. She attacked the last stretch, hurtling herself up to the summit.

The hill crested to a ridge of black rock, and Regina stopped upon it. Lightheaded and exposed to the wind, she breathed and tried to gain her bearings. Only then did she see the drop-off before her, a cliff to the mere hill she'd scaled. She prodded herself toward the edge and peeked over. Her nerves jolted her back fast.

The muddy, dull Monongahela snaked under the cliff. Car-specks crawled along a highway on the far side. The stacks of the Works were downstream on her side, shrunken by perspective. Upstream the river curved around a peninsula that housed the big rusty cube she recognized from yesterday.

The song kept playing while Regina watched the building. It looked like another hunk of neglect, nothing more, but she had to wonder. Twice she followed the song to a height she normally wouldn't climb, and twice her trip ended with a view of the cube. What if it was some kind of giant music box, long silent and newly sprung?

As if to answer her, the song played louder, forcing her to cover her ears. The cube's color changed gradually but clearly. Its rust darkened to black then lightened to gray then brightened to silver. The sun struck it with a glare. She closed her eyes, and they watered to recover.

The song stopped. The echo of the last note trailed off, replaced by the wind and the whoosh of distant traffic. Regina lowered her hands and dared to squint at the cube. It had returned to its usual orangish self.

She waited and gave it time to toy with her again. The cube didn't respond. No chameleon trick, no song. It left her alone to her sweat and galloping heart, alone on a cliff and no longer trusting her senses.

Tail beating, squealing with relief, Bullet rushed her when she jumped the creek. She crouched down to him with apologies for leaving. He forgave her with face licks and kept licking until she kissed his forehead.

This had to stop, Regina thought, this chasing a song no one else could hear, let alone seeing things that disappeared in a blink. But who could she tell? Everybody already thought something was wrong with her, from the other kids, her teachers, and Principal Klemko to Dr. Wohler and Dad. That was bad enough, but if she told anyone the truth, she'd be in the biggest trouble ever. Dad might even get rid of her like her real parents did, take her back to the orphanage for a refund.

No, she decided. Better to keep this to herself. If something was wrong with her, she would handle it, and nobody needed to know. In the meantime, it sure wouldn't hurt to have some earplugs.

6. Broadway

"Yes, Dad," Regina said, phone in hand, sprawled on her bed with her stuffed animals Mo the Orca, Slick the Dolphin, Wubby the Penguin, Roo-Roo the Kangaroo. While Dad talked (and talked), she fished a few dollars of her allowance from the stash in Roo-Roo's belly pocket.

"Okay, Dad," she said, gaze wandering from her posters of Sailor Moon and Princess Mononoke to the Catwoman action figure on her dresser. When Dad asked how that three-page report was going, she imagined Catwoman cracking her whip at him, making him cower.

"Great. Everything's great. See you when you get home." She hung up and checked the red digits of her clock-radio. 12:07. Plenty of time to go to Pharm-Rite, come back, and do his stupid report.

Regina stepped around the stalled projects on her bedroom floor: her would-be airship, made with a bendy-straw frame and plastic-wrap skin, damaged since the time she launched it out the window; her ant farm, lifeless since the time she fed the ants baking soda to see if they would turn purple like Toby from homeroom said; her 50-in-1 electronics kit, wired to function as a metal detector, its cardboard body smashed since the time Bullet rolled off the bed and landed on it.

She stopped by the living room to say bye to the dog, but he had fallen asleep. He looked too blissful to disturb, paws twitching like he was dreaming of running. She closed the door behind her very gently.

Regina reached Broadway fifteen minutes later. Dad was always comparing it to what it was when he was young and complaining about how rundown it had become. He took its failings personally, but to Regina the street was kind of neat. She had no memory of it thriving, so it left her to wonder what it might have been like, providing hints with its empty storefronts.

She passed Candy World and the gingerbread man painted on its front window, Sally's Deli and its marquee advertising chip-chopped ham and bottles of pop for 25¢, Susie Jo's Salon and its rows of space-helmet chairs, a branch of First Trust bank and its marble columns wrapped with razor wire.

The next block felt relatively lively. Murdoch's Pawn Shop and Campizi Pizza were still open, almost as open as the mouth of the old guy asleep behind the pizzeria's register, a fly buzzing around his head. Regina watched him long enough to confirm he wasn't dead and continued on past Club Climax, the place with a mirrored female silhouette on its door. Muffled oldies pounded behind its black-tinted windows. Some rock band from the '80s, Regina guessed, the kind with guys who wore makeup and sprayed their hair.

She came to MacAdder Plaza, Broadway's public square. A statue of Raymond MacAdder stood upon a pedestal in the center, and benches curved around the pedestal in a semicircle. Regina had seen the statue from Dad's car a hundred times but never up close, and that felt like reason enough for a detour.

The copper MacAdder grew to superhuman size as she neared him. His beard reminded her of Santa Claus, although he was neither fat nor jolly. He wore a long heavy coat and posed with his hands on his hips. His face had the grim look of a taskmaster, but that hadn't stopped birds from pooping all over him.

A metallic squeak sounded from the neighboring building. Regina turned around, startled to see the basement door of Ribbitski's bar opening. A black guy climbed up out of the hole, wearing a dirty winter coat and frayed tossle cap. His gray dreadlocks mingled with his beard, which had scraps of paper in it. Duct tape held his left shoe together.

Regina was tempted to hurry away, but the guy didn't try to approach her. He left the door open and limped toward a bench.

"You like Ray Mac, huh? Better kiss him goodbye while you can. They tearin' him down soon, him and his whole damn town. I'm talkin' demolition. Boom! They blowin' it up, you watch. They got plans for the Downs, *big* plans.

"Think I'm kiddin'? I seen 'em myself. They call themselves 'Condor.' They ride around in a van, takin' pictures, sizin' up buildings to blow. I even seen blastin' caps in that van. Those boys ain't playin'. Know what I'm sayin'?"

Regina stared at him, not knowing what he was saying.

"Shit, I'm confusin' you and never introduced myself. The name's Mason."

Regina continued staring at him and said, "I'm not supposed to talk to strangers."

"Smart girl. I can respect that. Lots of creeps out here. Tell you what. I ain't gonna grab you, offer you candy, ask you for nothin'. Won't say another word if you don't. I'm only here 'cause here's where I gotta be."

Mason reached inside his coat, pulled out a cup and piece of cardboard. "Vietnam Vet -- Please Help" read its black magic-marker lettering. He propped the sign against the bench leg, set the cup next to it, and sat.

Regina looked back to the statue and snuck a few glances at Mason. She didn't trust him, but he did make her curious. And she doubted he could move quickly enough to kidnap her.

"I thought everybody liked Raymond MacAdder. Everything's named after him," she said.

"True. Whole town's built with his money, plaqued with his name. But not everybody liked him. He made lots of enemies, got a lotta blood on his hands. You wanna know, go up the library and talk to Tom. He tell you *all* about Ray Mac and whatever else you wanna know. The man's a walkin' history lesson. You tell him Mason sent you. He tell you what's what."

Regina had encountered Tom before and didn't care for him. He seemed like a guy who talked down to people because they weren't as smart as him. However, if Tom knew anything about the cube at all, it might be worth the trip.

"Between me and you, I'm no fan of Ray Mac," Mason continued. "Never hired no brothers in his lifetime. Long after he kicked it, we *still* had to fight to work at the Works. And now his time's up, simple as that. New money comin', new power. History's nothin' to the Almighty Buck. If it was, you be seein' a totem pole and tepees in this square."

He yawned and lay down on the bench. "So the money's comin' back on Ray Mac now, erasin' his ass. Let it, I say. About damn time."

Three blocks beyond the Plaza, Regina closed in on the Pharm-Rite, which was set back from the street by its large parking lot. She saw no cars in the lot, only a man and two kids. The man looked as raggedy as Mason and pushed a shopping cart full of cans around the building. He wore a blue flannel shirt and a Steelers hat, his face wrinkled like a raisin. His cart bucked, and he stopped to kick its wheel and talk to it. The kids were skateboarding by the front door, where they had set up a ramp with plywood and bricks. They took turns doing jumps and stumbling off their boards upon landing.

Regina hesitated at the edge of the lot, not sure about those kids. They were big and possibly mean and kept using the F word. She considered turning back but scolded herself for being chicken. Maybe they won't bother me, she thought, and proceeded with dread.

"Yo!" one of them said soon enough. Regina kept her head down, kept walking. "Yo! I'm talking to *you!*" They skated over and blocked her way.

One kid was white with tattoos that colored his arms. A dozen chains hung from his belt, clinking around his jeans. His hair was dyed black except for a blond stripe down the middle. The other kid was brown with cornrows and wore his jeans low enough to show off his boxers' waistband. "Scarface" read the text on his t-shirt, which depicted a guy screaming and firing a machine gun. Both kids' eyes were glassy, and they both smelled like an odd non-tobacco smoke.

"We saw you watching us like you was afraid. And you should be, 'cause we're fierce fire-breathing motherfuckers," the tattooed kid said. "Why you here?"

"Shopping," Regina said.

The kids looked at each other and laughed.

"A customer! Aww, shit! A real, live customer! Get a picture of this, yo," the cornrowed kid said.

Regina didn't know what was so funny and resumed walking. The kids kept pace, skating alongside her.

"You got a name, pastyface?" the tattooed kid said.

"No," Regina said.

The kids laughed at that, too. The tattooed one said, "I'm Skunk. He's Jamal. We're just messing with you. We're not gonna do nothing."

"Why ain't you at school?" Jamal said.

"I'm suspended," Regina said.

"Damn! A hard case. My kind of kid!"

A girl stepped out of the Pharm-Rite and lit a cigarette. She was seventeen or eighteen, Regina guessed, as old as the boys. Her blue hair was shaved bald on the sides. Three rings stuck out of her eyebrow, one through her nose. She wore a black t-shirt with a cartoon cat on the front, a plaid skirt, ripped fishnets, combat boots.

"These clowns giving you a hard time?" she said to Regina.

"Ooh, look at the big manager, asserting her authority," Skunk said.

51

"Yeah, Kim. You sold out. Once you got promoted, you turned all corporate and shit," Jamal said.

"You just don't like taking orders from a woman. Get over it, boys. World's changing," Kim said.

"Woman? All I see's a blue-haired dude with a face only a magnet could love," Jamal said, and laughed with Skunk.

Kim flicked her cigarette at them, which only made them laugh harder. "Can I help you?" she said to Regina.

"Do you have earplugs?"

Kim held open the door even though a handwritten sign taped to its glass read "Store Closed. Thank You For Your Business."

"Ignore whatever they said. They're annoying but harmless," Kim said as Regina entered.

The store looked like someone had run through its aisles with outstretched arms, determined to knock everything off the shelves. Hair brushes and clips and curlers and perm kits blanketed Aisle 1. Toothbrushes and toothpaste and soap and deodorant cluttered 2. Diapers and paper towels and toilet paper swamped 3 with puffy whiteness. Skulls and anarchy A's sparkled on the floor of 4, each image drawn in glue and covered with glitter.

"The sign says you're closed," Regina said.

"We are, and we aren't. The CEO got slammed with a bunch of charges last month. The company was supposed to fold, and everybody quit but us. But then nothing official happened. Nobody ever came for my keys. I called headquarters, got the voicemail, left messages nobody answered. Whoever's in charge forgot about us. So we keep showing up, waiting to see if we're getting paid or what."

They came to Aisle 6, Cold Remedies, which had been looted half-bare. Kim found a pack of earplugs and handed it over.

"All yours, on the house. This place doesn't need your money. It needs someone to use this crap before it ends up in a landfill."

They headed back to the exit, but Kim blurted, "Oh, fuck!" and stopped short of the door. Regina froze, too, and followed Kim's eyes to the door's glass. A police car had turned off Broadway and into the lot. It sped toward the store, swerved out of sight.

Pharm-Rite had one front window, a horizontal strip set high in the wall. Kim hurried to it and stood tall enough to see outside. Regina needed more height, so she stacked plastic shopping baskets by the window to improvise a lift.

Two policemen had exited the car, leaving its doors open. Regina recognized them as the same ones who gave Dad a hard time, Officer Valducci and Chief Kagan. Valducci shoved Jamal to the car hood, bent him over, patted him down. He squeezed Jamal's privates and smacked the back of his head. Jamal tried to say something, and Valducci hooked an arm around his neck and hauled him to the ground.

Kagan pushed Skunk against the trunk of the car. Regina couldn't hear the chief's words through the glass, but his red face showed that familiar rage. He went to the kids' ramp, picked up the plywood, and heaved it away. Then he took Skunk's skateboard and threw it across the lot, too.

The chief thrust his chest in Skunk's face, yelling with spittle flying, and Skunk shrank back like Dad did. Meanwhile, Jamal lay facedown, covering his head with his hands. Valducci put his boot on Jamal's knuckles and kept shifting his weight, teasing like he might stand on Jamal's head.

While the policemen were threatening the kids, the raggedy man in the blue flannel pushed his cart toward the scene. He stopped by the car, observed, and made no move to leave. Valducci glared at him, and Kagan approached him.

Unlike Dad and Skunk, the raggedy man didn't flinch when the chief screamed in his face. Regina wondered if the raggedy man might be deaf. He didn't even react when the chief yanked the cart from him and overturned it, spilling its cans everywhere.

53

The chief pointed at the mess, spat something angry about it. Both policemen then went back to their car, said some parting words to the kids, and tore out of the lot.

Jamal stayed down, still shielding his head. Skunk looked at his friend and their dismantled ramp and looked ready to cry. Only the raggedy man seemed unaffected by what happened. He righted his cart and went about regathering his cans. Crouching to reach for a few, he faced the window.

Regina couldn't be sure, but she thought he might have spotted her. It was hard to tell with his hat's visor shadowing his eyes, but he did pause. Then he lowered his head and continued the cleanup. She stepped down from the baskets, gut-sick from what she'd seen.

7. Sacred Heart

Colton parked his Lexus in the lot alongside Sacred Heart, a century-old church in the Slopes. Its terra cotta roof and twin spires made it highly visible for several blocks in all directions. Its loudspeakers made it easy to hear, too: canned bells every hour, every day, from dawn to nightfall. On his way to its basement door, Colton passed a sandwich board sign that read "Welcome! Wednesday Night Bingo! 6:00 to 10:00!"

A fog seared his eyes and sinuses upon entry. Dozens of players hunched over cafeteria tables, blowing as much smoke as the Works' stacks ever did. Their haze shaded the overhead lights, stained the white walls gray, coated every surface with sticky residue.

Dolores the organist moonlit as the bingo caller. She presided over the game from a platform in the corner, turning a crank that turned a cylinder full of ping-pong balls. She stopped, opened a hatch in the cylinder, and pulled out a ball. Leaning into a microphone by her side, she said, "B-4. B-4. B-4 you call out, make sure you have a bona fide bingo. B-4."

A few players chuckled and ended up coughing. If any of them noticed the mayor by the door, they didn't care enough to acknowledge him. This didn't bother Colton, who understood game-time focus even if the game was bingo. He scanned the room and saw Grady in plainclothes, alone in the back corner.

"Where's Vic?" Colton said, sitting opposite the chief.

"Ribbitski's. Want me to call him?"

"Don't bother. This shouldn't take long."

"Christ, I hope not. Why do we gotta meet here, anyway?"

"The priest's request. You know how he is. Maybe it's his way of keeping us humble."

"Fuck him. He's the one who needs humbled."

"Careful, Chief. We're talking about a man of the cloth."

"He doesn't work, he pays no taxes, he's against the war, he's never fucked a woman, and he flits around in flowing robes. You call that a man?"

"I know you hate him, and you always have. But could you try to be respectful? For me?" Colton said.

"You're the boss," Grady said, and slouched deeper in his chair.

"I-22," Dolores called. "I-22. Two little duckies. Quack, quack, quack. I-22."

Colton looked at the neighboring table, where bewigged and wizened geriatric women chatted with cigarettes on their lips. Next to them blobbed an obese woman so bloated she needed a chair for each ass cheek, her muumuu spotted with fast-food grease. A few seats away, a haggard mom tried to hold a baby, play the game, and reason with a five-year-old brat all at once. The baby wouldn't stop crying, and the brat wouldn't stop running up and down the aisle, saying, "You can't catch me! You can't catch me!"

At the end of the table, directly across from Colton, a shriveled little man bent over his cards. He wore bulletproof-thick glasses and a golf hat. His head kept bobbing, and his hands shook with Parkinson's. It took him so long to pick up and place each chip, Colton guessed he was playing several numbers behind the calls.

These were Colton's people, the Downsers, and he couldn't see them without seeing his own failure. They'd filled the stands to cheer him as a boy, voted him to power as a man, and look where he'd led them. To a smoke-choked basement, gambling away their dying dollars and kids' lunch money. Two terms, and what had he accomplished?

Sometimes it depressed him that he'd stayed when so many had left. He could have gone anywhere after college, but he came back. The move felt noble in his twenties, like he was showing loyalty to his family and declining town. Now in his forties, Colton often second-guessed his path. Maybe loyalty had been his excuse for cowardice, for lacking the balls to leave the place that comforted him, the one place where his name commanded respect.

Some champion still lived in him, enough to fight such self-doubt. Colton would never quit on the Downs, refused to believe he couldn't rescue it. He'd pulled off enough last-minute comebacks to know there's always a way. You keep playing your hardest, and the breaks will come. Just last year, in fact, a huge game-changer arrived in a surprise visit.

At first he thought it was a joke. When his receptionist buzzed his line and said two FBI agents would like to see him, he laughed and told her to make some fresh coffee. Her pause and the way she said, "No, really, Colton" corrected him right quick.

Names and sums flashed through his mind. He'd taken kickbacks from Julius Construction, Kenney Asphalt, Stratus Ironworks, and Chemicore, always Chemicore. The slumlord Schultz who owned half the Flats, Ribbitski to keep his poker machines. And those were just the ones who'd paid him that week. There were others, not to mention his own dealings with council...

Shit, he thought, paralyzed in his chair. *Shit!*

Two men entered his office. They showed badges, introduced themselves as Agents Martinez and Poole. Martinez had a round face and spiked hair, was pudgier and younger than Colton had expected. Poole, on the other hand, had to be pushing retirement; his suit alone looked older than Martinez. His face was weathered, shoulders rounded, hair thinned to a wispy comb-over. They took their seats, and it soon became clear that Martinez would do the talking, Poole the quiet watching.

"Do you have a moment? We'd like to ask you a few questions," Martinez said.

"Am I under investigation?"

"Should you be?"

"No," Colton said. "But it's not every day the FBI comes to Burdock Downs."

"These are strange days, Mr. Mayor, but you can relax. No need to call your lawyer. We're not investigating you, though we are interested in your town. It appears that Burdock Downs has been economically distressed for many years: saddled with debt, continually losing population, its median income and property values stuck somewhere between nil and zilch. Its business district is a dilapidated eyesore. A large section, the Flats, has more vacants than residents. Environmentally, it hasn't begun to recover from the steel era. Is that an accurate assessment?"

"One could see things that way," Colton said.

"In your opinion, would Burdock Downs stand to benefit from an extensive federally funded redevelopment project?"

"Probably. What exactly are we talking about?"

"How do you feel about the War on Terror, Mr. Mayor?"

Colton hesitated, thrown by the odd shift. "I'm a patriot. See, look," he said, and tapped the American flag pin on his lapel.

"And Guantanamo Bay?"

"Hey, whatever it takes. Like the president says, it's time to take off the gloves. I don't care what you do to terrorists. Do what you gotta do, fine by me. But am I missing some connection here? I don't see what Gitmo has to do with Burdock Downs."

Martinez looked to Poole, who gave him a nod to continue.

"Mr. Mayor, what I'm about to tell you is confidential. The fact of the matter is that we're looking for a location to stage a highly classified operation. We want a space in which we can work without scrutiny or interference. With its warehouses, transportation lines, and state of neglect, the Flats section seems to suit our purpose.

"We can't divulge details of the operation itself. I can only tell you that it involves security and is rather unpleasant. The more sensitive among us might even consider it unacceptable. We risk the press, your colleagues, business owners, and the general public noticing our arrival and questioning our activities.

"Therefore, we need cover, which brings us back to redevelopment. If we were to act as a contractor and undertake major construction here, no one should suspect that we're doing anything else. This is where your cooperation could help. Think of the redevelopment as a productive diversion. Sell it to your people, and you give us valuable leeway.

"Granted, you would concede some power in allowing us to conduct our business as we see fit. In return we're offering you a brand new Broadway. Such a coup just might save your town, Mr. Mayor. Any questions?"

Colton sat there stunned and trying to comprehend what he'd heard. "This can't be legal" was all he could say.

"The Attorney General has signed off on it," Martinez said. "I do find it amusing that you would raise such a concern, seeing as how you've accepted so many contributions from serial polluters and tax delinquents like Chemicore. And how you're the mayor of Burdock Downs when you reside in Gladbury Parke."

Colton looked from man to man to the floor. He gulped and said, "I can explain. I –"

"It's better if you don't," Poole said.

"I thought you weren't –"

"We needed to know who you are. That doesn't mean we're charging you," Martinez said. "But that could change if you were to tell anyone about this conversation, including your wife and lawyer. In time we might permit you to reach out to a few close associates. For now we insist on discretion."

Martinez and Poole rose to their feet, both standing over the mayor.

"A representative from Condor Development Corps will contact you within the week, assuming you're willing to cooperate. Are you willing to cooperate, Mr. Mayor?"

"Bingo!" Grady shouted.

Dolores squinted at the chief through the smoke. Players shot skeptical and annoyed looks his way.

"My bad," Grady said with a smirk, and the players groaned.

The priest arrived shortly after ten, entering from a door by the platform. Within minutes someone called a real bingo, and the players started for the exit. Colton watched as almost all of them stopped to talk to the priest on their way out. The priest listened with patience, gazed with empathy, shook the men's hands, hugged the women. The players liked and trusted him, showed more warmth toward him than any mayor. That impressed Colton enough, but it downright amazed him when he remembered the priest as a kid. The players knew him as Father Andrew, but to Colton he would always be Andy. Painfully shy Andy, who never raised his voice or looked anyone in the eye, now pitching sermons and pressing the flesh. Knowing how much Andy had grown, and what he'd grown to become, Colton couldn't help but admire him.

One player, the old man with Parkinson's, lagged behind the rest. He was still gathering his cards and chips after everyone else had left. Andy stopped by and talked to him, told him not to worry about cleaning up, even helped him to the door.

"Laying it on pretty thick with the sainthood bit, don't you think?" Grady said to Colton, who said nothing.

And then some of us never grow, the mayor thought. Some of us become what everyone knew we would from the time we were kids. Some of us accept our birthrights and follow our fathers, left to wonder what else we might have done. Say that much for the priest: at least he had the balls to become what he wanted, far from his family and the Downs, at least for a while.

Andy seated himself across from Colton, two chairs away from Grady. Quite the pair, Colton thought, two men coexisting in a constant chill. The priest was thin with glasses and wavy gray hair, the chief bulky with a buzzcut. The priest placid, the chief tense with resentment. The priest thoughtful and deliberate and considerate, the chief likely to say and do what he wanted and fuck you if you didn't like it. They tolerated each other only by avoiding each other.

Colton didn't kid himself about Andy and Grady. He knew it wasn't his charismatic leadership that brought them together nor decades of friendship; it was Condor's promise of a fat payout. Even so, they looked to him to begin, his authority unspoken and understood. He pulled a map of the Downs from his jacket pocket and spread it upon the table.

"So we're all on the same page," Colton said, and pointed to a spot in the Flats. "Condor has set up its base here at the old Happ's plant. They're closing off these blocks of Broadway over the weekend. Demolition scheduled for Monday. These blocks next month, the rest in December. Construction will start right after the holidays. First with the plaza here, then the new buildings here, here, and here. And you're making a face, Father. What's up?"

"It's not about the demolition or construction," Andy said.

"Then what is it?"

"We might have a problem, Colton. I've been hearing some grousing about last night. The community's disturbed to learn that you've had so little contact with Condor. That you hadn't even met the CEO until the meeting. As for Waters himself, let's just say that he didn't charm them."

"I'll admit that Waters threw me. The Condor reps said he's eccentric, kind of a recluse. I never thought he'd show up. And I don't know what I imagined him to be like, but it wasn't who I saw last night. That's for sure."

"He looked like a little punk bitch. I could break his neck like that," Grady said, and snapped his fingers.

61

"There must be something hard about him, or he wouldn't be where he is. You saw what he did to Bixler. That wasn't a hatchet job, that was a buzz saw," Colton said.

"And if Waters could do that to Bixler, how do we know he won't do the same to us?" Andy said. "We've all made mistakes, committed sins that would hurt us if brought to light. I'm sure Waters could find them if he looked hard enough, went back far enough."

"What are you getting at?" Colton said. "That I had too much fun as a kid? Threw too many interceptions? What?"

"Not just you. All of us," Andy said, and lowered his eyes to the map.

"I know what it is," Grady said. "Father's keeping some altar boys we don't know about. Hiding 'em under the tablecloth, slipping 'em some Jesus Juice when nobody's looking."

"Leave it to you to find the humor in child abuse," Andy said, not looking at Grady.

"Yeah? And what are you gonna do about it? If the dress fits –"

"Stop it! God damn it! Both of you, stop it!" Colton said. "I don't like what I'm hearing here. I don't like the bickering, and I *hate* the fear. If I understand you, Father, you're asking if I trust them. I have to, don't I? They knew I wasn't pristine when they came to me, but they made it clear they'd lay off so long as I cooperated.

"Why? Because they don't care about me or you or anything we've done in the past. Their priority is their operation in the Flats, whatever the hell it is. They're spending the money, they're putting on this Condor circus to cover their own asses. We're just small potatoes helping it along to help our bankrupt town. Nobody could fault us for that, right?"

"Bixler did, and Bixler paid. That's what he got for crossing me one time too many. We're not mourning Gus Bixler at this table, are we? Should we go upstairs and light a candle for him? There was always some risk to this, Father. You knew that going in. It takes balls to play this game. Now's not the time to lose them."

"I'm asking valid questions. You don't have to bludgeon me with the macho jock talk," Andy said.

"Then let's be clear. If the community's as antsy as you say, it's your job to reassure them. Don't forget that I brought you in, Father, because you're so good at telling people what they need to hear. But if *you're* antsy, then you'd better tell me right now. Are you really gonna back down when we're so close to... to..."

"The goal line?" Grady suggested, amused by Colton's glare.

Andy looked down to the map again. "Of course I'm with you, Colton. I never said I wasn't."

Colton took a breath and slackened. "Sorry, Father. Sometimes macho jock talk's all I've got. It's a limitation I've learned to accept.

"You're not wrong to ask questions. And you did give me an idea. Maybe we should try to approach Waters while he's in town, reach out to him in some way. Invite him to a private function. I'm sure he'll decline for the sake of security, but the gesture can't hurt. If he does show up, maybe we'll learn something about him. Like it or not, we're in bed with him now."

8. Library

Regina ate her Choco-Rox cereal and pretended not to notice Dad watching her. She kept her eyes down to the table and her three drawings: a section of the Mon as seen from a hilltop, the river curving around a peninsula that housed a cube-shaped building; MacAdder Plaza, its statue looming over a man asleep on a bench; two police officers beating up two kids in a parking lot while a raggedy man pushed a shopping cart.

They weren't her best work, but Regina still liked them enough to feel slighted when Dad hadn't complimented them. She stopped eating, met his look, and said, "What?"

"Don't 'what' me. You know what."

"You said a three-page report. You never said it had to be written."

"Aren't you clever? You were supposed to think about what you did in school. What do those pictures have to do with that? I didn't ask for a comic book, Reggie."

She looked at the drawings again, refrained from defending them.

Dad finished his coffee, left the cup in the sink as always, and stooped to kiss her cheek on his way out. "Same plan as yesterday, and you're not off the hook. Three pages, written. With words. In English."

Regina listened to his departure. Top door, footsteps, bottom door, car engine. Once he was gone, she fetched her shoes and jacket. Bullet perked up with a squeal, eager for another run at the squirrels.

"Not yet, boy. But I'll come back as fast as I can, I promise."

She climbed Elsinore Street in the Slopes, Broadway behind her and MacAdder Library ahead. The building took up an entire block, its stone walls giving it the heft of an ancient temple. A bronze lion stood guard by the broadside wall and overlooked the hill. Twin lionesses flanked the front doors, facing Elsinore on their bellies like Sphinxes. An engraving above the doors read "Free to the People."

Regina entered the main floor, walked past long tables and hardback chairs. The room invited her to look up, up at the high bookshelves she could never hope to reach, up to the second-floor walkway circling overhead, all the way up to the diamond-shaped skylight.

Tom was seated behind the information desk, reading a newspaper. He was older than Dad, with bushy gray hair and beard, wearing a brown cardigan. He was so focused on that paper, he didn't notice Regina standing just a few feet away. There was no one else in the library, no sound but Tom grumbling to himself through gritted teeth, "Fuck you, Cheney. Go have another heart attack, you evil fuck. Fuck you, too, Dubya. Monkey-faced moron piece of shit."

Turning the page, he glanced up and did a double take.

"Oh! Hello there! Guess I, uh, guess I didn't see you come in. Wait, I know you. You're that kid who likes those Japanese cartoons. Jenny, is it? Jessica?"

"Regina."

"Close enough. What do you need? Looking for a book?"

"No."

"Noooo. Who reads books anymore, huh? No, we got cable TV, video games, the Internet, and the attention spans of gnats. Great. God bless America." Tom grabbed and rustled the newspaper. "Hear that, Dick? You got what you wanted. You got your hive. A generation of illiterates good for nothing but consumption. You win, oilman. You win!"

66

He tossed the paper aside and looked at Regina. "So I guess you want to use the computer? Go shopping online? There it is. There's your golden calf. Go. Throw rose petals at it."

"I came here to ask you something. Not to get yelled at."

"Who's yelling?" he said, deaf to his own volume.

"A guy named Mason said you know all the history of Burdock Downs. So I thought maybe you could tell me about a building. The one that sits out on the river, like it's stranded on its own island. Looks like a big rusty cube."

"I know Mason, all right. He wanders in sometimes when the weather's bad. Poor soul. A true casualty of the Machine. And of course I know that building. MacAdder's Folly. Why does it interest you?"

"I don't know. It speaks to me in a way."

"You know anything about Ray Mac himself?"

"He built the Works, got rich, put his name on everything. And not everybody liked him."

"What about this building you're standing in, Regina? Know anything about it?"

"It's a library. It has books," she said warily, thinking he was messing with her.

"It has something else, too," he said, and jingled a key ring on his belt.

Tom went to a door stenciled "Staff Only," unlocked and opened it to a dark hallway. Once he found and flicked the light switch, he walked ahead and didn't stop. Regina hesitated, for she didn't fully trust him, but she was too curious to dawdle for long.

The corridor's brass light fixtures matched the library's style. However, most of the bulbs had burned out, and the brass hadn't been polished in her lifetime. Dead roaches littered the floor, and dead spiders dangled from cobwebs above, swaying as she passed. Around a corner and through another door Regina went, and stopped, jarred by the abrupt change. She'd gone from a cramped and drab hallway to a spacious and brightly lit room draped with a curtain of ivy green velvet.

Tom waited for her by the far wall, holding a rope that hung from pulleys overhead. He worked it down, hand over hand, the same way she operated the Bullevator. The curtain parted to reveal a theater, and he had led her onto its stage.

Regina faced the seats, rows upon rows receding beneath a balcony. Crown molding topped the walls with a sculpted floral pattern. The ceiling curved up in a dome, and its chandelier bloomed with a swirl of glass petals. The seats and walls were dark green, the woodwork brown. Between its color scheme and plant theme, the theater evoked a forest.

For all that, one detail captured Regina's eye. The floral pattern banded across the balcony, breaking for a lion head in the center. The beast had faded under the dust. His mane had grayed, face paled to beige, eyes gone opaque. He mimed a roar minus an upper fang, splinters marking the loss. She found him pitiable, especially compared to his bronze siblings outside.

"Whoa," Regina said. "I had no idea this was here. Any of it."

"Pretty cool, isn't it?" Tom said, and joined her at center stage. "It was something back in the day. People would come from around the world to perform here. Symphonies, ballets, plays. Magic shows, lectures, debates, you name it. And free admission, too, if you worked in the mill. Compliments of Ray Mac himself."

"That was nice of him," Regina said.

"That's what he wanted everyone to think. He used to brag about all the wonderful opportunities he gave his workers to live full, meaningful lives. Self-development, he called it. The idea was to exercise both your body and mind. If you busted your tail in the mill but had access to Art and Culture, you'd somehow become a better person. The Works brought the work, this place offered the rest. That was the idea, at least, but this was never just a gift. His workers paid for it, all right. Believe me, they paid.

"Anyway, you can see that nothing happens here anymore, and nobody cares. The Foundation barely keeps it standing, and the Downsers don't miss it. They have their Steelers football. That's all they need."

"What's up with the lions?" Regina said.

"That involves a bit of MacAdder family history. I'd hate to bore you with it."

"I asked because I want to know."

"Do you now?" Tom said, and met her stare with a smile. "All right, then. Way back in the 1830s, before Ray Mac was born, there was an enterprising Englishman named Knox Barlowe. He owned the Magical Menagerie, a collection of wild animals he'd imported through London. Big cats like lions and tigers, antelopes, a few zebra, an ostrich, kangaroo, chimps, boa constrictor, even a crocodile. Keep in mind, this was before there were a lot of zoos. So for most people, the Menagerie was their only chance to see these animals.

"Barlowe toured them all over Great Britain, raked in a lot of money. During a stop in Glasgow, Scotland, a young man named Angus MacAdder approached him. Angus had come from a family of sheep herders in the Highlands. He'd moved to Glasgow to support his poor parents by working as a shipbuilder.

"Angus was hooked the second he saw the Menagerie. Forget shipbuilding; he knew right away that he wanted to join Barlowe's crew. Barlowe was reluctant, but Angus convinced him he could handle any animal without fear. So Barlowe hired him as the wrangler's assistant, and within a few years Angus took over when the wrangler retired.

"Time passed, and Angus met a lass named Nessa. They married, had a son named Raymond. She and the baby stayed in Glasgow while Angus traveled with the show.

"Meanwhile, the public's taste was changing. Just seeing animals in cages didn't impress people anymore. They wanted to see the animals *do* something. They wanted action, spectacle. So when Raymond was four years old, Barlowe staged a special event called 'lion baiting.'

"Barlowe and Angus brought their lion Brutus to a field in North Wessex, where Barlowe's new partners had set up a tent and cage. These partners bred Staffordshire Bull Terriers, which are basically pit bulls. The plan was to have three dogs fight Brutus before a paying audience.

"Well, it didn't go as planned. Barlowe and Angus had never seen Brutus defend himself but assumed he would. The breeders thought the dogs would do some damage, put on a good show, but still die. Instead, it turned out that Brutus just wasn't aggressive. The dogs attacked and attacked and tore him up, but he wouldn't fight back. Angus even jabbed him with a sharp stick, but that didn't rouse him, either.

"The dogs mauled Brutus' paws, gashed his face, took a chunk out of his flank. Barlowe stopped the fight to save him, which really ticked off the bloodthirsty mob of an audience. Made them mad enough to throw rocks. So the Menagerie fled the field, heckled and pelted all the way.

"Late that night, when Barlowe finally stopped the wagons for a rest, Angus went to check on Brutus. And guess what happened."

"Brutus had died?" Regina said.

"No. Good guess, but no. Brutus wasn't dead, just different. All that power and anger the crowd wanted to see, it was like he'd withheld it from them. Like he'd stored it, waiting for the right moment. Like he'd remembered the hurt of the stick-poke more than all the dog bites. I say "like" because who can ever know what an animal's thinking? The point is, when Angus reached in between the bars to give Brutus a chicken, Brutus skipped the bird and went right for Angus' arm. He bit down and ripped it off at the elbow.

"Angus was lucky to survive, but Nessa and little Raymond might've wished he hadn't. He returned to them a broken man, good for nothing but getting drunk. He took to beating Nessa and wasn't above hitting the boy, too. Nessa didn't put up with it, though, bless her heart. She squirreled away the money she earned at a textile mill and got in touch with family who'd come to America. She made the jump when Raymond was six, taking him with her and leaving Angus to rot in Scotland.

70

"Many years later, after he made his fortune, Ray Mac built buildings and decorated them with lions. People noticed this and asked about it. He claimed to trace his ancestry back to a clan with lions on its coat-of-arms. It was one of his favorite lies. Of course he never mentioned the story of Brutus and his father," Tom said, and gestured to the lion face in the balcony. "So there you go. A glimmering tile in the grand mosaic of history."

"I don't get it," Regina said. "Why would he keep reminding himself of something so bad? You'd think he'd want to forget it."

"I can't read Ray Mac's mind any more than I can read Brutus'. I guess we'll never know what these cats meant to him. That's a funny thing about us, Regina. We're always telling each other something about ourselves, whether we want to or not. Whether we're conscious of it or not. Through our words, how we act, how we make ourselves look, by what we create and leave behind. We may not even know what we're saying, and there's no guarantee anyone's getting the message. But we keep sending it anyway, fueled by our constant need to communicate."

Tom closed the curtain, turned out the lights. Regina followed him back through the hallway, silent and trying to understand what he meant. When they returned to the library, she remembered her original question and reason for this visit.

"Thanks for showing me all this, Tom. But what about the building I asked about?"

"Persistent, are we? I like that," he said with a chuckle. "I didn't show you around just for the fun of it. I wanted to get a read on you, see if you have a mind that likes to learn. To see if you have something going on in that little coconut, and I think you might."

Tom scanned the empty room with shifty eyes and lowered his voice. "The question is, can I trust you? If I lend you something most people don't know about, will you promise to keep it safe?"

"Maybe. What is it?" Regina said.

"Normally I favor books, but sometimes you gotta go audiovisual." Tom opened his desk's bottom drawer, reached behind folders, dug under papers, and fished out a videocassette. Its cover depicted Raymond MacAdder, the words "Robber Baron!" splashed across his face in red text. In the background, three cartoon pigs in top hats gorged on a trough full of cash, their cheeks bulging, bills sticking out of their mouths.

Regina reached for the cassette. Tom jerked it back.

"I mean it. The Man's already breathing down my neck for the stands I've taken. You can't let anybody see this. If somebody does, God forbid, you can't tell them where you got it. I'd get fired for lending you this."

"Why? Is it dirty?"

"Ha! Hardly! No, it's nothing but the truth, and sometimes the truth is a dangerous thing. Are you prepared to face it?"

Regina reached for the cassette again, and this time he let her have it.

"Thanks. I'll keep it secret," she said, and took a closer look at the cover. "Tom? If you hate Raymond MacAdder so much, why do you work here?"

"Because I refuse to slave my life away to some soulless corporate Moloch! Here, at least, I can share some knowledge and serve the community, even if it's under the MacAdder banner. I didn't sell out, damn it! I'm still in the fight!"

Tom sank into his chair and deflated with a sigh. "Oh, what happened to us? We had such beautiful hair! What happened to our Garden? Gotta get back to the Garden."

He closed his eyes and hummed a melody. Regina wondered what he meant again, but Tom didn't look to be answering any more questions. He continued his humming, punctuating it with mumblings about bombers turning into butterflies. She took that as her cue to leave.

9. Robber Baron

Regina sat on the living room floor with a peanut butter sandwich, Animal Crackers, and a glass of milk. Bullet sniffed the picnic and settled beside her with a grunt. She hit the play button on the remote, and the TV screen brightened to white.

A graphic of a black fist appeared over the words "Black Hand Productions." The film opened with black-and-white footage of a steamship approaching the Statue of Liberty. A synthesizer droned in ominous tones fit for a horror movie, and the narrator spoke.

This is the American Nightmare, the story of how one man made a vast difference for the worse. How greed corrupted his soul and conscience, turned him into a monster who valued money above all else. This is the story of Raymond MacAdder.

He was born on February 6, 1841, to Angus and Nessa MacAdder in Glasgow, Scotland. Angus was a lion tamer who lost an arm to one of his imprisoned, mistreated animals. A drunken failure of a man, Angus took out his frustrations on Nessa and Raymond until they fled to America in 1847.

The ship dissolved to a painting of a port. A river forked off into two branches, outlining a wedge of land. Steamships and barges traveled the water while columns of smoke arose from factories crowding the wedge. A charcoal haze hung over the scene.

They arrived in Pittsburgh, Pennsylvania, joining Nessa's relatives in that city's Scottish community. They found little comfort in their new home, struggling to support themselves like so many before them. Nessa worked in a glass factory while Raymond swept chimneys.

Dissolve to a sepia-tinted photo showing several boys Regina's age. They wore soot-blackened clothes, and their faces were dirty and grim. The text "Raymond MacAdder, age 11" appeared under one particular boy.

Cut to a woman in her thirties wearing cat eye glasses and a red sweater with a black blazer. She also held a wineglass sloshing with dark drink. Text identified her as "Dr. Kyra Viskovich – American Studies, University of Pittsburgh."

"No question it was exploitation," she said. "You think there were *laws* to protect these kids? Hell no! Since they could squeeze into chimneys, their size made them a commodity. Plus they were cheap labor, starved for any table scraps that fell their way. Today we know that frequent exposure to soot causes scrotum cancer. But back then? Who knew, who cared? Just shove 'em in a smokestack and pay 'em peanuts. If their balls grow tumors, oh well. Get more kids."

Cut to another photo, this one showing a young man seated at an office desk. He was tapping a telegraph key, which Regina recognized from her 50-in-1 electronics kit. A visor obscured his eyes, but his nose and mouth gave him away as the chimney sweep grown up.

MacAdder resolved to escape the life of manual labor that had worn down so many of his peers. When he wasn't cleaning chimneys, he spent his high school years running messages between local businesses. Privy to gossip and the latest job openings, he learned of a telegrapher position at the Keystone Railroad office in 1859. MacAdder immediately applied to the superintendent Arthur Kittener in person, impressing the executive with his assertiveness.

The camera pulled back to reveal an old man standing behind MacAdder. He had white mutton chops and a rotund build that stretched his vest. Checking the younger man's work, he seemed confident that all was going well.

Cut to Viskovich, who said, "Historians like to paint it as a surrogate father-son relationship. The wise elder schooling his youthful charge, imparting sage wisdom on the lad, grooming his heir. Blah, blah, blah. Those same historians tend to ignore evidence that Kittener was buggering MacAdder, who gladly bent over and took it for the sake of promotion.

"Here's what we know. Once Kittener hired MacAdder, Mrs. Kittener complained to her friends that her husband spent too much time with the boy. Meanwhile, MacAdder shot right up the Keystone ladder, from telegraph operator to second-in-command in a few short years. And then Kittener died of a heart attack while on a 'business trip' in which he shared a hotel room with MacAdder.

"Hey, no accusations, no judgments. Just sayin'. It's not like MacAdder would've been the first, or last, to screw his way to the top."

Cut to silent-movie footage of a train speeding into a tunnel, through plains, and slowing to a stop in a station teeming with people.

MacAdder became Keystone's superintendent upon Kittener's death in 1864. Despite the shareholders' concerns about MacAdder's age, he soon proved to be more skilled than his mentor. During his tenure, he would guide the railroad to unprecedented profits.

Cut to an old, balding man with sleepy eyes. His mouth drooped at the corners, and his jowls flapped against his turtleneck. "Prof. Alan Maxwell – History, Duquesne University" appeared as he spoke.

"What did this twenty-three-year-old wunderkind do that his competitors hadn't? Rigorous cost analysis. He tracked the performance of every man and machine. He knew what every employee was doing, where and when and to what capacity his trains were running. He knew what everything cost and sought more efficient practices to limit those costs.

"A man obsessed with efficiency often shows keen interest in technology. MacAdder was no exception. He demanded the newest, fastest engines and largest cars for maximum capacity. But then he faced a problem: most rails were made of iron, which couldn't support his increasingly heavy trains. Seeking a stronger rail, he turned to the steel industry."

Cut to interior footage of a steel mill. A blast furnace poured a stream of molten iron. A man in silhouette stood by a vat of the glowing brew, stirring it with a pole. Machines rolled the white-hot liquid into sheets, cast it into beams.

Steel. The backbone of America's industry. The bedrock of her prosperity. The blunt instrument of her empire.

"But what did MacAdder find?" Maxwell said in voiceover. "Rampant inefficiency. Steelmaking requires limestone, iron ore, and coke, which is a byproduct of coal. These raw materials were embedded throughout the Great Lakes region and Appalachia. First you had to mine the minerals, then bring them together and heat them to refine the iron. Then you had to reheat the iron to further purify it. Then you had to mold your metal into a useful shape.

"MacAdder saw lags in every step of the process, from mining to combining to burning to transportation. Middle men controlled the supply lines, and mill operators produced far below capacity to protect their equipment. MacAdder sensed that if he took the plan he'd perfected at Keystone and applied it to steelmaking, he'd make a killing."

Cut to a map of Pennsylvania. A dot marked Pittsburgh at a point where three squiggly blue lines converged. The lines represented rivers. The Allegheny came down from the north, the Monongahela up from the south, both meeting to form the Ohio, which flowed westward. A second dot marked Burdock Downs along a bend in the Mon.

As the 1860s drew to a close, MacAdder left Keystone and invested much of his wealth in steel. He built a mill in Burdock Downs, a town outside of Pittsburgh. Here MacAdder would realize his dreams of efficiency, cost control, and on-site integration.

Dissolve to a photo of the Works, which looked dinky compared to the version Regina knew. It was just a cluster of brick buildings, lacking its current barn-like structures, towering blast furnaces and conveyers, big rusty ducts. She only recognized a row of stacks near the river. Otherwise, the photo could have been showing any factory anywhere.

The Works' location, between the Monongahela river and a Keystone line, ensured the rapid transit of materials at a bargain. The proximity of its furnaces and converters also drastically shortened production time. MacAdder pushed his equipment with no regard to its limits, always eager to upgrade should it break down.

This ingenious blend of design and execution paid off, as the Works quickly surged past its competitors. By 1880 it rivaled the output of Great Britain's entire steel industry, making MacAdder one of the wealthiest men in America.

Cut to Viskovich. "A heartwarming fairy tale, isn't it? The self-made man with a vision. He comes to this country a poor immigrant boy, works hard, builds a business, earns a fortune. All the individualist Horatio Alger nonsense you can shovel.

"The truth is more brutal. MacAdder's workers endured hellish conditions. They were constantly exposed to poisonous waste gases, not to mention oceans of molten ore. A furnace could malfunction and shower them with liquid death at any moment. One slip, and they might fall into a vat of the stuff. These guys were clocking twelve-hour days, seven days a week. No vacations, no sick days, no pensions, no health coverage. If a man was injured or killed, and many were, his family had no safety nets."

Cut to a photo of men leaving the mill. They were a crowd of tired bodies with grimy clothes and skin, eyes in a trance. Not a smile among them, Regina noticed, but also more mustaches than she'd ever seen in one place. Every other guy seemed to have one.

Workers. The true heroes of America. Determined to feed their families while maintaining their human dignity, MacAdder's employees unionized, forming the Fair Labor Alliance in 1881. When their collective bargaining agreement expired in 1886, the union proposed a forty-hour work week and a pay raise proportionate to the mill's soaring profits. These were reasonable requests by any reasonable measure.

77

Cut to a photo of MacAdder, bearded and resembling the Plaza statue. He stood near a long window, the incoming light casting half his face in shadow. A cigar smoldered between his fingers. His hard stare cut through the smoke and leveled contempt at the camera.

During the course of his rise, MacAdder had forgotten the plight of the common man. He flatly rejected his workers' wishes and suggested they take a pay cut instead. In his words, "They should appreciate the opportunity I've given them, but they mewl like ungrateful babies. Do they not know how utterly replaceable they are?"

Confronted with such callous opposition, the union staged a strike on June 26, 1886.

Cut to a photo montage, each image dissolving to the next: a crowd of men gathered before the mill's entrance, shouting with raised fists; a mother and five children among the men, the smallest daughter holding a sign that read "Fair Pay – No Less"; a one-legged man on a crutch, hobbling in a picket line, a boy walking alongside the man and holding his hand.

Gunshots.

Cut to a photo of men with rifles stepping off a train. A flaming barge on the Mon. A man lying in a street, blood gushing from his head. Children running and screaming toward the camera, a mob of adults brawling behind them.

MacAdder dispatched a squad of armed Pinkerton agents to secure the Works on July 10. Today's historians still disagree as to who fired the first shot, but none can deny the final result. An eruption of violence claimed the lives of ten workers and nine Pinkertons. Shocked by the workers' resistance, the Pinkertons fled Burdock Downs in a shameful display of cowardice.

Dissolve to a photo of men dressed like Civil War soldiers, marching in formation, rifles on their shoulders, Stars and Stripes flying at the head of their column.

MacAdder then appealed to Governor Robert Pattison, who deployed a state militia of two thousand men to restore order. By July 13 the militia had imposed martial law on Burdock Downs after gunning down four more workers. The strike was broken, the union defeated. MacAdder's workers would return to the mill on his terms.

Cut to Viskovich, who said, "After such a tragedy, you'd think MacAdder might have learned something. Might have become more introspective about how he was treating others. But no. All he learned was that he'd won and that guns solve problems. From there it was full-blown hubris, full speed ahead to his Folly."

Cut to a photo of a stone wall with an archway in its center, turrets on its corners. Dissolve to a large brick building, a loading dock jutting out across its frontside. Horse-drawn wagons lined up along the dock while men rolled or carried barrels inbound or out. Dissolve to a courtyard with cannons and pyramids of balls in the foreground, the brick building and stone wall in the background.

In the wake of the strike, MacAdder developed an interest in the arms industry. Noting Europe's rising militarism and the U.S. government's ongoing clashes with Native Americans, MacAdder hoped to capitalize on the world's insatiable demand for weapons. In 1894 he built the Alexandra Arsenal in Burdock Downs, two miles upriver from the Works. The facility was named after the twenty-year-old Alexandra Kaye, whom the fifty-three-old MacAdder married earlier that year. It would produce rifle cartridges and artillery shells.

Cut to Maxwell. "It was an experiment, a chance for MacAdder to test his strategy in yet another industry, and it started auspiciously enough. The arsenal matched most of its competitors within two years, and the Spanish-American War generated a windfall in 1898. But then came another labor problem."

Dissolve to a photo of girls gathered on the loading dock. Children younger than Regina sat along the edge, their feet dangling. A row of teens stood behind them, a woman in a suit off to the right.

With most local men employed at his mill, MacAdder hired a female team for the arsenal. 'The Boom Girls,' as they were nicknamed, spent long hours rolling brass and packing it with gunpowder and lead. Despite the hazardous nature of such work, MacAdder paid the Boom Girls half the salary of their male counterparts in the Works.

The camera closed in on the woman in the suit. She had a pale, frosty beauty with sharp cheekbones and dark hair. Her gaze retained its captivating power a century later.

As his wife fell ill with tuberculosis, MacAdder conducted a romantic affair with Evelyn Lakatos, an arsenal employee. In 1901 he promoted Lakatos to an executive position overseeing the arsenal's operations. At a time when men dominated the business world even more so than today, Lakatos' ascent was considered highly unorthodox if not reckless.

However, the risk paid off. Just as the young MacAdder excelled at Keystone, Lakatos defied her own skeptics. The arsenal's production and profits climbed steadily on her watch, and its workforce developed a strong loyalty to her.

Cut to Maxwell. "You might describe the MacAdder-Lakatos relationship as 'stormy.' She had no problem standing up to him on behalf of the Boom Girls, advocating shorter workdays and more stringent safety measures. They argued on the lab floor more than once, openly before the Girls, and yet MacAdder never disciplined Lakatos.

"Some historians believe that MacAdder truly loved Lakatos and couldn't bear to punish her. Others think he might have met his match, as Lakatos was known to be very smart and strong-willed. The most colorful explanation is that MacAdder feared Lakatos' mother, Saraya, an alleged devotee of the occult. MacAdder alternately refers to Saraya as a Satanist, a pagan, and 'that damned witch' in his journals. Unfortunately, we know little else about Saraya, except that her influence in Evelyn's life was much stronger than MacAdder would have liked.

"All this speculation might be amusing, but let's not forget that MacAdder was a businessman first and foremost. He might have loved Lakatos, but he certainly wouldn't have promoted her if he didn't think she would succeed. As for his leniency with her, we can safely assume that was a business decision, too. Whatever his thinking, the tragedy of 1907 rendered the arsenal's politics irrelevant."

Fade to black.

The sound of an explosion, followed by screams and roaring fire.

Fade in on a photo of the arsenal grounds. The brick building had been destroyed, reduced to ash and rubble. Cart wheels, rims, and axles were scattered among cannons and balls, bricks and charred wood. Crows picked at a horse carcass.

July 27, 1907. The Alexandra Arsenal suffered one of the ghastliest accidents in American labor history. According to a federal investigation, gunpowder had been accumulating between the flagstones of the arsenal's access road over time. On that fateful morning, a horse's shoe sparked off the stones, igniting a fire that caught the powder kegs stacked upon the main laboratory's dock. The resulting blast set off the powder magazines, secondary labs, and barracks in a devastating chain reaction.

Dissolve to the photo of the girls on the dock. The camera panned over their faces in closeup. They seemed happy to be together, happy to be photographed. They seemed like friendly girls who might have been nice to Regina if she'd lived among them.

The human toll was staggering. Forty-eight were killed in the laboratory explosion alone. Another twenty-four later died from burns and wounds. Dozens more were severely injured for life. The fatalities included Lakatos, her mother, and nearly all the Boom Girls.

Cut to Viskovich. "MacAdder received a telegram and hurried from his Pittsburgh mansion to see the damage firsthand. True to form, he thought of his money first. He could have respectfully buried the dead. Instead, he ordered his minions to flush the bodies into the river with water cannons.

"MacAdder claimed he did this for sanitary purposes. That was the spin. But years later, his goons admitted that he'd ordered them to leave nothing to bury because he didn't want to pay for so many funerals."

She looked at the camera with a smirk and said, "Welcome to the dark side of capitalism, kids."

The camera stayed on Viskovich as she gulped down wine and continued, "I'm not so sure it was an accident. I don't mean to sound like Oliver Stone, but it's fishy. I don't *know* that MacAdder sabotaged his own lab to get rid of Lakatos and her mother, but isn't it *convenient* that their threat to his power was so *efficiently* dispatched that day? The government said it was an accident? That means nothing. We know they were in his pocket, and we know what MacAdder thought of his 'utterly replaceable' workers.

"Really, would it surprise you to find out he torched the place himself? If MacAdder thought he could've come out ahead, would you really put it past him? I'm not advancing conspiracy theories here, I'm just sayin'. Just sayin.'"

Dissolve to a photo of the scorched peninsula, the river in the background. The stone wall, archway, and turrets lay collapsed in the foreground. Workers swarmed the ruins, removing debris.

The arsenal was a total loss for MacAdder, and he never attempted to replace it. He chose to build a different structure altogether, leaving the rest of the site barren.

Dissolve to another shot of the peninsula. The workers were gone, the grounds cleared except for the cube. It wasn't dark with rust but bright and shining, as silvery as it had appeared to Regina yesterday. The image froze her, stopping her cupped hand full of Animal Crackers halfway to her mouth.

The press dubbed it 'MacAdder's Folly,' for it came at a steep cost to its creator. Its completion took five years, eight different construction crews, and thirteen million dollars. MacAdder himself steadfastly refused to discuss the structure. His intent in erecting it remains a mystery to this day.

Cut to Maxwell. "It's one of those great boondoggles. Here you have this master industrialist, this icon of pragmatism, and what does he do? Squanders millions on a huge useless cube. Nobody even knows what it's supposed to be. Is it a monument? A piece of modern art? Did MacAdder even know what it was?

"I don't ask that facetiously. The arsenal disaster consumed MacAdder. His physical and mental health quickly deteriorated post-explosion. Dementia plagued his final years, and the Folly was quite possibly the result of his addled state."

Cut to a photo of MacAdder in a wheelchair. He was hollow-eyed, frail, and wrapped in a blanket that failed to hide his withered condition. A nurse was pushing him through a garden, maneuvering among rows of flowers. Blurred leaves framed the shot as if the photographer had been hiding among trees.

In 1908 MacAdder retreated to a mansion near the town of Stillwater, New York. He spent his last six years bound to the estate. He was also very much alone, as Alexandra had died in a sanatorium shortly after the move. They had no children.

The camera closed in on MacAdder's face.

Mortality scared MacAdder into a flourish of generosity. He sold the Works to Carlisle Steel in 1910 and donated the payout to Burdock Downs. His foundation funded new infrastructure and provided capital for a business district, school, and library. He also penned essays praising the virtues of his workers.

Ultimately, however, MacAdder's late bid for atonement neither saved him nor changed the past. He died on February 10, 1914, at the age of seventy-three. No one attended his funeral.

Cut to Viskovich. "He was an ugly old goat. For decades he was notorious for buying sex from his female workers and fathering children he didn't support, all while his poor wife was coughing up blood in a TB ward. He was throwing fistfuls of money at prostitutes right up to the end. And you know what his autopsy showed?" She held up a hand, spread her thumb and index finger slightly apart. "Three-inch penis. Really. Remember that next time you see a picture of him.

"I don't care how much sucking-up he did in his senility. His gifts don't erase the Strike of '86, the Disaster of '07, and his overall greed. And if you visit Burdock Downs today, you won't find a bustling metropolis, to put it kindly. Oh, MacAdder definitely has a legacy, but it's not the one he wanted."

Dissolve to a split screen of two photos previously shown: workers leaving the mill on the left, MacAdder smoking a cigar on the right.

Viskovich continued in voiceover, "He illuminates this country's fundamental divide between the wealthy elites and the rest of us. When it came down to treating people like people or protecting his money, he chose the money. He drew the battle lines so clearly a child could see them. The super-exclusive, all-powerful, privileged white male patriarchy on one side, and everyone who's ever had to work for a living on the other. I guess we should thank him for that.

"Yes, thank you, Raymond MacAdder, for being everything it's okay to hate."

Dissolve to white. A graphic appeared, showing a black hand pointing at the camera.

Which side are you on? the narrator said.

Fade to black.

10. Singles Bar

Off-duty and out of uniform, Vic Valducci knew something was wrong when he'd entered Ribbitski's. It was a Thursday night, but the place was empty. No Stan Probanic weighing down the corner stool with his bowling-ball gut. No Hildie Krotto parked at the poker machine in sweats, showing her ass-crack. No Steve Lowry passed out by the glass-block window, drool dripping down his chin. Not even Frankie Ribbitski, bartender and owner, white t-shirt stained yellow at the armpits, head bald and liver-spotted.

Vic sat upon a stool and scanned a room full of familiar sights. Above the liquor bottles were photos of the young Frankie home from Korea and Frankie's son between tours of Vietnam. Thumbtacks pinned an American flag over the photos, its loose edge fluttering from the ceiling fan. On another wall a poster of the Twin Towers hung alongside Frankie's hardhat from his days at the Works. The TV was perched up in the corner, flashing with commercials.

He knocked on the bar and called Frankie's name. Nothing pressing awaited him at home, just microwave pizza and a rerun of *Bassmasters*. But he'd come to Ribbitski's to drink, not to admire the decor. The eleven o'clock newscasters chatted about the upcoming Steelers-Chargers game. Otherwise, the bar was silent.

Vic noticed a glass left on the poker machine. One of Hildie's highballs, ice not yet melted. Drops of liquid had landed on the screen, magnifying its pixels. Someone had left a cue and a few balls on the pool table, too, having quit midway through a game. A toppled stool lay near the jukebox, a man's shoe nearby.

Vic called Frankie's name again, louder, and heard movement in the back room. He'd left his duty belt in the car and considered leaving to retrieve it. The back-room door swung open before he could move, however, and the person who emerged wasn't Frankie.

Lonnie Waters wore ripped jeans, a black AC/DC t-shirt, and a dirty apron. Strands of reddish-brown hair hung about his face. "Frankie's indisposed at the moment," he said, and poured a shot of Grey Goose for Vic.

"How'd you know?" Vic said, meaning the drink.

"I'm observant."

Staring down shitbags came with the job, and Vic could do it as well as anyone. He'd arrested countless junkies and drunks and a handful of wackjobs in his seventeen years. His experience filed Waters with the wackjobs. Waters didn't just meet Vic's stare but seemed to welcome it, smirking as if the two men were sharing a funny secret.

Vic blinked, looked to his drink. He had to remember that Waters outranked him, Grady, even Colton. Whatever this was, it called for tact. "Everything okay here? Place looks a little roughed up," he said.

"You're wondering why I'm here," Waters said. "I was hoping to find a lady. Maybe I picked the wrong place."

"Yeah, this ain't that kind of bar. It's more of an old-man joint," Vic said.

"Then let's pretend. Let's imagine a woman walks into this fine establishment. She doesn't have to be a model. Not a knockout or a fox. Not a hot bitch, as you might call her, but passably attractive. Not ugly, better than plain.

"Let's say she sits right here. And over there by the pool table, four guys are watching her. Of course they're watching her. No way any pussy's coming in here without them appraising it, judging it. 'I'd do it.' 'I wouldn't.' 'Gimme another drink, and I would.' Standing there holding their dollar drafts. Some stubble, guts, love handles. Such manly American specimens.

"One of them makes eye contact, decides he'd do it. Now, here's where it gets good. Picture his approach, how he walks with confidence. No hunching, no head down. Can't look timid in this game. Chin up, eyes locked on hers, and easing onto that stool right there beside her. If she doesn't have a drink, he orders one. If she does, he asks her something.

"And really, it doesn't matter what he asks. You don't need dialogue to enjoy this scene. Just watch him gaze so *deeply* into her eyes while she's talking. He nods a lot, smiles, leans closer by degrees. He's doing his damnedest to show interest in what she's saying, even if it's a bunch of trite crap about her job, her dog, her family, where she's from, the weather. None of it matters. He wants to fuck her, that's all, and he doesn't care if he's being subtle about it.

"But she's not interested. She may be alone, and not so hot, but she just doesn't feel like riding this guy's cock tonight, spoilsport that she is. So she drops some hints of her own. Mentions a husband or boyfriend, maybe a child. Says she has to wake up early, and oh, my, would you look at the time.

"That's when the guy's face is priceless, that moment when he realizes he's not getting any. And yet he lingers, still nursing his beer, still gazing at her, still rapping. Telling his stories, telling his jokes. Though it obviously ain't gonna happen, he's gotta keep working it. While it might be important to keep his pride, it's more important to get some if he can. To not give up so easy. If he could just keep her there, keep hammering away, maybe just maybe she'll submit to his charms.

"But nope. No thanks and goodnight. She picks up her purse and leaves him to his bros. They tweak him a little, sure, but mostly they talk about what a cunt she is. Who needs her anyway? She wasn't even that hot."

Waters let his eyes drift away from Vic, and said with a note of regret, "Just think, this is happening in some bar somewhere as we speak, and we're missing it."

Vic downed his shot with nothing to say. He didn't want to be there and sensed that Waters knew it. He tried to think of an exit line as Waters poured another.

"On the house, of course. A privilege of the badge. For all the good work you do."

"Thanks," Vic said, edgier than intended, and looked to the TV.

"It's *The Tonight Show with Jay Leno*! Tonight's guests: George Clooney, The Blue Man Group, and The Pussycat Dolls..." said the off-camera announcer. Leno walked out onstage to wild applause and squawked through his jokes. The studio audience roared with every punchline. Vic felt Waters watching him in a lull that grew more awkward as Leno's monologue went on and on.

"So, what happened to Frankie?" Vic said, hoping a different topic might help.

"Tell me, Victor, what kind of women do you like? Athletic? Petite? You like 'em chunky?"

"Athletic's good."

"Good, *good*. Personally, I'm not attracted to women. Now, don't go grabbing your pepper spray. I'm no faggot, either. No, I don't get off on cock. What I like is pain. Better yet, the anticipation of pain. The look on a man's face when he knows he's about to get fucked and fucked hard. Especially a man who thought he had power. One who's used to doing the fucking."

"Why are you telling me this?" Vic said.

"A September night twenty-five years ago, in the playground behind Suncrest Kindergarten. There was a fire, beer, a spirited debate about AC/DC. A girl named Maura joined you and your friends, and I know what you did to her, Victor. I'm here and telling you this because she was my sister."

It took Vic a few seconds to remember, but he did. He knew the night and could still see the girl. He'd tried to bury the memory and never talked about it with anyone. Not when she ended up dead in the river a few months after that night, not in all the years since. The mere mention of it now froze him from his toes to fingertips. His throat dried and tightened. He wanted to drink but couldn't grip or lift the glass.

Waters watched Vic all the while, savoring his discomfort. A smile tugged at Waters' lips, drawing lines that aged his face. His pupils seemed to swallow their irises, turning his eyes to voids as the bar's door opened and closed.

Vic forced himself to turn partway around, enough to see the figure entering the bar. At first glance he saw a six-foot-tall body with broad shoulders and cut muscles and assumed it was a man. However, this new stranger had a square-jawed woman's face. She wore black leather boots and pants, a studded dog collar fit for a pit bull, and a white tank top stretched tight by her torso.

The woman hadn't entered alone; she was dragging an unconscious Frankie Ribbitski by the ankle. The seventy-five-year-old scraped the floor, face bruised, eyes and mouth duct-taped shut. She crouched, grabbed him by the throat, and hoisted him onto the pool table in one fluid move. Balls clacked with the impact. One hopped the bumper and hit the floor rolling.

She walked over to the bar and leaned against it, next to Vic, eyeing him with cold regard. Up close her figure looked curvier, her face softer. Her lips and cropped hair shared the same black-cherry color. Long lashes set off her blue eyes. Blood speckled her tank top and hands. Vic still wasn't sure that she hadn't been a man before. Hell if he knew anything anymore.

"Victor, meet Mirzeta," Waters said. "Look how athletic she is, and exotic, too. She's Bosnian, in case you're wondering. She was eleven in Srebrenica in '95, where she lost her mother, father, brother, and sisters. When the Serbs tried to have their way with her, she resisted. For that they took her voice and so much more. So, even though you don't know her, I think she knows you and your kind very well. Is that fair to say?"

Vic looked to his glass. He lifted it with an unsteady hand and gulped the shot. After setting down the glass and letting the alcohol burn down his gullet, he said, "What do you want from me?"

"Hit her."

"I can't – no, I can't do that."

"Sure you can, tough guy. Go on, take a swing. I know you have it in you. Or do you only get aggressive when your bros are there to back you up?"

Stay calm, Vic thought. Whatever you do, stay calm. No sudden moves. He pressed his hands to the bar to still their trembling and said, "I need to leave."

"Funny. My sister once said the same thing. But hey, it's okay. You can go. We're not vindictive people here. I just want one thing from you, Officer. Just one thing."

Waters pulled a cell phone from his pocket and held it close to Vic's fear-stricken face. Its camera flashed. "There, now that's a picture. Yes, sir, I'll be masturbating to that one long after you're dead."

Vic had no chance to answer. Mirzeta threw a left hook that broke his jaw. He dropped off the stool, landed with a thud to rattle every glass in the place. She stomped, boot heel pulping his eyeball in its socket. Stomped again, cracking his front teeth. Again between the eyes, bashing his skull against the hardwood. Vic blacked out, and she kicked his temple anyway. And kicked his ribs just to feel them give.

"Hey, easy now. I have to mop that up, you know," Waters said.

Mirzeta stood over the body, weighing whether to kick it again.

Waters stepped out from behind the bar, took her hand, and brought it to his lips for a kiss. "Easy," he whispered. "Easy, my lovely."

Mirzeta searched his face for any sign of insincerity. Seeing none, she blushed and gave his cheek the gentlest caress. He closed his eyes and licked her bloody knuckles.

11. The Folly Beckons

The red digits of Regina's clock-radio read 1:46 when the phantom song woke her. Chord, chord, notes flowing downward, chord, chord. Disoriented at first, she needed a moment to realize where she was and what was happening. Chord, chord, she stumbled to her light switch, scanned the room for her earplugs, chord, chord.

Regina ripped open the pack, took out two foam cylinders. She pinched and rolled them, jammed them in her ears. They made no difference. The song played through the earplugs at full volume.

Bullet slept on the floor as oblivious as always, and nothing else in her room had visibly changed. But this was her one private space, not an outside place like school or the Heap. If the song could follow her here, how could she hope to escape it?

Regina considered waking Dad but thought better of it. Seeing no other choice, she turned off the light and buried her head under pillows, blankets, Mo the Orca, and Slick the Dolphin. And still she heard the synthesized violin.

It stopped at 2:04. Regina lay awake and awaited its return, her fear turning to anger. She didn't know how to get to the Folly or what good it would do, and she didn't care. She was sick of being bullied from afar. At least she might confront the source, see it up close. She owed herself that much, her thumping heart marking every second of a sleepless hour.

"Dear Dad," she wrote at the kitchen table as the Cavalier sputtered away. "Hopefully you'll never read this. But if you do, I went to MacAdder's Folly, the cube-shaped building on the river. If I'm not home when you are, something happened to me between here and there. XOXOX – Regina"

By eight o'clock, she was on Broadway with a water bottle and flashlight in her backpack. She passed the Plaza and Pharm-Rite and didn't see Mason or the skateboarding boys. Not that it mattered; she was in no mood for chitchat anyway. Nor did it matter that she was heading for the Flats, which Dad had always told her to avoid. From what she could see, the Flats filled the space between Broadway and the Mon. If she had to cross that space to reach the Folly, so be it.

The Flats' numbered streets ran north-south, gridded with east-west avenues named after presidents. Regina took a left onto Sixth Street because it looked like a straight shot to the river. With Broadway behind her and Garfield ahead, she approached a brick building painted yellow. An air conditioner sagged out of its front window at a perilous angle. "Repent and Be Born Again!" proclaimed text on its side. An old man sat on the stoop with a CD boombox on his lap, blasting a sermon. He wore a hospital gown and sunglasses and rocked back and forth to the cadence of a prerecorded preacher.

"And on that great day, when the Lord God shall look upon us and all our deeds, large and small, the powerful and weak shall be judged equally!" cried the preacher.

"Amen! Amen!" the old man answered with the congregation as Regina passed. "You tell 'em!"

"And it won't matter, children, what make or model you drove, or how voluminous your bank account was, or how high upon the hill your mansion stood. You will answer to the *Lord*!"

"Amen! You tell 'em, brother! You tell 'em!"

The street decayed as she strayed farther from Broadway. Between Garfield and Grant stood a row of houses gutted by fire. They'd lost their roofs, windows, doors, and porches, and yet Regina sensed they weren't empty. She couldn't help peering into their gaps and shadows as she walked by, thinking she glimpsed movement or spying eyes.

Three teenage kids leaned against a garage across the street, on the corner of Grant. A sickly-thin woman was trying to talk to them. Her clothes hung loose, and patches of her hair were missing. One kid kept telling her to fuck off and go away while the others ignored her.

"I know I'm ugly," she said. "Just close your eyes. I'll suck your dick for five. Just gimme five."

"Get the fuck outta here. Nobody wants your nasty crack-smoking lips on their dick."

"I oughta kick you. You a *mean* motherfucker. It ain't funny. It *ain't* funny!"

The kids and woman quieted when they saw Regina, who didn't dare make eye contact, and resumed their dispute behind her as she continued toward Lincoln. Regina noticed that everyone she'd seen in the Flats was black, which reminded her of the time she asked Dad why all their neighbors on Pike were white.

"Because the Downs is segregated. That's one of its charms," he said.

Sensing sarcasm, she asked what "segregated" meant.

"It means the black people stick to one part of town, like the Flats, and the white people stick to another, like the Slopes or Pike, and they don't hang out together much."

"Why?"

"Because the Downs is fifty years behind the times."

"So how come you always tell me not to go to the Flats?"

"The Flats are rough, but that doesn't mean black people are bad. Don't think like that."

"But why are the Flats worse than the rest of town?"

"It's not about race, it's about money. The whole town's broke, but the Flats are the poorest part of all. And when some poor people get really desperate, they do things they wouldn't normally do, like turn to crime."

"So poor people are criminals, and most poor people are black?"

"No. No! Poor people aren't necessarily criminals. And black people aren't necessarily poor or criminals. You have no reason to fear poor people and/or black people. No reason to treat them any differently than anyone else."

"Can we take a walk around the Flats then?"

"No."

"Why not, if there's nothing to fear?"

"Do you bring up this stuff at school?"

"No."

"Good. Don't."

Regina stared at Dad and waited for a real answer.

"There's a lot to it, Reggie. It's complicated. Someday I'll tell you all about racism and classism, the cycle of poverty, and the drug trade. But tonight I'm tired. Just don't go to the Flats. That's all you need to know."

He never did revisit the topic, and she never asked her next question, about why they didn't have any Hispanic or Asian neighbors, either. The Royal Dragon and Señor Taco take-out joints on Broadway were the only signs that such people had ever lived in the Downs, and both places were out of business.

After Lincoln, Sixth Street traded homes for warehouses. Every one seemed huge to Regina, each occupying its own block and rising high enough to dim the sun. Seeing little variety in their boxy shapes, she focused on their textures and colors: sky-blue corrugated metal for BD Valve Co., tan-painted cinder block for Rieger Appliance, basic brick for Drax Vending, checkerboard of rusty aluminum and plastic siding for Schorlach Welding Supply.

She came to the Happ's Ketchup plant on the corner of Sixth and McKinley. Unlike its neighbors, Happ's had a distinctive sign. A large mural on its facade showed a bottle spilling a river of the red stuff, which in turn spelled the company name in gloppy letters. It was also the only place with any activity on its loading dock. A fat white guy with a hardhat and clipboard stood by a van while two skinnier guys tried to lug a box into it. All three men wore navy blue coveralls. The van was also navy, "CONDOR" printed on the driver's door.

"Hurry up! We don't get it rigged by noon, the boss is gonna be pissed!" the fat guy said.

Regina paused to watch them from across Sixth Street. The fat guy spotted her and lowered his clipboard. She averted her eyes to a jeep, the only other vehicle parked at the dock, and noticed its bumper sticker. A space alien with antennae, blocky like an old video-game graphic. It was an odd bit of cuteness out of place with everything around it, and she had to wonder what it meant to the jeep's driver.

"Whatta ya lookin' at?" the fat guy said to her.

Regina hurried onward, knowing she'd heard of Condor before. She couldn't remember where, though, as Happ's and the rest of the Flats fell back behind her. To open air and the railroad tracks she went, along the Mon shining with morning light. The Folly awaited upriver, and she trusted the tracks would lead her there.

Within minutes she reached a spur that curved off the main line and followed it onto the peninsula. Its rails soon cut out, both mangled into backward-bent loops of jagged steel. The cube kept growing with her approach, and yet it also seemed to melt; its rust had spread outward in all directions, staining the surrounding ground. The temperature dropped, and the river wind sliced through her kelly green jacket. Her breaths froze as she finally stood an arm's length from the Folly.

Regina looked around. Nothing but rocks, river, and woods from where she stood to the Downs, which had dwindled to a miniature. Even the Flats warehouses had shrunken to specks. Drifting clouds darkened the Mon. Fog materialized over the water, obscured the far bank.

The Folly revealed nothing up close. She circled it and found no seams, no cracks, no trace of an entrance. It presented itself as a monolith, perfectly impersonal aside from a lion head sculpted into the landward wall. Even that detail was easy to miss, as it blended into the surface so well. At a glance anyone might have mistaken it for mere corrosion. It was also set unusually low for such a decoration, low enough for Regina to meet its eyes on the level.

He was a twin to the lion in the theater balcony, miming the same roar. She reached up and traced his pupil, ran her fingers down the bridge of his nose, poked his nostril. She flicked her nail to his chin, pressed the point of his fang.

And that was all the Folly offered. No answers, no way to end the song or know when it might return. She'd marched so far on so little sleep, and for what? So this structure could tower over her, dwarf her with indifference.

Regina picked up a rock and threw it at the cube. She picked up another and fired it harder, and another. The rocks clunked off the metal and made no marks.

"I hate you! Leave me alone!" she screamed.

"I hate you! Leave me alone! I hate you! Leave me alone!" her voice echoed through the river valley.

"Just stop, please. I'm begging you to stop. What'll it take to make you stop? What do I have to do?"

Still nothing. The wind chilled her to a shiver. Cars whooshed by across the Mon, and she wished she could have hitched a ride with one to flee far from the reach of the song. She picked up one more rock and wound up to throw.

A chord halted her. It wasn't the song, just one sustained chord, and it seemed to come from the lion's mouth. Regina dropped the rock and gave him a long nonplussed look.

She prodded herself toward him while the chord continued to play. Shaking with nerves as much as cold, she raised her hand to the space before his mouth. The chord lowered in pitch, and a breath warmed her skin.

Regina jerked back. The chord stopped. Her heart drummed as hard as it had when she couldn't sleep. She closed her eyes and whispered, "I'm dreaming. I know I'm dreaming, and I'll wake up."

In her blindness, she heard the chord again. Telling herself this wasn't happening, this couldn't be happening, she reached for the mouth anyway. Again the pitch lowered, and again the breath puffed warmth. Even so, she thought, dreaming or not, I can still control what I do.

Regina opened her eyes. As both sound and sensation intensified, she slipped her hand into the lion's mouth. She touched metal, about a foot deep in his throat, that moved with her push.

"Holy crap!" she said, and yanked her hand out.

The chord stopped. The warmth left the air. There was only the lion, silence, and her own hesitance. She gulped and told herself to try again.

Regina fed her hand into his mouth once more. She hit the pit of his throat, and it budged like a plate held in place by a spring and hinge. Standing on her tiptoes to reach deeper, past the displaced plate, Regina felt a lever granulated with rust. She gripped it and gave it a pull.

The lever resisted but grated toward her. Regina let go and staggered back with a brush-burned hand. Before she had a chance to inspect her skin or think about what she'd done, the Folly began to stir.

A series of clicks sounded behind the wall. They started slowly but sped up to a patter. Then a much lower, heavier sound followed as ancient machinery awoke from an eon of slumber and groaned into motion. The ground vibrated under Regina's feet. She stepped back and back, her balance wavering.

Vapor jets burst through the wall with a hiss. Regina dropped to the ground, sprayed with a mist of dust and rust. She covered her head as the groan strengthened to a roar. All at once the barrage stopped. When Regina looked up, she saw that two panels had slid apart to leave an opening in the Folly wall.

She glanced around for witnesses. The Downs, the far bank, the rest of the world was far off and unaware. It did occur to her to run for help, but she had a feeling that would go the same way as the song. She would hurry all the way back to the Downs, drag Dad or someone else here. The wall would be sealed, the lion's throat immovable, and she would look crazy. She was afraid to enter but even more afraid of the passage closing before she could, never to reopen.

Regina's curiosity brought her to her feet. She unzipped her backpack, took out the flashlight, and took a breath. Whatever awaited within MacAdder's Folly, she chose to face it alone.

12. The Blood Trade

Regina stepped into the passageway and upon a metal plate that sank with a click. She waited. Nothing else happened, so she proceeded. The door panels slammed shut behind her and trapped her in total darkness. She turned on the flashlight, but its beam landed nowhere and revealed nothing.

"Oh, no! Oh, no, no!" she whispered in a panic.

A light shone down from above, and others followed in succession, each activating with a *pfoom!* Light after light, *pfoom! pfoom! pfoom!*, lighting to form a glowing spine overhead. The spine illuminated a tunnel that trailed far beyond the dimensions the Folly showed the world. The tunnel walls gleamed with the silver color she'd seen from the hill by the Heap, and their curve gave the passage a circular shape.

Regina gazed at the riddle before her, buzzed with adrenaline. The tunnel led to a distant pinhole, and it might have been her only way out. If not, she thought, Dad better find that note and come with one heck of a rescue crew. She bagged the flashlight and ventured ahead.

Soon the tunnel played a strange game. Regina felt resistance as she walked, the air thickening in her path. She stopped, backed up, and sensed similar resistance from behind. This wasn't a hard barrier but a flexible invisible membrane that stretched with her progress. Stranger yet, it gained density even as it kept stretching.

She pressed her palms against it, testing it, and finally charged it. The membrane ruptured with a flash, causing her to close her eyes as she stumbled into open space. Squinting, opening her eyes to a sunny morning, she found herself in the Little League field behind Pike. She wore a different t-shirt and jeans, no jacket or backpack.

Bullet waddled on the outfield grass. He chomped a dandelion stem, releasing airborne seeds. The breeze carried a few to his nose. He sneezed and snorted.

I've seen this before, Regina thought, and not in a dream. I've been here. This happened in June. I remember this happening in June. As in a case of déjà vu, she anticipated what came next an instant beforehand.

A baseball flew past her and barely missed Bullet's head. Three junior-high kids came jogging after it, laughing. Two girls and a boy. One girl wore a pink baseball cap and glasses, hand still in her mitt. The other wore a purple t-shirt and black sweat pants. The boy was dressed for basketball more than baseball in his tank top and baggy shorts.

"You call that a dog? I got a pit. He'd rip that fat bitch to pieces," said the girl with the pink hat.

"Look at her. Look how scared she is!" giggled the one in purple.

"I said, 'My dog would rip yours to pieces.' I'm talking to you." She shoved her mitt in Regina's face. "What? Can't hear you! *What*?!"

"Leave us alone," Regina heard herself mutter exactly as she'd muttered the first time.

"What? Can't hear you! Speak up, you ugly little freak!"

"Are you retarded? You look so retarded."

"What's your puppy's name?" the boy said between laughs.

Last time I hurried home, Regina thought, and felt her body repeating that action. She couldn't stop it if she tried. She was stuck within a shadow version of herself, reliving the past with hindsight but powerless to change it.

"What's your mutt's name? We're *talking* to you!" said the girl with the pink hat.

"Told you she's retarded," the girl in purple said as Regina hooked up Bullet's leash and led him away. The kids followed her, and she quickened her pace. Bullet struggled to keep up, the leash making him gag.

"Yo, your dog's *dead*. Put that shit to *sleep*. Let it go," the boy said.

"Look at her running away. Look at her!"

"What, you scared? I didn't even touch your ugly face. But if I see you again, I'll fuck you up, you little bitch!"

Regina retreated just as she had in June, just as afraid, but knowing this couldn't be happening because it already happened. The kids stayed in the field, calling after her just like before. She and Bullet climbed the hill to the duplex just like before.

When she walked through the front door, however, she arrived in the kitchen. No hallway, no lugging Bullet up the steps. He was on the floor, but she was no longer holding his leash. Night had fallen outside, and the overhead light was on. Regina was wearing her Powerpuff Girls pajamas, which she hadn't worn in years. She had outgrown them, but now they somehow fit again.

She had no idea how she'd gone from downstairs to upstairs, from morning to night in a blink. The déjà vu lingered; she knew she'd been there before and not just because it was her kitchen. She knew she'd lived that particular moment but didn't know when.

The hallway door was open, but there was no sign of the Bullevator on the steps. No rope, pulley, gutters, or wagon. Schoolbooks lay on the kitchen table, and she recognized the topmost one as her first-grade Reading workbook. It was left open to a page of fill-in-the blank exercises, pictures of simple things (boat, car, house, airplane) labeled with her own shaky handwriting of four years ago.

She went to the dim living room, which looked similar to its current state. It had the same sofa, TV, and coffee table with a chipped leg, but she hadn't seen its burgundy curtains for a long time. Nor the brass lamp on the end table, which Dad had pitched when it stopped working. But there it was again.

Regina heard voices through the open windows. She turned down the TV, listened to familiar bits of conversation, and remembered. This was the night when Amy left, never to come back. They were outside, Dad and Amy, on the porch. Regina peeked around the curtain and could see the porch roof and streetlit Pike but neither person.

"So that's it. Just like that. Three years and goodbye," Dad said.

"You had to see it coming, or at least you should've," Amy said.

"I'm sorry I'm not the happiest guy, but I was always good to you, wasn't I?"

"You're never happy, and you never will be. I can't help you with that. Your life is not my fault, Shelton. Getting you to do anything, or enjoy anything, it's like doing push-ups in wet cement. And I'm tired of it. I'm worn down and worn out."

"What about Reggie? What should I tell her?"

"Tell her she'll understand one day. Tell her not to major in poetry. Tell her to avoid depressed guys."

"Three years, Amy."

"I can't take them back, either," she said. A car door opened and shut. An engine started.

Regina ran back to her room. It was past her bedtime, and she certainly wasn't supposed to be eavesdropping. She left her door open a crack, enough to spy through as Dad plodded up the steps. He entered the kitchen and dropped onto a chair by the table. For a whole minute, he held his face in his hands, and then he lowered them to show glassy eyes.

Seeing this again, Regina felt the same mix of shock and gut-hurt. This was her Dad, who'd always been so big, strong, and wise. He would never cry, and yet there he was, doing just that. He looked weak and beaten, and the sight choked her up as it had before.

Say something to him, she thought. Go out there and make him feel better. Tell him he's a good dad and you still love him. Say something!

She could neither speak nor move. She could only do what she'd already done, which was nothing. Bullet came over and sniffed Dad's leg. Dad wiped away a tear with the back of his hand and leaned down to pet the dog. Another surprise, since Dad never seemed to pet Bullet or even like him very much, but it happened. On that night it happened.

Regina retreated from the doorway. The slit of kitchen light disappeared and stranded her in darkness once more. She touched no walls or bed or anything else, only the floor underfoot. It tilted backward abruptly and jostled her off-balance. She staggered, windmilling her arms. It tilted forward just as fast and threw her down. Regina closed her eyes as she landed. Wake up, she thought. Wake up! Please, God, wake me up!

She opened her eyes to a landscape of damp blue rocks that sloped down to a pond. Beyond the water stood a glass wall. Two more glass walls extended past her on either side, their surfaces filmed with scum. As bizarre as this new locale was, it didn't frighten her nearly as much as her own physical change. Regina lay naked and belly-down, and she couldn't stand no matter how much she willed herself to do so. She was able to crawl, and that was all, for her body had reverted to its infancy.

Okay, she thought, I'm still dreaming. I know I am, and I know I'll wake up. No need to panic, won't panic. But where am I, and why am I a baby again?

The walls rose above her with no visible limits. A white banner hung high upon the left wall, on the outer side of its glass. Made of paper and as large as a tablecloth, the banner was marked with writing she couldn't decipher. Otherwise, the world outside was a blur of flat rock and rusty mountain.

She squirmed around in a half-circle to face a jungle of giant plants. Bright yellow stalks led skyward, sprouting with orange branches and green leaves the size of dinner plates. She crawled up the slope and toward the plants, which had a waxy texture.

Damp blue rocks. Glass walls. Aquatic-looking plants. What is this place, she thought, some kind of weird greenhouse?

She continued through the jungle, scraping upon the rocks until she struck a fourth glass wall. Sensing that she was boxed in, she let out a baby's cry. Regina told herself to stop it and stay calm, but her baby-self only cried louder, belting out a piercing wail.

Her tiny hand grasped for a tree leaf and managed to grip it. She pulled, and the plant swayed with her force. It felt rootless and elastic, too willing to bend, but the baby Regina didn't care. She wanted out and was determined to climb, trying to use the plant to scale the wall.

Regina knew that wouldn't work but was helpless to stop her baby-self. She grabbed the next-highest branch with her other hand, and the plant fell upon her. She thrashed her hands and kicked her feet against the plants. She cried her throat to a hoarse burn and clawed at the glass.

Close your eyes, baby, Regina thought. Go to sleep. This can't last. This can't be how it ends.

Of course she could be wrong. Maybe she never would wake up, with no way out of this baby-body or glass prison. The possibility was almost enough to panic Regina, but she still refused to believe this wasn't a dream, that she had no measure of control. She concentrated on her fatigue and need for sleep, and her body seemed to respond. The baby tired and lulled off.

See? I'm home in bed, Regina told herself. I never left my room, and when I wake up, my room will be the next thing I see. My name is Regina Gundy, I am ten years old in the year 2005, and I live on Pike Street in Burdock Downs. When I open my eyes, that's where I'll be.

She opened her eyes to the Folly tunnel. She lay belly-down on the metal, her current self again. The spine of lights glowed behind her, trailing off to the distant point from which she'd started. Before her was a stone chamber and a doorway open to steps that only went down.

Regina slouched against the tunnel wall. She was done. Exhausted, defeated. The thought of taking those steps made her want to lie down again. She might have, too, if the song hadn't played. This time it sounded without echoes or otherworldly tones, closer and purer than ever before, every note drawn from the strings of a real violin. This time I'll see who's doing this, she thought, I swear I will.

She pushed herself to her feet and plodded onward to the chamber. Through the doorway and down the short flight she went. On the bottom step she stopped, overwhelmed by her new surroundings.

Stone walls didn't enclose the space so much as fade toward each other. They never met in corners; gaps of darkness were their only borders. Moss webbed their surface, and black liquid glistened through their pores. Regina saw no doors, windows, or ceiling, and yet a bluish light shone down from overhead. She could only glance at it, as its intensity was blinding.

Dozens of figures lay upon the floor. They were all asleep and all females. Some curled up or stretched out alone. Others held hands or nestled together. Their ages ranged from about ten to sixty, but there was little variation in their clothes. They wore either smocks or heavy wool dresses ingrained with dirt, and most had their hair pulled back. Regina recognized them as the Boom Girls, but they weren't the only ones before her.

Two figures were seated at a table beyond the sleeping Girls. One slouched on its elbows and wore a burlap cloak and hood that concealed its features. The other was a woman with pale skin and black hair who wore a suit. Evelyn Lakatos, Regina thought, noting that she appeared to be asleep, too.

A tall, thin girl stood by the table, between the two seated figures. She wore a pearl dress, and a matching ribbon held back her copper hair, and she was quite pretty, and Regina didn't care. What mattered was that she was playing a violin, face tilted downward and eyes closed, deftly gliding the bow and fingering the strings. Finally and at last, Regina found the source of the phantom song, and for a moment the sight transfixed her.

Despite her nerves and sweat, dry mouth and racing heart, Regina moved toward the girl. She navigated her way through the sleepers with measured steps. As she reached the table, the violinist noticed her and froze.

The song fell to silence. Evelyn opened her eyes. Upon seeing Regina, she bolted up to her feet, and her chair rattled upon the stone floor.

Regina heard movement behind her and looked back. The Boom Girls had also stirred from their sleep. They sat up, rubbed their eyes, yawned, and became aware of her. Their faces registered shock, confusion, disbelief. Their whispers blended to a murmur.

One girl, younger and smaller than Regina, broke from the crowd. She had pigtails, brown eyes, and a cute freckled face Regina remembered from the video. "Are you real?" she said as she poked Regina's arm. The contact felt solid, and Regina didn't know how to respond.

"She *is* real! I touched her!" the girl announced, and more of her cohorts immediately pressed in on Regina.

"Stop it! Stand back, all of you!" Evelyn said, and the Girls obeyed without exception. "Who are you, and why are you here?"

"I'm Regina Gundy. I came because I heard the song, her song," she said, and pointed to the violinist. "I heard just a little at first, then more and more. Then I couldn't stop hearing it no matter what I did, so I followed it all the way here. It's a beautiful song, it really is. But, um, could you please stop playing it for a while, please? Pretty-please?"

The violinist blushed, and the Girls' voices overlapped: "She heard the song!" "She couldn't have heard it!" "She said she heard it!" "How else could she find us?"

"Quiet," Evelyn said, and again they obeyed.

"Look, I *know* I'm dreaming," Regina said. "I know this can't be real. You're Evelyn Lakatos, and you're the Boom Girls. I know all about you. You're..." 'dead' was the word, but Regina couldn't bring herself to say it. "You're famous."

"Oh, are we?" Evelyn said. "And what of your ancestor Raymond MacAdder? Is he famous, too?"

"Ancestor? He's not my ancestor."

"He must be, for you to have heard the song. For you to find your way here, to see us as we stand before you. You must have MacAdder blood."

"I'm adopted. I don't know who my parents are. But I... I really don't think so," Regina said.

"Let's find out, shall we?" Evelyn took Regina by the hand and led her to the cloaked figure at the table. "Mother? It's time to wake up, Mother."

The figure leaned out of her slouch with the sound of cracking bones. Gnarled hands emerged from the burlap and reached up to pull off the hood, revealing a face that petrified Regina where she stood. Mother was not hideous, disfigured, or grotesque; it was her resemblance to Regina that stopped the girl short of the table. She had Regina's pale skin, abundant hair, and gray stare. The same eyebrows, nose, cheekbones, and chin. Her features had aged – her hair was white, skin wrinkled, teeth absent or craggy – but the similarity was undeniable.

I can see it, Regina thought. Why can't anybody else? It's like looking in a mirror that adds sixty years to my reflection.

If Mother had comparable thoughts, she didn't share them. She simply gave the same inscrutable gray stare Regina had so often given others. Evelyn tugged Regina to the table, enabling Mother to clasp Regina's free wrist. Mother jerked Regina's hand to her mouth with surprising quickness and strength and slurped her tongue between Regina's fingers.

Regina winced at the wet squishing, the trail of spit left upon her skin. Evelyn nudged her even closer to Mother, who bent forward and planted her nose on Regina's neck, dabbing it with cold slime. Mother sniffed and released Regina with a dismissive grunt. She then spoke to Evelyn in a language Regina didn't recognize, her voice a gravelly rasp.

Evelyn nodded knowingly and looked to the Girls. "Mother Saraya has spoken. This child is a MacAdder."

Regina scanned the Girls, whose stares grew wary if not hostile. One scowled and spat on the floor. The girl with pigtails and freckles shook her head, disappointed. Another hissed, which sparked off scattered shouts: "Throw her in the pit!" "To hell with her!" "To hell with all MacAdders!"

"What?! I didn't do anything to you!" Regina cried. "I don't know anything about being a MacAdder. Just let me go home!"

"You're cursed, child," Evelyn said. "Your ancestor was a vile bastard, his sins too numerous to list. If you know who we are, you may know what he did to us. On the day the laboratory exploded, he refused to dignify us with a proper resting place. He chose the river instead. Mother was here with us, the last to fall. She saw the desecration of our bodies, and with her final breath, she ensured that we would have justice. Oh, yes, we *will* have it!"

"Yes! Yes!" "Hear, hear!" "Die, MacAdder!" "Burn in hell, MacAdder!"

Evelyn silenced the Girls with a raised hand and lay that same hand on Regina's shoulder.

"MacAdder built this place as a monument to his guilt, thinking he would come here to curry favor with his god. All he did was provide us a confined space in which to pool our energy. He discovered that for himself and scurried off like the coward he was. For each of us, we take one of his. For every generation grown from his seed, one MacAdder must pay his debt until we are all counted."

"Just let me leave, please! I want to go home," Regina said, her voice breaking.

"You have two choices. You may leave, but you will experience the slow, tortuous disintegration of your mind. The song was the beginning. You will see sights that will tempt you to pluck out your eyes, that will violate the boundaries between dream and reality. These illusions will haunt you as long as you live, driving you insane or to an early, unnatural death like so many MacAdders before you.

"Or you may choose the more merciful option, your submission to a power greater than yourself and all of us. Offer yourself to the emissary of our lord, and you will feel no pain, Regina, only eternal peace."

She led Regina away from the table and the Girls, approaching an opening in the floor Regina hadn't noticed before. It was circular and rimmed with metal, twice the size of a normal manhole. Evelyn stopped about ten feet from it, as did Regina. She heard water rushing somewhere in its depths, smelled a noxious mix of smoke and rot. Evelyn urged her on with a soft push. She moved a few steps closer to see what she could see but halted when she heard a moan.

A slug-like thing appeared, poking up over the rim. It swelled, gathering strength to lift itself, and oozed up onto the floor. Its grayish flesh grew more transparent as it inched into the light. Cloudy liquid sloshed around within it, and within the liquid swam a half-dozen human eyeballs. Regina stood paralyzed before the thing, both awed and horrified, unable to move or look away.

"Don't fear it, Regina. It's only a servant," Evelyn said behind her.

It continued to creep up from the hole, dripping with river water. There was no way to gauge its size, to know how much larger it would grow or how far it stretched down the hole. Its eyeballs clustered together, all returning Regina's gaze with different-colored irises. From some unseen orifice it bellowed with a hundred wounded voices. Its acrid smoke-rot odor grew stronger with the outburst, and motes of burnt matter thickened the air.

"Don't move!" Someone grabbed Regina by the arm and yanked her back several steps. "Look at me. Look at me!"

Regina looked up to a girl in modern clothes: t-shirt, jeans, Cheetah sneakers, a blue satin jacket embroidered with a rainbow. She cupped Regina's chin in her hand and said, "Don't you dare give yourself to that thing. It's suicide, you hear me? Stay back, don't look at it. It'll sink back down."

The girl then said to Evelyn, "What is wrong with you?! You would feed her to that thing? She's a child!"

109

"She's a MacAdder! And what are these?! These *aren't* children?!" Evelyn said, gesturing to the Girls. "You picked a fine time to find your courage, didn't you, you selfish bitch? Go back to your corner, go wallow in your self-pity."

The girl said to the others, "If we let this happen, what does that make us? Then we're no better than what we're against. And how many years have we been stuck here? Torturing the MacAdders hasn't changed that. Killing this girl won't change it, either. Face it, the curse was a mistake, and now it's turned us into a lynch mob."

"Stop talking like you're one of us, Maura. You're not, and you never will be. Don't forget it," Evelyn said.

Some of the Boom Girls applauded. One whistled. A few called for Maura to be quiet, stand down, go away.

Maura continued undaunted, "For all your talk of justice, you're not being square with the girl, Evelyn. She has a third choice, doesn't she? If she's the one who heard the song, the one who made her way here, then she can break the curse. Can't she?"

"She's obviously not capable," Evelyn said. "Yes, she's just a child. So how do you expect her to make the trade? You know she can't. I did not treat her cruelly or dishonestly. I was only expediting the inevitable."

Maura glared from Evelyn to Mother. "Please settle this."

Everyone then looked to Mother, who'd been watching the argument. She rasped her pronouncement, crumpling as if every word strained her.

Evelyn took a breath and reddened as Mother concluded. "Very well," she said to Regina. "Maura is correct. You do have a third choice, a provision we call 'the blood trade.' Once per century, a subject of the curse has a chance to end it. The song called you here because you are that subject.

"You may free yourself, and all of us, on one condition: you must bring a tyrant to this site. Someone who has shed blood for personal gain,

110

wasted lives for pleasure, wrought destruction on a whim. Someone who is a living equivalent of your ancestor. Deliver such a soul to us, and you may keep your own while we pass on."

"But how could I do that? I don't know anybody like that," Regina said.

"That's your problem, not ours," Evelyn said. "Also, consider that if you leave now, the illusions will savage your mind until you bring the tyrant. If you attempt to bring anyone else who doesn't fulfill the trade, you will never exit this space again. You can neither fool us nor escape us, Regina, but you can choose your path. What will it be?"

"I want to go home," Regina said.

"Of course you do. You know the way," Evelyn said.

Regina looked from her to Mother to the crowd of Boom Girls, sensing condemnation at worst, gloomy pity at best. She looked to the manhole, empty again, and to Maura. Together they started for the steps.

"You saved me," Regina said.

"No, I didn't. I gave you a chance. That's all I could do."

"How did you end up here?"

"Let's not talk about that, okay? Go home, figure out how to live. And hopefully we'll never see each other again," Maura said, and walked away, vanishing into one of the dark gaps between the walls.

Regina ran up the steps, afraid the others might change their minds about letting her leave. She retraced her route through the tunnel, which felt much shorter this time with no membrane or déjà vu. The plate by the door sank underfoot with a click, and the door panels groaned, roared, and rumbled apart.

She jumped out to daylight and a restored morning. It welcomed her with the same fog and cold air, the same rocky earth as before. Same river, tracks, and distant Flats. Metal slammed against metal behind her, and she looked back to a resealed wall with no seams, to the lion face sculpted in rust. Same as before, same as before, showing no sign that she'd passed through his door, same as before.

13. Vigil

Three mornings after Regina's trip to the Folly, an audience had gathered before a stage on Broadway. Red, white, and blue crepe streamers drooped along the front of the platform. The Stars and Stripes hung from a pole on one rear corner, and Locust County's green and gold flag hung from the other. A podium stood in the center. Members of the Burdock Downs High marching band filled the rest of the stage, playing Sousa's "The Washington Post." The sun glinted off their brass instruments and buttons.

The crowd numbered about a hundred. It included retirees like Mrs. Bidwell and the Goleski Sisters, broke drunks like Mason, bored kids like Skunk and Jamal, and one reporter in the form of Jerry Kropke.

Sawhorses penned in the crowd from behind. A long, evacuated space stretched from the crowd to a barricade posted with signs that read "ROAD CLOSED – DEMOLITION." Beyond the barricade was a blast zone containing the blocks Colton had shown in his presentation. Zelda's Gift Cards, Morton Hardware, Sugar Polly's Bakery, Slappy's Tavern, and Sunny Dawn grocery had been stripped to girders and bricks, their doom pending.

Waters observed the crowd from within Orslovski's Barber Shop, a long-dead business behind the stage. The shop still had its mirrors and chairs, the former cracked and the latter covered with bits of fallen ceiling. Tufts of hair littered the floor, but they all belonged to rats or raccoons these days. Waters' walkie-talkie crackled in his hand, and a man's voice called, "Boss, you there?"

"Talk to me, Scott," Waters answered.

"It's all rigged up and ready to go, just like you asked."

"Good. See you in a minute, then."

"Boss? Are you... you sure about this?"

"See you in a minute."

Colton appeared by the front door, and Waters showed him in. The mayor watched his steps, minding his best Italian loafers. Grady entered as well, in uniform and exuding contempt. He'd chased more than a few junkie squatters from Orslovski's over the years and wouldn't have been surprised to find syringes on the floor.

"Mr. Waters," Colton said, and extended his hand. "How's everything going?"

"As planned. Just getting into my pitchman character, thinking about what to say."

"You're going to speak?"

"Would you rather I didn't?"

"No! Of course not!" Colton glanced at Waters' too-big Condor t-shirt and jeans, his long hair and dark-circled eyes. "Not at all."

"I have to introduce you, you know. I'd hate to see you go out there naked. And please don't be insulted if I leave during your part. It's nothing personal. Security measures and such."

"Okay. I was, uh – there's something else I wanted to ask. I know this might sound silly, but my wife is throwing a dinner party on Friday. I'm sure you're busy and have a lot going on, but we figured since we're kind of in business together –"

"Can I bring a date?" Waters said.

Colton nodded and said, "Sure. Yeah. Great. We'll see you there."

"Lovely." Waters started for the door but stopped short and looked back to Grady. "By the way, Chief. You may have noticed that Officer Valducci hasn't reported to roll call lately."

"No kidding. Not since Thursday. Can't find him anywhere," Grady said.

"You can stop looking for him. I recruited him for a special detail."

"Vic? You serious? With all due respect, Vic's no Navy SEAL."

"He's doing fine. You'll see him soon. I apologize for any inconvenience," Waters said, and exited.

Colton sensed Grady giving him a look and ignored it to focus on his own reflection in the mirrors. He checked his hair, straightened his tie, practiced his smile.

The band stopped playing as Waters took the stage. He adjusted the podium microphone downward, creating a feedback screech that killed the crowd's tepid applause.

"Thank you, thank you. Lonnie Waters, CEO of Condor Development Corps. Some of you may remember me from that eventful meeting last week. Yes, in just six days, Burdock Downs went from hopeless hand-wringing malaise to this glorious renaissance you're about to witness. In just six days, we freed ourselves from the shackles of those limp-wristed red-tape bureaucrats over at council chambers. In a perfect world, we'd line them up against that wall right over there, and bam! One shot to the back of the head. Problem solved, China-style.

"And, you know, we could learn a lot from China. You don't see them wasting time with namby-pamby regulations and crybabies whining about their civil rights. No, you go ask any Tiananmen Square student or the Dalai Lama, and they'll tell you China's a winner because China gets *results*.

"But I digress. My message here today is quite simple, people: hope, freedom, change, freedom, tax cuts, don't trust your government, trust the market, freedom."

"Whoooo! Freedom!" screamed a guy in the crowd. A few others clapped or whistled. The rest of the audience stared at Waters in silence.

"And not all politicians are pathetic weasels. In fact, you have an exemplary one right here in Burdock Downs. A true man's man with

115

aspirations. A strong leader with a strong chin and steel in his spine. Most importantly, he's a winner. Never forget, he led *your* Burdock Downs Spartans to not one, but *two* championships back in the day. Here he is again, the ol' Colt Rifle him– oh, wait. Before I forget, I wanted to mention that I'll be unveiling my sculpture garden here on Broadway on Halloween. That's exactly three weeks from today. Sculpture garden, Halloween. Save the date.

"So, where was I? Oh, yeah. The mayor. Colton Hauser, everybody. Let's hear it for the champ."

The band played the Burdock Downs fight song, "Marching Spartans," as a red-faced Colton emerged from Orslovski's. He stepped up onstage to applause and waved to no one in particular. Grady took the stage, too, which prompted Jamal and Skunk to slip away from the scene. Scott, the fat man Regina had seen on the Happ's loading dock, brought the detonator box to the podium. He also handed a hardhat to Waters, who hadn't yielded the podium just yet.

"Who wants to see the ol' Colt Rifle fire off one more shot, just like old times?" Waters said, and the audience cheered as he placed the hardhat on Colton's head. He then slapped the mayor on the back and left the stage with Scott.

"Thank you, everyone. Thank you, Mr. Waters," Colton said, and looked around for Waters, who had already disappeared. "That was... um... I can't follow up that. All I can say is that I promised you three Rs, my friends: rebirth, regrowth, recovery. Today I am very proud and honored to deliver on that promise. Will you join me in welcoming Burdock Downs to our new, young century?"

Yes, said their applause. Yes, we will.

"Then you may want to hold your ears," Colton said with a smile and began the chant, "Ten... nine... eight..."

The crowd chanted along with him, "...seven... six... five..." turning away from the stage to face the blast zone, covering their ears as advised, "...four... three... two... one!"

Colton pressed a button on the box, which triggered a flash and resounding boom. All of Broadway shook, and the tremor spread throughout the Downs: up to the library, where Tom paused in his reading; out to the Flats, where the kids leaning against the garage stopped harassing the homeless woman and wondered if they'd heard thunder; on the riverbank, where the Mon splashed onto the mud with unusual force; even to the duplex on Pike, where Regina was talking to Dad on his daily check-in call.

Dust massed in a gray cloud as structures crumbled. Bricks spilled and piled. Steel beams fell with a clangor. When the last echoes had faded and the haze had begun to thin, two blocks of Broadway lay devastated.

The crowd cheered but not as loudly as Colton expected. Soon the applause turned to gasps, concerned murmurs, and phrases like "Oh, my God!" "Wrong side!" "Wrong buildings!" Someone clearly said, "Jesus Christ! They blew up the wrong blocks!"

Indeed they had. Zelda's Gift Cards, Morton Hardware, Sugar Polly's Bakery, Slappy's Tavern, and Sunny Dawn remained standing. The blocks across the street – home to the still-in-business Murdoch's Pawn Shop, Campizi Pizza, and Club Climax – had been annihilated. The strip club's demise seemed to affect Jerry Kropke more than anyone else. The old hunchbacked *Dispatch* lifer dropped his notepad and pencil, gawking at the ruins in a remembrance of lap dances past.

Still wearing the hardhat and holding the detonator, Colton also stared at the smoldering blunder. He did not blink as cameras beeped, flashed, and captured his shellshocked face. Nor did he move, nor even breathe, as a tear beaded in his eye.

He paced in the basement of Sacred Heart, slammed his fist on a table, and paced. Grady and Andrew were seated at that table, and both picked a focal point to pass the moment. A flimsy tin ashtray for the chief, the cylinder full of bingo balls for the priest. Both also snuck glances at the mayor when they thought he wouldn't catch them.

Andrew noted the sweat stains on Colton's white shirt, the slight hitch in his walk, even his double chin, all of which conspired to make him look weak. At the same time, fury also turned Colton's handsome face ugly. If the last meeting had shaken Andrew's faith in the mayor, this one was hammering it.

Colton wheeled around and slammed the table again, flipping the ashtray. "That *smug* motherfucker! At least he could've dressed like an adult!"

"Maybe he'll dress nice for the dinner party," Grady said.

Colton sank into a chair and slumped forward, palming his brow.

"You know I could track him, see what he's doing around town. Hell, I got a friend of a friend in the FBI. Say the word, Colt, and I'll have him check up on this guy."

Colton said nothing, just kept slumping.

"What do you think?" Grady said to Andrew.

"You're asking me? As I recall, I raised my concerns about Waters when we last met, and you both accused me of lacking the manhood to play this game. Well, how's that game going for you now, boys?"

"You're in this, too, *Father*. If this thing goes bad, you think you're gonna walk away clean? Unh-unh. Don't think so. I'll see to it that you don't."

"God damn it, Grady, shut up!" Colton said. "We stick to the plan. We stay patient. I'll see Waters on Friday. I'll deal with him then."

"Colt, that's twice he's made you look bad in public. How much of this are you gonna take? We don't even know what he's doing at the Flats. His people blow up the wrong side of the street, then run off and don't answer your calls. And this secret mission shit with Vic? What the fuck's up with that?"

"I'm telling you, we stay the course. Leave Waters alone. If he finds out we're spying on him, then we're really fucked. No. We can't risk that.

"It's no secret those buildings were coming down next year anyway. So we accidentally jumped ahead of schedule. It's embarrassing, but it's not a dealbreaker, okay? We stay the course. We stay patient," Colton said to himself as much as anyone, staring through his men to that distant but ever-billowing dust cloud.

Hours after Colton and Grady had left his church, Andrew stepped out carrying a small candle in his jacket pocket. He cut across the Slopes to Sheridan Street, which wasn't the most direct route to his destination. However, it did take him past two specific houses, which was part of the ritual.

He passed his parents' place, now occupied by a young couple with a red Kia. Andrew's parents never wanted to live anywhere else even as the Downs emptied around them, even after decades in the Chemicore mines gave his father black lung. It seemed the medical bills would force his parents out in 1990, but a newly elected councilman named Colton Hauser rescued them. While Andrew was a young priest in Colorado struggling to keep a small parish solvent, Colton had covered the Dorovich expenses plus a live-in nurse, no questions asked. Neither Andrew nor his parents were in a position to refuse the help. You might call that an act of the good Colton, the generous and loyal friend you would forever treasure.

The second noteworthy house would always remind Andrew of the other Colton, the one who wasn't so lovable or easy to forgive. Nobody was living there anymore, not since the girl's grandmother died in 1994. To anyone who didn't know better, it was just one more rundown house in a town full of them. One more rat-trap with busted-out windows, flaking paint, and missing shingles.

There were circumstances, he told himself as he crossed the railroad tracks, still climbing Sheridan. Colton, Grady, and Vic would party at Suncrest all the time. They drank a lot of beer and screwed around with a lot of girls. They were all kids, remember, seventeen or eighteen at the oldest. Whatever judgment they had didn't stand a chance against hormones and alcohol.

They hadn't known how fragile she was. They knew about her mother, but she didn't even seem sad about it. She seemed so confident when she showed up that night, so unafraid of them. Like she knew what Colton wanted and was willing to give it to him. Like she knew what she was doing.

It was 1980. If you have to call what happened a date rape, go ahead and call it that. But nobody was using that phrase then. *You heard her say, 'Stop.' You saw her try to push Colton away.* And it wasn't so simple. Why didn't she scream? Why didn't she fight? She seemed to put up token resistance to show she wasn't easy, but then she lay down for Colton anyway. Lay down for Grady and Vic, too, and never screamed, never fought, never tried to run. *Because she was afraid like you were afraid. You heard her say, 'Stop' and 'I want to go home.' You saw her push her hand to Colton's face, and you did nothing. You did nothing, and nothing will ever change that.*

After Vic finished with her, she vomited and passed out. They didn't know what to do then, hadn't thought that far ahead. Andrew volunteered to take her home, having driven that night. Colton and Vic carried her to the car and dropped her in the backseat as thanks.

Andrew knew her address and that she lived with her grandmother. *Because you watched her, didn't you? Once you noticed her helping her grandmother carry groceries into that house, you looked for her every time you walked past. You even followed her home from school a few times, keeping your distance. You never did try to talk to her. Never had the nerve.* The house was dark when he pulled up to it. He assumed the old lady was asleep and felt safe enough to take the girl inside. If she had lived with her parents, especially a dad, he might not have been so bold.

Andrew dragged her out of the car and to the porch steps. He fished her keys from her jacket pocket, opened the door as quietly as he could. She was still blacked out and couldn't stand, let alone walk. It took all of his strength to carry her up the steps and into the house.

He paused on the living room threshold. The TV was on but muted, its light too dim to be seen outside. A red-haired kid was sitting on the floor before the screen, joystick in hand, playing *Space Invaders*. He was small, couldn't have been more than ten. A pale little pee-wee dressed in dark sweats. His game character, a green spaceship, moved laterally along the bottom of the screen, dodging bombs dropped by a descending wave of aliens. His ship returned fire with each touch of the joystick button, blasting his enemies to cosmic dust.

If the kid heard Andrew come in, he didn't let it distract him from the game. Nor did he turn around as Andrew brought the girl to the living room sofa. Andrew hardly wanted to talk to the kid, but the situation demanded a word.

"She had a little too much to drink. Don't tell grandma," he said, trying to sound lighthearted.

The kid continued to ignore him. The aliens kept advancing and bombing. His ship kept dodging and firing back. A purple mothership traveled across the top of the screen but exploded with a direct hit from the kid.

"Looks like you're doing pretty good there, buddy."

The kid turned partway around. Andrew saw only half his face, the kid's eye like a black marble in the TV light. "I'm not your buddy," the kid said with venom in his voice.

He glared at Andrew and never looked away. even as alien bombs struck his ships. The girl shifted on the sofa, mumbled, but didn't try to rise. Snoring grated from another room in the house. The clock on the mantelpiece ticked toward one-thirty. The screen turned yellow to signal Game Over, and still the kid glared at Andrew, daring him to say something else.

Andrew backed out of the room and felt a chill all the way to the car.

He paused upon the summit of Sheridan, where it intersected with Foster. Both houses had shrunken and blended into the others far behind him. Time accelerates and memories may fade, but guilt remains. The guilt of failing to support a dying parent, of letting aggressors prey upon the vulnerable. Guilt makes you paranoid, willing to consider the impossible. *The kid knew. There was no way he could've known, but he knew.* It compels you to revisit your crime scenes long after the rest of the world has forgotten.

Dusk was falling upon Foster as Andrew continued toward Suncrest. If the street had changed, most of the differences escaped his eyes. He saw the same houses and woods, the same potholes, the same building tucked away in the same dead end, albeit with different graffiti. Locust County Public Works had painted over Suncrest's walls about fifteen years ago, only to clear the space for the next generation. Andrew couldn't understand the new designs ("Wu-Tang"? "Jay-Z"? "Niggaz4Life"?) and assumed they had something to do with rap, which he was admittedly too old and white to appreciate.

He arrived behind the building, where the playground had been and where kids still came to drink, judging by the bottles and cans strewn about. The County had removed the swings, monkey bars, and slide for their jagged rust; gaps in the asphalt marked their absence. The pavilion and picnic table were gone, too, leaving only the concrete floor-slab.

Candle in hand, Andrew went to the far corner of that slab. A blotch of wax coated the concrete, twenty-five years of melted and weathered penance. Someone had carved a message into the wax since his last visit, the first time anyone had bothered to do so. He lit the candle with a match and aimed it to see the etching. In neat capital block letters that must have required time and care, it read "JEREMIAH 16:17."

Andrew scanned the surrounding woods, as frightened as he'd been once before, so long ago in that very place. He heard whispers in every movement of the trees, glimpsed stalkers in the shadows. Of course he knew better. He was doing nothing but scaring himself; no one else was there, no one was watching him. *Then who wrote this? Someone who knew you'd come here, who knew what that chapter and verse would mean to you.* No, he thought, no one knows what happened here but me and the other three, and no one cares but me.

"No one," he whispered.

"My eyes are on all their ways; they are not hidden from me, nor is their sin concealed from my eyes."

"No one," he repeated, aloud and defiant. "No one!"

14. Research

Tom was sitting at his desk, hunched over the *Burdock Downs Dispatch* once again. This time he was working on its crossword puzzle as Regina approached him. Seeing no one else in the library, she took the *Robber Baron* videocassette from her backpack and placed it on the desk.

"How'd you like it?" he said.

"I didn't, but it was useful. Now I need to know something else," she said, and went to the nearest computer.

Tom watched her log on, jaw clenched and fingers pecking the keys. The sight of her taking herself so seriously amused him, all the more so when she met his stare and said, "What?" with an edge in her voice.

"Good morning to you, too," he said.

A search engine awaited onscreen, its field blank and cursor blinking. Regina entered the words "satin blue jacket rainbow," which in turn produced hundreds of images. She scrolled through rows and rows of clothes, through dozens of stills from *The Wizard of Oz*, even through pictures of the Columbus Blue Jackets hockey team. Several eye-straining minutes later, she found one promising photo and clicked on it.

The search engine gave way to uBuy, an auction site. An enlarged version of the photo appeared, showing a teenage girl modeling a blue jacket. Aside from its color, the jacket had snaps down the front, a rainbow over the hip, and elastic-knit cuffs, hem, and collar. Its similarity to Maura's jacket was telltale enough for Regina.

"Vintage Spectra jacket!" read the caption below the photo. "Pre-owned but looks like new! Perfect for '80s karaoke night! Rad retro! $70.00." Further down the page, a list detailed the jacket's measurements, materials, condition, and year of production. 1979.

Regina typed "Cheetah sneakers" into the uBuy search bar. A column of photos came up, the topmost showing cheetah figurines and stuffed dolls. Cheetah-skin shoes and purses followed, then cheetah print blouses and pants and pillows and blankets and bed sheets. Down she scrolled, seeing nothing resembling Maura's shoes until the fifth page, the 247th result. The pictured shoes weren't an exact match, aquamarine to Maura's red, but worth a click.

"Gotcha Cheetahs?" the caption read. "Never worn, never removed from their box! Don't be fooled by the fakes. Authentic from the Cheetah company's final line! Super rare, super collectible. $400." The specs list dated the shoes to 1982.

Regina walked back over to Tom's desk. "A girl named Maura died in the Downs, sometime between 1979 and 1982. I don't know her last name, but I want any information you have on her. Any newspaper articles, anything."

"Should I know why you're so interested in this person?"

"I met her ghost the other day."

"Sure you did," Tom said with a smile. "Well, Halloween is coming, you know. Perhaps I can recommend some Henry James? Or some Shirley Jackson?"

"I'm not joking today. I want information. Can you help me?"

"Sheesh. Aren't we the little fascist this morning?" Tom picked up his desk phone and punched in a number. "Hello, Gladys? Tom Sligo over at the MacAdder library in Burdock Downs... Not bad. How about yourself?... Oh, dear. Sorry to hear that... That is awful...

"Uh, listen, Gladys, I'm calling because there's a girl here with an unusual query, and I was wondering if you could help us out. She's looking for a death certificate... No, doesn't need a copy, just wants to confirm a name. But there's a catch. She doesn't know the last name, only the first name and approximate date...

"I know, not your typical genealogy thing. It's her homework, though. She's supposed to research and debunk a local urban legend. Something about the ghost of a girl who died around here.

"Would you? You're the best... Okay, you ready? First name is Maura. Sometime between '79 and '82 or thereabouts. Right here in the Downs... Whenever you can, dear... Can't thank you enough... You, too."

He hung up and said, "That was Gladys Maythorpe at the Department of Health in Harrisburg. One of the last great civil servants. If she can't find it, it doesn't exist."

"Thank you," Regina said, and returned to the computer.

Demolition was on her mind after what had happened on Broadway yesterday. Dad had come home griping about some construction company blowing up a few blocks, the wrong blocks, and the ton of complaint calls he'd received as a result. Together they'd watched the six o'clock news, "Big Bomb On Broadway" being the lead story. Regina had even glimpsed the wreckage from afar on her way to the library.

To pass the time until Tom's friend called back, she went to the VidiVista video-clip site and watched controlled explosions. Empty hotels, skyscrapers, and stadiums poofed into dust clouds. Bridges dropped into rivers. Oil derricks and air traffic control towers toppled. Recorded on cell phones, the clips were grainy and shaky and had annoying off-camera commentary, but Regina still found them captivating. She felt an odd satisfaction, maybe even a small thrill, in seeing such huge structures come thundering down.

VidiVista listed related clips in a sidebar, some labeled in a language she didn't recognize. Arabic, she guessed, curious enough to click on one.

The video began loudly, with a mob of people burning an American flag. She lowered the volume as the video cut to a masked man wearing sunglasses and scolding the camera in his language. Cut to a U.S. helicopter crashing, to a mob dragging charred bodies through a Middle Eastern street. Cut back to the masked man still ranting and wagging his finger. He stood in what looked like a basement, with a black, white, and green flag behind him.

Dissolve to another masked man in another basement. The camera moved in close to a worktable upon which he'd laid out a cell phone, wires with alligator clips, and AA batteries. He took the phone apart, cut a hole in its casing, and reassembled it. Explaining his technique as he proceeded, he inserted two wires in the hole and connected one to the batteries. From what Regina could tell, and knew from her 50-in-1 kit, he was creating a circuit using the phone as its switch.

She didn't understand why until the video dissolved to outdoor footage of a sunny desert. One masked man held the phone, batteries and wires, all bundled to an artillery shell with duct tape. He placed the bundle in a roadside hole, and two more men swept sand over it. Dissolve to a closeup of someone's hand dialing a number on another phone. Dissolve back to the desert. A caravan of American military vehicles sped along the road until a flash cut them off. One vehicle burst into flame and black smoke. The others swerved around it and kicked up dust. The video looped the explosion, showing it over and over again, and ended with a freeze-frame of the blast.

Regina looked around the library. Tom was still working on his crossword, absorbed in his effort. An old woman he'd called Mrs. Bidwell was browsing the New Arrivals shelf. Regina could have done somersaults and jumping jacks, and neither grown-up would have noticed.

She rewatched the video, her captivation turning into something else. The explosion neither satisfied nor thrilled her. If anything, it repulsed her to know the people in the vehicle were probably killed. Likewise for the copter crash and charred bodies. Yet Regina knew she was seeing something forbidden, like an R-rated movie. She knew Dad wouldn't let her watch such a thing and that Tom would've disapproved, too. As gross as the video was, it gave her the chance to put one over on those guys, and that would always appeal to her. She watched it a third time.

Ready for a less-foreign video, Regina scrolled down the related-clips sidebar and found one labeled "The Trinity." She clicked on it, wondering if it had anything to do with Trinity, her favorite character from *The Matrix*. Three photo portraits of white men filled the screen instead. One was clean-shaven with short hair, the second had long hair and a beard, the third had a mustache. The name "McVeigh" lit up below the first, "Kaczynski" the middle, "Rudolph" the third. Kid Rock's "American Bad Ass" pounded the computer speakers, audible even at low volume.

"Freedom Fighters and True Patriots who stood brave in the face of tyranny" read text below the names. "Do YOU have the courage and will to follow their lead? Find out at ivoryeagle.com"

She began to type that name in the address bar when Tom's phone rang.

"MacAdder Library, Tom speaking... You don't say... Huh. Interesting... Okay, give me a second." Pen click, scribble. "Gladys, you're a paragon. I owe you one, dear."

Tom hung up and looked at Regina. She waited for a smart remark, but for once he had nothing to say.

They went upstairs to the looping walkway that hovered over the main floor. She followed him past shelves of reference books to a machine on a table. It had a glass screen like a computer or TV, control panel with buttons and dials, and plastic body gauzed with dust.

"Have a seat and don't touch anything," Tom said, and disappeared into the aisles beyond the table.

He came back minutes later with a palm-sized reel of film. The machine's screen lit up blank and white when he hit the power switch. He pulled a tray out from beneath the screen, loaded the film, replaced the tray. The blank whiteness became a gray blur. Turning a dial, he focused that blur into the front page of the *Dispatch* dated February 26, 1981.

"Whoa, cool," Regina said.

"Yes, microfilm is cool," Tom said. "Tangible media. Tangible! That's where it's at. Not all this wifty digital nonsense you kids use, rewiring your brains so you can't process or retain anything anymore."

He showed her how to move the film with the panel buttons, scrolling newspaper pages across the screen. She scanned the front page ("Works Announces More Layoffs"; "Reagan Claims Reforms Will Cut Inflation"; "Boy, 9, Robs New York Bank";) and went to the next.

The weather. A map of the U.S. dotted with little happy-sun faces and snowflakes. Letters to the editor, a cartoon of the Grim Reaper looming over the Works. "Hauser Vows to Reverse Downs Exodus"; "Polluted Creek Cause For Concern"; "Kagan Says Crime On The Rise."

It wasn't until Page 8 that Regina found the headline "County Coroner: Girl's Death Was Suicide." Below it was a yearbook photo of a smiling Maura, captioned "Maura Dougal was a senior at Burdock Downs High School." The byline credited the article to Jerry Kropke.

"Locust County Coroner Rodney James has determined that Maura Dougal, 17, drowned herself in the Monongahela river last week. Dougal's grandmother reported her missing on February 19. A Chemicore barge operator discovered her body two days later. Burdock Downs police disclosed that Dougal's body had been anchored to the riverbed with a sack of bricks, which raised questions of foul play.

"'There is no longer any doubt,' James said yesterday. 'Our autopsy, along with a thorough police investigation, indicates the decedent ingested a large volume of barbiturates hours before her death. A neighbor witnessed the decedent taking the bricks from a vacant property earlier in the week. We've also confirmed that the decedent had taken the sack and clothesline from her grandmother's basement. All evidence points to suicide, premeditated and deliberate.'

"Dougal's mother had been killed in a drunk-driving accident last year in Pittsburgh. Dougal and her brother Oscar, 10, had moved to Burdock Downs to live with their grandmother, Martha O'Donnell. Friends and relatives claim that Dougal seemed to have adjusted to the tragedy prior to her own death.

"'She was depressed when her mother died,' said Kristin Platt, a classmate from Pittsburgh. 'Who wouldn't be? But when I last talked to her, she was doing so much better. She was coping really well. I can't believe she would [kill herself], not Maura. She was always so strong.'"

Regina felt her throat tighten, a shudder in her chest. She closed her eyes, unable to look at the photo of Maura anymore, and told herself not to cry. Not there, not yet, not in front of Tom.

He leaned in closer to the screen. "Hey, I think I remember this now. It happened ages ago, and my memory's not what it was. But I remember it being sad when it happened. It was one of those – hey, are you okay?"

"Yeah. Great," she said, eyes still closed.

"Will you tell me the real reason you're looking this up?"

"I already did."

Regina stood up and ran from Tom before he could say anything else. Down the steps, out the front doors, out onto Elsinore she ran, bronze lions shrinking behind her. Lightheaded, sweaty, and breathless, she ran like running could erase that smiling face from her mind.

15. Doing Some Good

Bullet waddled on the Little League field, a panting mass of slobber and fur. He paused every so often to look back to Regina, wary of her ending his fun, but he needn't have worried. She was in no hurry to return to the duplex. Staying home only kept her mind on Maura and the Folly. Being outdoors and active helped her to feel a little less trapped, at least.

So they took in the sunny October noontime. The dog was excited and trying to move faster than he could, the girl sleepwalking in a listless daze. She followed him from the field to Cherry Way to the woods, where he attacked his favorite tree with all the stealth of a lawnmower.

A squirrel was perched upon the lowest branch, some ten feet off the ground. At first it ignored Bullet's yelps, but then it dropped twigs and bits of bark on him. Bullet managed to lift himself onto his haunches, clawing at the trunk with his forepaws. He was vertical but earthbound. The squirrel climbed down just enough to tease the beagle into a squealing, shaking rage before scooting back up with a flick of its tail.

While this routine played itself out, Regina noticed something much more unusual. A vehicle was parked on the dirt road, up ahead near the Smash Heap. From a distance it looked like the jeep she'd seen at the Happ's Ketchup plant. Closing in on it, she confirmed it was the same by its space-alien bumper sticker.

Regina continued past the jeep and stopped in shock upon reaching the Heap. Her once-secret playground greeted her with a rainbow makeover, splashed with jarring colors. The shack and wrecked Plymouth were still there but spray-painted yellow and brown. The bathtub had turned purple, the TV pink. The fridge wore orange and black stripes. The box spring had traded its rust for lime green. The drab filing cabinet had brightened with swirls of copper and amber. The clothes dryer shone with silver smudges on sky blue.

A person was lying on the ripped-up sofa, now painted fire-engine red, sneakered feet propped up on the armrest. He or she played a handheld video game that obscured his or her face, clicking its plastic buttons with a mad patter. The person noticed Regina and lowered the game. Between his long reddish-brown hair, skinny build, and sunglasses hiding his eyes, it took Regina a moment to decide he was a guy. His age remained a question to her. It could have fallen anywhere from twenty to forty.

He sat up and set the game aside. "Hello, munchkin. What brings you here?"

"I come here all the time. Did you do all this painting?" she said.

He looked over to the spray-paint cans piled in a wheelless wheelbarrow. "That would appear to be the case, yes."

"Why?"

"It's one way to remember the dead. You know what a coral reef is? At the rate we're killing them, there won't be any left by the time you're my age. When I happened upon this place, I saw it as a postconsumer reef. The reef we made and deserve. Here, try it with these."

He took off his sunglasses, blue-lensed wraparounds, and held them out to her.

Regina didn't move to take them. "I'm not supposed to talk to strangers."

"Fair enough," he said, and set the glasses down beside the game.

She stared into his dark-circled green eyes and saw someone who'd been hurt and expected to be hurt again. There's beauty in his face, she thought, enough that he would've made a very pretty girl. Part of her wanted to touch that face, and the idea of touching it sent a tingly sensation through her. Another part of her said there was something wrong with him, something not to be trusted. Maybe it was the way those unblinking eyes met hers and seemed to laser-cut right through to her confused mind.

Whatever he saw in Regina, it made him smile. "So you're just going to stand there and stare at me? I know I'm debonair and all, but you're starting to creep me out."

She might have backed off if Bullet hadn't come schlepping along the dirt road, drawing the guy's eyes from hers. Bullet licked Regina's hand and went over to the sofa to sniff the guy, who stooped to pet him.

"Affectionate fellow. Does he have a name?"

"Bullet."

"I see. And do you have a name?"

"No."

"I'm Lonnie Waters, and I run a company called Condor. We're doing all kinds of big, important construction projects in your town. Now, now. Don't thank me. Just know that I'm a public figure and nothing to be afraid of."

"I heard your company blew up Broadway."

"Just some of it."

"The wrong part of it."

"There may be a kernel of truth to that, but what's it matter? Our country, the good ol' U.S. of A., has been dropping bombs on people for the last two-and-a-half years. People who did nothing to us. We've killed thousands of them, crippled and maimed and displaced thousands more, and I don't see anyone in Burdock Downs crying about that. But they lose a few blocks of rat-infested storefronts, and they're bitching and whining like it's a national tragedy. Does that seem right to you?"

It didn't, but Regina also didn't want him to think she agreed with him. So she said nothing.

"Anyway, I didn't blow up Broadway just for fun. I freed up space for something special. New buildings aside, I'm working on a sculpture garden to replace MacAdder Plaza. If you like animals, you should check it out. It's going to have four awesome specimens, brought to you by these very hands."

Regina looked at those hands, marked with bruises and scabs, back to his eyes. "You run a construction company but do art, too?"

"I wanted to be an artist from the time I was your age. Acting, painting, sculpting, I loved it all, but other stuff got in the way. So yes, now I run Condor for a living and 'do art' on the side because that's what I really care about. You'll see when you grow up that most people don't get to do what they want for a living."

"What 'other stuff' got in the way?" Regina said.

"Personal stuff," Waters said. "Stuff I don't discuss."

"You carve stone, cast metal?"

"No, I'm trying something more experimental. Temporary. Working with what you might call 'organic materials.'"

"Can I watch you work? I promise I won't bother you."

"Thanks for your interest, but no. Sorry. Not possible. I have my secret techniques, and I prefer to keep them secret."

"I can keep a secret."

"You're curious. I admire that. I really do. But how can I trust a girl with no name?"

Regina had no answer and didn't try to think of one. Instead, she approached the sofa and took the sunglasses. Upon donning them, she surveyed the Heap and viewed Waters' project as he'd suggested.

The tub and TV lost their corners and edges, warped into pink and purple boulders. Fridge stripes and filing-cabinet swirls mingled as plants among the Heap's weeds. Box-spring coils blurred into a bed of shells encrusted with barnacles. Silver smudges flashed past like a school of fish when she glanced at the dryer. The sunken rowboat of a Plymouth lay wedged against the sandbank shack.

136

Regina stepped away from Waters and Bullet and wandered toward the aquatic plants. They reminded her of another illusion, the jungle where she struggled among yellow stalks and orange branches and green leaves that had a waxy texture. Where she was trapped within glass walls as a baby. Regina reached out and touched the same filing cabinet and fridge she'd always known at the Heap, much to her relief. She dragged her fingertips along their metal just to confirm reality because if she needed anything these days, it was more reality, not less.

Waters' cell phone buzzed in vibrate mode. He pulled it from his back pocket and flipped it open to read a text. Regina stood nearby and Bullet lifted his leg to wet the toaster oven while Waters thumb-typed a response. No sooner had Waters clapped the phone shut than another text vibrated it again. With a put-upon sigh, he went about typing another response. Then the phone beeped, and he rose to his feet to take the call.

Regina took off the sunglasses while he was distracted. She reached back discreetly and dropped them in her jacket's hood, concealed by her hair. Waters continued talking, pacing around the sofa, paying more attention to Bullet than her.

After a few minutes, he hung up and pocketed the phone. "So, you're the audience. What do you say?"

"I don't know. Can't tell if I like it or not."

"Does it make you feel anything?"

Regina gave a one-shoulder shrug. "Sad, mostly, and a little afraid. Afraid that nothing's what it looks like, and sad that I'll never see a real coral reef. But if yours is all I get, I guess I'll settle for it."

"Fear and pain are essential to life. If that's what you felt, then I did some good here." Waters picked up his video game, scanned the sofa and Regina. "Where'd you put my glasses?"

"On the sofa while you were on the phone," she said.

"Oh, yeah?" Waters said, sounding skeptical. He fed his hand between the cushions, pulled out nothing but wads of stuffing. "Okay, then.

As much as I'd like to stay and chat, I can't. I'm a very busy man, munchkin. The pleasure was all mine."

Till next time, Regina thought, and bit down her smile as he started for his jeep. Bullet waddled over to her, and together they watched Waters rev the engine and swing the vehicle around on a U-turn, churning up dirt and dead leaves.

16. Dinner Party

The grandfather clock in the Hauser living room struck eight, every chime a reminder that dinner was supposed to begin at seven. Grady, his date Nikki, and Chemicore president Ogden Wiems paused their conversation. Andrew stood nearby, sipping his water and observing his fellow guests.

Grady looked far from comfortable wearing a suit. His coat appeared to be too small, his tie too tight around his thick neck. He fidgeted, too, with one meaty hand balled up in his coat pocket and the other vise-gripping Nikki's wrist. She was in her early twenties, a generation younger than Grady and a fraction of his size. A hundred pounds and five foot two in heels, Andrew guessed. She kept glancing at a mirror on the near wall, but Andrew didn't perceive vanity from her. If anything, she seemed to be uneasy with her makeup, especially the patch of foundation meant to disguise a bruise near her eye.

Ogden Wiems III (or "Oggie," as he insisted everyone call him) was a fixture at Hauser socials. He had been a close friend and backer of Colton's father and continued his support through the son. Tall and burly with a full head of white hair, Wiems had the red complexion of a heavy drinker. He also spoke with booming volume, quite assured that everyone knew who he was and valued his opinions. Grady and Nikki deferred to the Wiems mystique, letting him dominate the talk, nodding along to his every declaration. Andrew, whose father had worked and arguably died for Chemicore, was less receptive.

When the chimes subsided, Wiems resumed sharing his geopolitical expertise. "And that's why it's a mistake to trust the Jews," he said, third glass of Knob Creek in hand. "Here we are, shelling out all this money to prop up their state, and what are they doing? Not keeping the Arabs in line, obviously. And if they're not keeping the Arabs in line, what good are they are to us? Ask yourself, who *really* stood to benefit from 9/11? The Jews! The towers come down, where does the money go for security, intelligence, stability? Think about it. Same Judases they always were. Right, Father? I don't have to explain this to *you*, do I?"

"Well, I – I don't – I don't agree, Mr. Wiems. I don't think that's –"

"Hey, Lorna!" Wiems called, having no time for dithering. "Lorna, I don't think this Waters bozo's showing up. I'm hungry, and I say we eat!"

Lorna Hauser emerged from the kitchen trying to smile. Back in Andrew's high school days, Lorna was the consensus pick for prettiest girl in the Downs. She was still beautiful, Andrew thought, if not more so with age. It wasn't just her Scandinavian blonde hair and blue eyes, fair skin, and face Hitchcock would have obsessed over. As her pastor and confessor, Andrew knew the private Lorna as few could. She was a kind and gracious wife, generous parish donor and volunteer, loving mother to her children. That she secretly loathed Wiems, Grady, and Vic – calling them "disgusting," "repulsive," "amoral," "assholes," and "pigs" at various times – didn't strike Andrew as a flaw.

"Oh, Oggie, you're really too much. Would anyone else like a drink?" she said.

"I'm not kidding," Wiems persisted. "If you ask me, every second we wait's just another slap to Colt's face."

All eyes turned to Colton, who lingered by the dining room windows. He looked sharp enough in his white shirt with French cuffs and gold links, but there was a nervousness in his posture and every gesture.

140

With an overeager laugh and shrug at Wiems' remark, he gave the impression of being self-conscious before an audience.

"I'm sure there's a good reason for the holdup. He does have a lot of – there he is! He's here!" Colton said, and hurried to the vestibule. Upon opening the front door, he backed into the living room, face ashen with humiliation.

Waters entered wearing jeans and sneakers, a midnight blue smoking jacket, and black t-shirt with the text "Heckuva Job" across the chest. Mason followed in the same dirty winter coat, frayed tossle cap, and duct-taped shoe Regina had seen him wearing last week, his beard and dreads likewise unwashed. His smell wafted in with him, its blend of b.o., booze, and piss overpowering every aroma from the kitchen.

"How's all y'all doin'?" he said, as jovial as could be.

The Hausers, Andrew, Grady, Nikki, and Wiems answered with silence.

"Good!" Waters said. "Glad to hear you're all good. This is my date, Mason, everybody. Mason, this is Mayor Colton Hauser. His luminous wife, Lorna. Ogden Wiems, president of Chemicore. Chief Grady Kagan. And what's your name, darling?"

Nikki muttered her name.

"And Father Andrew Dorovich, Burdock Downs' very own saint in the making."

"I wouldn't say that, but I am pleased to finally meet you, Mr. Waters. And you, too, Mason," Andrew said.

"Yes, of course," Waters said. "You'd think we would've met by now."

"Miss Lorna, I don't know what you're cookin' in there, but I can't wait to get some," Mason said. "Believe it or not, I ain't had a decent meal in weeks."

"I believe it. Decent meals don't fall out of Dumpsters," Grady said.

"Now, chief, that was uncalled for," Waters said.

141

"I don't care. It's bad enough I have to see him on the street. I'm not gonna eat with him."

"Yes, you are. If I can eat with you, you can eat with him," Waters said, and looked to Nikki. "Darling, did you bump into a door?"

"I, um..." She glanced at Grady and blushed. "I did."

"I bet you did. In these uncertain times of aggressive doors, it's a good thing you have a strong, brave man like the chief to keep you safe," Waters said.

Grady turned as red as Wiems.

Lorna sensed that someone had better say something and broke in with a buoyant "Dinner's ready, everyone! Let's all have a seat, please."

Wiems was seated at the head of the table, Andrew across from him. The Hausers, Grady, and Nikki along one side, Waters and Mason the other. Two empty chairs on the Waters-Mason side were the only hint of the Hauser children, Taylor and Jayden, who'd been sent to the sitter's in advance. Andrew said a short prayer, and everyone began to eat the antipasto.

No one spoke while Grady scarfed down the artichoke hearts and goat cheese. His face remained red, eyes fixed downward, Adam's apple pulsating with every gulp. His palpable anger cowed his entire side of the table.

"Mmmm-mm! *That's* what I'm talkin' about, Miss Lorna!" Mason said.

"Thank you," she answered with a forced smile.

Wiems gauged this scene with waning patience. He didn't know why everyone was tolerating this Waters and his colored accomplice or why Colton was behaving so passively and utterly failing to assert himself. If anyone was going to take charge here and be man enough to call a spade a spade, it would have to be Ogden Wiems III.

He cleared his throat with authority and said, "So, you're Lonnie Waters, are you? You're supposedly redeveloping Broadway? I have to say, I'm not impressed with you, your company, or your work."

"That's unfortunate because I'm so very impressed with you, Ogden," Waters said. "It's remarkable what you've done. The steel industry went broke, and so you became the top player in the Downs by default. You've undermined and strip-mined a quarter of Locust County to oblivion, and you still dump your toxic waste-water into the river. Thanks to you, every creek around this town's a healthy shade of orange.

"I especially respect how you treat your employees. A dozen men killed in a shaft collapse in '82, eighteen dead in a methane explosion in '87. Another explosion in '90, fifteen dead. Another collapse, seven dead in '97. And that's not counting everybody who's come down with black lung over the years or all the skulls and kneecaps your hired thugs cracked when it came time to break up some strikes.

"Chemicore rakes in tens of millions of dollars and pays no taxes, and follows no safety or environmental regulations, because you own every politician you need from here to Harrisburg to DC. And while you're strokin' 'em off with barrels of grease, you're not paying a red cent in benefits to the people who die in your mines for a lousy buck, people who have nowhere else to go for a job. That takes real moxie, bro. What a world this would be if we all had your ambition and will to succeed."

Waters rose to his feet and raised his glass. "In fact, I propose a toast to Ogden – excuse me, *Oggie* – Wiems. Many may see him as an old washed-up lush or a pompous fraud or an impotent cuckold whose wife gets boned by his own brother. But not me! I look at him and see so much less. To Oggie Wiems: a rapist of Nature, exploiter of men, and living proof that you can't inherit character. Cheers."

No one joined Waters in the toast. He drank up and sat down.

Wiems stood, his face purplish with rage. "I demand an apology!"

"I'm not supplying one," Waters said.

"I won't stand for this. Colton, I won't stand for this!"

143

"Then sit down and shut up," Waters said. "Or walk. There's the door."

Wiems stormed away from the table.

Colton jumped up to follow him. "Oggie? Oggie! Don't go, Oggie!"

Wiems ignored him and slammed the front door in his face.

Another lull befell the party, every tick of the grandfather clock audible. Colton dragged himself back to the dining room and stood there, hands on hips, breathing like he'd jogged a mile. His guests pretended not to notice him even as he leveled a death stare at Waters.

"Food's great, by the way," Waters said to Lorna, who looked to her husband, her eyes pleading for him to please do something already.

Colton leaned down to Waters' ear and whispered, "Can I see you alone?"

"Can I see your trophies? I'd love to see your trophies," Waters whispered back.

Their departure left Mason alone on one side with Grady, Nikki, and Lorna across from him and Andrew at the head. No one spoke or looked at each other. The grandfather clock struck to mark the quarter-hour. Lorna moved to collect the plates. One course down, four more to go.

Colton led Waters downstairs to a basement game room. They passed a big-screen TV and pool table en route to a bar in the corner. Colton poured a rum and Coke for himself, heavy on the Bacardi and sloppily enough to wet his cuff. While he cursed and looked for a towel, Waters wandered over to the trophy case along the near wall.

Brass figures gleamed in their poses: a pair of quarterbacks dropping back to pass, arms cocked and balls loaded; a running back dodging a defender; a generic player raising his arms in victory. A helmet occupied its own shelf, nicked-up white with a green center stripe and Spartan-sword logo on the sides. A matching jersey lay upon the shelf below, laundered and folded to show the 7 on its chest.

144

"Wow, would you look at that. You were a real superstar, weren't you? And you've kept it all very pristine. You must be proud, still?"

"Mr. Waters, we need to talk about our project," Colton said, and approached him.

"Yes, yes. But tell me, what was it like to be you back then? To be so strong and athletic? To have so many people praise you for your talent, worship you for it? To run out onto a field and hear them all screaming and cheering for you? Sure, you took your hits, and it was never easy, or was it? You tell me, what was it like?"

"It was a long time ago," Colton said.

"But I have no frame of reference. I can't imagine. I mean, look at me. I'm just a little guy. A runt of sorts. I could never do what you did. I would've gotten killed or laughed off the field. So I'm curious is all."

Colton looked at the trophies. "I try not to think about it. World's full of sad ex-jocks clinging to the past. You know that Springsteen song 'Glory Days'? That about sums it up. Lorna's the one who polishes these. She keeps this alive more than I do, her and the kids."

"And I have to ask, what was it like having all those girls throwing themselves at you? I bet you had 10s and knockouts tripping over each other. There had to be at least one little firecracker before you settled down. One little hellcat who still makes you smile."

"Yeah, sure, there were girls," Colton said, and couldn't help but smile. "Some really cute ones, too. But honestly I don't remember those days so well anymore. My concussions might be catching up to me, or maybe I just moved on. Once I met Lorna, I never thought about anyone else. And the kids, I love 'em to death. All this stuff seemed important at the time, but I've grown, I've changed. I'm just a boring old dad now. Thank God for that, right?"

"I'm very happy for you on your journey of self-discovery," Waters said.

Colton took a drink, took a breath, and said, "What the hell was that upstairs? Gus Bixler is one thing, but I can't afford to lose Wiems. Do you have any idea how much ass I'll have to kiss to keep him? And what about Monday? Your crew screws up massively – *stupidly* – and guess who takes the heat."

"Kissing ass and taking heat. You are a politician, aren't you?"

"Yeah, but I'm not an idiot."

"Are we having a crisis of confidence, champ?"

"I could use some reassurance. I don't want to complain, okay, but I can only play the fool so many times. And it's been happening a lot lately. And sometimes I... If you'll excuse my language, sometimes I think you're fucking with me just to fuck with me."

"Now, why would I do such a thing?" Waters said.

"I didn't say you were. I meant that sometimes it seems like it. Like this is all a big joke to you."

"That would be one very elaborate and expensive joke, wouldn't it?"

"I know how I sound right now. I'm not saying I don't trust you. I just – I took a *lot* of heat on Monday. And now Wiems –"

"No, this is good, this dialogue," Waters said. "It's important that we communicate and understand each other. I hear and respect your concerns. I'm aware enough to notice that people don't take me seriously, and I can't say I blame them. Again, look at me. Why would anybody take me seriously as a man, let alone a man of consequence?

"But appearances aside, I am very dedicated to what I do, and I can tell you the site in the Flats is operational. I won't discuss the nature of the activities there, but my employers are satisfied with their progress. I've brought evidence of that progress if you'd care to see it."

Waters pulled a small plastic canister from his jacket pocket. He shook it, rattling its contents, and handed it over. Colton set down his glass and popped open the lid. He couldn't make out the contents, so he emptied the canister into his cupped hand. A clump of pebbles and curved dime-sized chips fell out, all crusted together with a sticky brown substance.

It took Colton a few seconds to recognize what he was holding. The pebbles were human teeth. The chips were extracted fingernails. The brown crust was dried blood. He dropped the clump on the bar with a "Jesus!"

Waters watched the mayor and savored every jitter, trusting his jacket to hide his growing erection. "As you said to Agents Poole and Martinez, we can't let those bastards win. Whatever it takes. Time to take off the gloves. Now more than ever and all that. Correct?"

Colton couldn't speak. He could only gape at the clump, his blue eyes wide and dilated with fear.

"Need more reassurance? I can show you more where this came from," Waters said.

Colton shook his head no, no more, no thanks, and absently wiped his hand on his pants.

Waters picked up the clump and dropped it in the canister, which he capped and pocketed. "Then let's rejoin the party. Lorna's delicious spread is growing cold."

17. Matinee

Regina went to the library on the following morning, regretting how she'd run out on her last visit. She figured she owed Tom an apology. He'd been helpful enough to lend his secret video and find that microfilm. Even if she didn't always like his tone, he did deserve better than a freakout.

He wasn't at his desk when she entered the main floor. A laminated sign held his place instead. "Be Back Soon. Thanks For Your Patience." She looked around and didn't see anyone else, either. There was no sound but her sneakers squeaking on the floor, no movement but dust drifting in the sunlight. The library was its usual lonesome self.

Might as well kill the time online, Regina thought, logging on to the nearest computer. The browser awaited, and she blanked for a moment regarding where to go, what to see, what might be interesting. She remembered her last session and typed "ivoryeagle" in the address bar.

The screen flashed, and the site loaded. The three faces of McVeigh, Kaczynski, and Rudolph reappeared, again with "American Bad Ass" punishing the speakers. Scrolling down, she came to a picture of an eagle who mimicked the bird on the dollar bill, wings spread and head turned. True to the site's name, this eagle was carved from the hard white stuff. His eye glowed red, and he clutched the Washington Monument with one foot and the Capitol dome with the other.

"Are YOU oppressed by the government and its so-called laws?" read text below the eagle. "FIGHT BACK! Sick of them taking YOUR money and giving it to immigrants and Welfare Queens? RESIST! Can you see the 'browning of America' is the ruination of America? DEFEND YOURSELF! Tired of being spied on, sold out, disarmed, unmanned? RECLAIM WHAT'S YOURS! YOU have the power to defeat any Enemy, but do you know how to use it?" A list of links followed the text: Pipe; Mail; Nail; Truck; Dirty; Molotov.

Regina clicked on Molotov because it sounded so odd, so foreign.

The screen flashed and showed photos of liquor bottles, gas cans, and a flaming building. A caption read "Molotov Cocktails are simple to make and can take out many soft targets. The materials are affordable and readily available. All you need" –

The phantom song jolted Regina from the screen. Chord, chord, notes flowing downward, chord, chord. It played from somewhere beyond the door labeled "Staff Only," once again echoing with synthesized tones. It also stopped as abruptly as it had begun, leaving her to wonder if she'd really heard it.

Regina scanned the room and saw no witnesses. She was about to call for Tom when the "Staff Only" doorknob moved. It turned slowly, very slowly, and inch by inch the door opened to reveal a woman in the corridor.

She wore a black hat, its brim as wide as the doorway. Her silk dress was also black and long-sleeved with a low neckline. A boa was draped over her shoulders, its feathers light blue. Her face was powdered pale, eyes heavily shadowed, lips and curls a licorice red. She looked to be about thirty and leered in a way that unsettled Regina.

"There you are, tootsie pie. What are you waiting for? Show's about to start. Come now, up with you. No time to lose," she said with a smoker's sandpapery voice.

Regina stared at her for a wary moment and said, "I'm not supposed to talk to strangers."

"Who says I'm a stranger, Regina? I heard the same song you just heard, and I know what it means. I can help you, but you have to come with

150

me quickly. Your doodads and your librarian friend will be here, but I'm not one to wait."

She turned away, and her footsteps trailed off. The door began to shut. Regina sprung up and ran to it, stopping it before it could lock her out. The woman was already halfway down the hall, and Regina hurried after her.

"But who *are* you?"

"Miriam if you want a name. A friend of your great-great-great-grandpa. I like to think I've aged gracefully," she said, and turned the corner to the next door.

Regina followed her through but grew disoriented. The very same door that led to the theater stage last week now led to the theater floor. That would have been weird enough, but every seat had been removed except for one. The lone chair faced the stage with no sign of the hundreds of others, not a single divot in the floor.

The rest of the theater looked much the same as last time. Bright house lights still reflected off the glass chandelier overhead. Sculpted floral patterns still crowned the walls. An open-mouthed lion head still fronted the balcony. The ivy stage curtains were still there, too, but drawn to frame a movie screen that Regina hadn't seen before.

"This isn't right. It's changed. The seats, the screen. It's not right," Regina said.

"It's better than right; it's impossible. Take your seat and pay attention," Miriam said.

Regina sat reluctantly, not trusting this strange woman but curious enough to listen to her. Miriam stood close by and reached down to clasp Regina's wrists to the armrests. At once Regina felt pinpricks on her skin where Miriam touched her, felt the armrests' cast iron turn to ice. She couldn't move her hands. Her wrists were frozen in place, numbed and held fast.

Regina wriggled and kicked and opened her mouth to scream, but Miriam grabbed her by the neck. The same pinpricks, the same cold shot paralyzed Regina's voice. Miriam pressed two fingers to Regina's lips and fused them shut as well. Regina fought harder, panicking and straining to wrest free, but her hands were hundred-pound weights. She doubled over, forcing gusts through her lungs to scream, but all sound died in her throat.

"Stop it," Miriam said calmly and repeatedly while Regina kept straining. "Stop it!" she finally shouted, harshly enough to seize anyone's attention.

When Regina dared to look up at her, a voice said, "There's no need to resist, no need to speak. We are in the confines of your diseased mind. We can talk with our thoughts."

Although Miriam leered down at Regina, her mouth didn't move with the voice. Nor was the voice hers; it was Evelyn's, distorted with the same spacey echo as the song.

"You! Why are you doing this?! Let me go!" Regina thought.

"Do you like Miriam? Do you find her alluring? She's a bit cheap for my taste, but Raymond certainly had a weakness for her. Oh, he was quite fond of the ladies. He had no qualms about indulging himself through them. Why shouldn't I enjoy the same privilege?"

"Evelyn, please, let me go!"

"I've restrained you for your own benefit lest you be tempted to leave prematurely. As I said before, the song is only the beginning. By fleeing your fate within our home, you've chosen to endure it out here in your waking life. Your predecessors never had that choice, and let's see how they fared, shall we?"

The house lights dimmed as a silent black-and-white movie began to play on the screen. Fade in on a tile floor. The camera glided over a mess of clothes to the claw feet of an old-fashioned tub. Upward the camera went, pulling back to show a woman lying in the bathwater, head and shoulders just above its surface. She had dark eyes and crow's feet and studied a single drop on the lip of the spigot. She watched it bulge and fall and another do the same and another do the same.

As yet another drop appeared, Evelyn's voice said, "Rose Stollmeyer, one of Raymond's bastard children. Here you see her on December 13, 1936, age thirty-four. She was adopted, like yourself, and never discovered her connection to the Great Man. Those who knew her said her brother's death in the First World War had been a factor. That her husband abused her before and after losing their fortune in the Depression. That she suffered several miscarriages. While all that may have been true, we know something else that drove her to it, don't we, Regina?"

The woman lifted her hands from the water. She held a straight razor and touched it to her left wrist. Still watching the spigot and rigidly focused on the drops, she drew the blade from wrist to elbow crook. Blood gushed from the slit. Eyes closed, she took the razor in her left hand and repeated the cut, right wrist to elbow crook. She never screamed, but the pain creased her face.

The camera lowered its view back down to the floor. The razor fell onto the tile, blade coated with blood. More droplets landed from above and collected in the grout.

Regina closed her own eyes too late, knowing there was no way to unsee what she'd seen. She didn't understand how or why anyone would film such a thing. The slash and the blood and the woman's hurt all looked real, but Regina told herself it was fake, it had to be fake.

"No, it's real, witnessed by the roving eye of the curse," said Evelyn's voice. "The scene has changed, mind you. Observe."

Regina squinted at a dingy living room in the aftermath of a trashing. The camera surveyed the wreckage: overturned armchair with torn upholstery, emptied liquor bottles on the hardwood floor, ants crawling on food scraps, pieces of a smashed lamp, splayed books with pages ripped from their bindings. The camera closed in on a pull-down bed, where a man sat hunched on the edge of the mattress.

He wore only an undershirt and boxers. His face was wrinkled and stubbled. His hands shook as he clawed his brow with crud-stained nails. Tears glistened in his eyes while he talked to himself.

"Douglas McGilney, May 8, 1962, age forty, grandson to MacAdder through another line. His family and friends assumed his service in the Second World War had disturbed him. They also blamed alcohol for his ill health and estranged marriage, his inability to work. There was something else troubling him, though, wasn't there? Here you see him praying, imploring his god to stop the visions, to have mercy on his soul. Do you think his god saved him, Regina? Do you think he went to Heaven?"

The man tugged the bedsheets aside and uncovered a snub-nosed revolver. He cocked the hammer, jammed the barrel up under his chin, and closed his eyes. Regina closed her own before he squeezed the trigger.

"I get the point!" she thought. "I get it! Stop this already, please!"

"Take heart, Regina. They weren't *all* suicides. Behold Nancy Murphy, August 11, 1979, age twenty-seven. She first heard the song and saw the visions when she was a child like yourself. After years of trying and failing to care for her, Nancy's parents committed her to an asylum, where she still resides."

Regina opened her eyes to a bright white room. A table and folding chairs were its only furniture, and a hoop of fluorescent light shone overhead. Two huge male orderlies in scrubs were struggling to restrain a woman in a gown while a bearded doctor in a lab coat stood off to the corner.

The camera pulled in, showing that half of the woman's teeth were missing. She raged and spat at the men, her eyes alight with hatred. One orderly grabbed her hands, the other her feet, and they pinned her facedown. She beat her head against the floor, screaming as the men tied belts around her wrists and shins. The doctor knelt beside the fray to needle-stick her arm, injecting a sedative.

Dissolve to the woman in a padded cell. She wore a straitjacket, and her head was shaved. A line of stitches curved across her scalp like the seam of a baseball. Saliva dribbled down her chin as she rocked from side to side, laughing and hitting her head against the padding. She aged a year with every hit, thumping her way through her thirties, forties, and fifties, trying to bash in her own skull all the while.

"You'll never find these stories in your history books," said Evelyn's voice. "Lacking the MacAdder name, these figures are lost. Nobody remembers them. Nobody cares who they were, how they lived or died. They had his blood, your blood, and they shared your curse.

"You needn't follow their path, Regina. This can end for you quickly and peacefully if you come back to us and accept your fate."

"No! No way. I'm not feeding myself to that thing you keep in the floor. I can find your tyrant. I just need time. Now let me go. LET ME GO!"

"Time? Oh, you have time. You have a lifetime of time. An endless stretch of the reality we give you, if you have the head for it."

Miriam removed her boa and playfully roped it around Regina's neck. She kissed her fingertips, dabbed them to Regina's lips, and started away.

"Wait! You're not leaving me here, stuck like this?" Regina thought.

"Another family friend will show you out," said Evelyn's voice as Miriam opened the hallway door and slipped out, hat brim grazing the jamb. The door closed, and Regina was alone but still captive.

A wooden crackling sounded behind her as if someone were breaking twigs by the fistful. The noise lasted for a few seconds and then stopped for a silence Regina didn't like. She twisted around as far as she could, enough to see the balcony.

The lion head was gone; a splintery hole marked its absence. Something was slinking around in the shadows down below, under the balcony. She heard a rumble from that direction, distant but drawing nearer, gaining the guttural texture of an animal growl. Two greenish-yellow specks lit up in the darkness, the eyes of a sculpted beast come to life.

This isn't real, Regina thought. I'm seeing him, but I know he's not there. This can't be real. He stalked toward her anyway, his mane, tail, sleek flanks, and muscular legs all taking shape as he emerged from the shadows.

He came closer yet, close enough that Regina could see his whiskers and feel her certainty waver.

The house lights brightened, and the animal vanished. Regina's hands lifted free. "Yes! Thank you! Thank God!" she said, voice restored, and leapt up from the seat. She threw down the boa and started for the door, but the movie screen stunned her to a halt.

It had become a large mirror, reflecting a magnified version of the theater. Even as Regina stood a few steps from the chair, she remained bound and silenced onscreen. The lion still prowled toward her from behind, as flesh-and-fur real as Bullet or any other animal she'd ever seen.

He pounced upon the chair. Regina screamed as the lion bit her double's neck. Screamed as he whipped his head from side to side, ripping hers halfway off. Screamed at the geyser spurt of her blood, at how the lion never let up but kept pulling and tearing until her head fell to the floor. Eyes closed, she screamed.

"Whoa, whoa, *whoa*!" Tom said, patting her shoulder. "Regina! What is it? What's wrong?"

She opened her eyes to him, to the library, to the computer and her timed-out session. She looked around and saw a woman, two kids younger than her, and a man older than Tom all gawking like she'd scared them. Sweating and short of breath, she said, "No. Can't be. Can't be! The lion, he killed me! I saw him kill me!"

"What are you talking about? What lion?"

"In the theater! Next door! I was in the theater! I was there!"

Tom's face changed from afraid to confused. He glanced at the onlookers and said, "Regina, dear, you've been here since I've come back from the men's room. Sitting right there in that chair, staring at that computer screen for the last twenty minutes. I even said hi to you, and you nodded to me. You haven't gone anywhere."

"No, it happened. I was there."

"Come on, let's go to the break room. I'll call your folks –"

"No! I'm not going anywhere with you or anybody else, ever!"

"Okay, then I'll – hey! Regina!" Tom called after her as she took off running for the doors once again.

18. Team Freak

Grady had never bought Waters as a fed, not from the first time he saw him at council chambers, not after the Broadway fuck-up, and especially not after Colt's party. Nor did he trust Waters to deliver a worthwhile payout. Waters was nothing but a punk, a little smart-shit begging to get punched in the face. Grady couldn't imagine why Colt was intimidated by Waters, and Colt refused to discuss the topic after the party. It was all too much and too far gone. If Grady was ever going to find out what Waters was up to, he'd have to do so himself.

So he'd taken a few vacation days to go hunting. In his defense, that wasn't a total lie; he just didn't tell anyone where or what he was hunting. While the Burdock Downs police department assumed their chief was stalking deer with a bow somewhere in the Pennsylvania mountains, he'd pitched camp in the Drax Vending warehouse.

Its owners went broke twenty years ago, leaving a padlock prone to bolt cutters and a floor full of dusty stock. Rows of gumball machines paralleled rows of helium tanks topped with plastic clown heads, gas-jet nozzles poking out of the painted grins. Crane games still housed stuffed bunnies and elephants in their glass bins. Coin-op space rockets, speedboats, and biplanes faced race cars and horses, all mounted on ancient motors and long past their last rides.

Drax could have been packed with leaking drums of napalm for all Grady cared. He'd only broken in for its location, its swing-out windows giving a vantage toward Happ's. Through one particular window he could observe both the front and loading-dock entrances of Waters' supposed base, and that's just what he did. Saturday and Sunday, dawn to nightfall, Grady spent hours perched upon a crate he'd budged to the windows, watching and waiting.

By Monday, his crushed coffee cups and fast-food takeout bags littered the floor, rats be damned. His back and neck ached, his eyes were strained, but mistrust and anger kept him there. Every time Grady pictured that midget bitch ("Darling, did you bump into a door?"), he felt strong enough to stay put and endure the boredom.

His patience paid off when Happ's front doors opened at 1008 hours. Waters came out wearing a baseball hat and sunglasses that hid most of his face, his long red hair giving him away. He turned the building's corner, climbed into his jeep parked at the loading dock, and drove off.

This fit the pattern. Waters had left Happ's on the last two mornings at the same time. On those trips, at least, he hadn't returned for about three hours. Grady had never seen anyone else enter or exit Happ's, nor had he seen any vehicles there besides the jeep. He'd come to suspect that no one else was in the place.

He downed the last of his coffee, tossed the empty cup, and picked up his duty belt. If anyone were to ask, Grady happened to witness a robbery and pursued the suspect into the Flats, saw him duck into Happ's. Not that Grady needed an excuse to go anywhere in the Downs. He was the chief of police, for Christ's sake.

Regina donned the blue sunglasses before her dresser mirror and said, "Look what I found. Mind if I come in?"

And then Lonnie Waters would smile, surprised that she'd found him, admiring that she'd cared enough to retrieve what he'd lost. Because she'd been so kind, he would welcome her into his studio and give her a sneak preview of his sculptures. They might even have lunch together if she timed it right, and he would tell her everything she wanted to know about him. Where he came from, what he was like when he was her age, what kind of girls he thought were pretty. She would reach up to his face and touch him while he was talking, and he would look in her eyes and know she was his friend.

She flicked a finger at the mirror, clinked her reflection between the eyes. You're being stupid, quit being stupid, she thought. He's a grown-up. He's too busy for you, doesn't care about you.

But this is your last day off. Tomorrow's back to school. You'll never get another chance to go there or see him again. Or would you rather stay here, cooped up in your room, doing nothing but waiting for the song?

Grady crossed the street to approach Happ's, its spilled-ketchup mural looming overhead. He tried the steel double doors and found them locked. No surprise there, no reason to give up. He went around to the loading dock and a more breakable-looking entrance.

Termite-ridden steps led up to the platform and a single wooden door. Grady leaned into it and felt enough give to know he could force it. He drew his Glock, backed up, and charged. The jamb cracked, brittle with rot, and the door flung open.

"Police!" he screamed, stumbling in. "Police! Hands up!"

Nobody. No alarms. No sound but the echo of his own words. Grady scanned the vast, well-lit space in disbelief. He saw no signs of security, not a single camera, and nothing to suggest this was a contractor's headquarters.

Instead, the place seemed to be staging an art exhibit. Velvet curtains sectioned off four separate areas, enclosing each with a distinct color. Blue curtains hung directly ahead, green to their left, yellow to the left of green. At the far side of the plant, red curtains walled off an area as large as the other three combined.

"Police! Come out, hands up!" he shouted once more.

No takers.

"Didn't think so," he said, but kept his weapon drawn.

Grady proceeded to the blue curtains, hearing a quiet blend of sounds as he neared. Electronic music, explosions, screeching tires, clanging swords, and grunts all overlapped at low volume. He felt around for a gap in the fabric and parted it carefully.

Five large flatscreen TVs were mounted to the wall to form an X with two screens on top, one in the middle, two more below. The center screen showed a close-up of a human eye with a blue iris. It darted in different directions, pupil dilating and contracting. When the eye blinked, the iris turned brown. Blink, and it became green. Another blink, hazel. Another, back to the blue.

Video games played on the other screens. Top left, two ninjas fought before a mountain temple, trading punches and leaping kicks. Top right, a car chase tore through city streets seen from a driver's point of view. Slower vehicles blurred and swerved past, pedestrians scattered, police lights flashed in the rearview. Bottom left, a knight splashed around in a castle moat, fending off goblins with a broadsword. Bottom right, a spaceship blasted though formations of enemy crafts in a psychedelic laser-light show, weaving and swooping with dizzying speed. Every game continued on and on without pause, prerecorded like the eye closeups.

Wires, controllers, and consoles cluttered the floor. Grady nudged the mess with his foot, seeing an old Atari among a PlayStation, Xbox, Nintendo, and Sega Genesis. An air mattress lay half-buried with handheld games. Most of them looked somewhat new, but he noticed one, *Electronic Quarterback*, that dated back to his own high school days.

This had to be a joke, right? He was supposed to answer to a loser who'd never outgrown video games? The chief felt a rush of vindication as he left the blue room. Wait till you see this, Colt, he thought. Wait till you see how bad you got played.

He grabbed the green curtain and swiped it open. Someone was there, someone as big as him, moving just as quickly as him. He raised his Glock, but that someone's face stopped him. Grady was confronting a dressing-room mirror, ambushed by his own reflection. A tackle box of makeup lay open on the table below the mirror, surrounded by trays of paints, jars of creams, eyeliner pencils, brushes, powder puffs, cotton swabs, sponges, bottles of rubbing alcohol and Spirit Gum.

Another table extended to the right, topped with two shelves filled with mannequin heads. The bottom-shelf heads wore wigs: the wavy blond of a pampered movie starlet; the gray scraggle of a back-alley bum; the jet-black slick of a corporate suit; spiky brown, curly white, even hot pink. The top-shelf heads wore latex masks: a dirty, deep-wrinkled face alongside a sickly junkie; an owlish grandma beside a doughy teenage girl; a leathery, sun-roughened woman next to a pale corpse like the floaters Grady and his men pulled from the river on occasion.

Above the shelves hung a framed movie poster. It showed a sad clown, his face white against a black background, and its text read "Lon Chaney in 'He Who Gets Slapped.'" Lon-Lonnie. Grady made the connection and was not amused. He looked over the masks and touched the wrinkled one just to feel its rubbery texture. He shook his head, now more vexed than vindicated. There was something else to this, he thought, something right in front of him, another connection. He could feel it, just couldn't make the pieces fit.

Grady moved on past the masks and came to clothes racks. Suit coats, dress shirts, ties, t-shirts, and flannels hung from one rack, dress pants and jeans from another. There was also a laundry basket full of hats down on the floor, a Steelers cap atop the rest.

That hat. Alone it meant little, for Steelers clothes were everywhere in the Downs. But it wasn't alone, and he'd be damned if he'd really seen it where he thought he'd seen it.

Grady holstered his Glock and picked up the hat. He rummaged through the shirts, searching for a blue flannel. And there it was, on a hanger but just as tattered as before. He yanked it down and went back to the mannequin heads, where he removed the scraggly gray wig from its head and fit it upon the dirty, deep-wrinkled mask. He capped the wig with the Steelers hat and held the flannel up to the mask, and Jesus Christ he was

163

right. Here was the bum from the Pharm-Rite parking lot when he and Vic last checked on those pothead kids. The bum who said nothing when Grady flipped his cart full of cans, who just stared like he was deaf or retarded.

"Motherfucker," Grady whispered. "Mother. Fucker."

Regina hadn't walked too far along Broadway since the demolition, hadn't seen the damage up close before. For two blocks, she passed fallen bricks and broken glass and recognizable debris. Sally's Deli marquee still offering pop for 25¢. The plastic bubble-helmets of Susie Jo's hair dryers. Stubs of First Trust's marble columns. An oven that had fired up countless Campizi pizzas.

The destruction saddened her in a way she couldn't explain. They're just buildings, she told herself. They were going out of business or empty anyway, like Lonnie Waters said, and it's not like anybody got hurt. She knew this, and yet she couldn't help but miss those places now that they were gone.

Condor Development Corps hadn't spared MacAdder Plaza, either. Its semicircle of benches had been uprooted, the statue toppled. Mason was standing by the statue, peeing with his back to the street. Regina heard the tinkle, saw the trickle wetting the ground. He zipped up and moved aside to reveal MacAdder's face newly baptized.

"Hey! I remember you! You don't talk to strangers!" he said when he noticed her.

"That wasn't nice," she said, still looking at the statue.

"Nice?! Open your eyes. Ain't nothin' nice in this place. And I don't care 'cause I'm gone!"

Mason pulled a wad of cash from his coat pocket and fanned the bills, showing all hundreds. About five thousand dollars, Regina guessed, distracted by his bloodshot eyes and alcohol smell.

"See that? Not bad for a night's work, huh? All I did was party with what's-his-face, that red-haired Condor white boy. Now Ray Mac and this here cracker-ass town can eat my shit! I got a bus ticket, and I'm gone! You ain't seein' me again!"

Regina wondered if she'd heard him correctly. If so, that must have been some party.

"Tell you what. You been civil to me, treat me like a human. So I got a partin' gift for you. Take these. I got no use for 'em anymore." Mason pushed his money into one coat pocket and pulled a key ring from another.

"Keys to the kingdom," he said, and gestured toward Ribbitski's. "Frankie's gone. Had an accident, ain't comin' back. He was a real bleedin' heart, Frankie. Let me rent out the basement so long's I played Stepin Fetchit for him. Who's playin' now, Frankie?! Who's moppin' your floors, scrubbin' your toilets now?"

He handed her the keys and limped off toward the street.

"Thanks, but what am I gonna do with a bar?" Regina said.

"Get drunk!" he said with a laugh, never looking back.

Grady left the green room and headed for the yellow, to hell with caution. If Waters were to catch him here, all the better. He'd take his chances against a little queer who played with wigs and makeup any day. Bring it on, he thought. You want to creep around and spy on me? You want to be a clown? Bring on your circus and all the artsy-fartsy bullshit you got.

He threw open the curtain and entered an operating room with a ceramic slab at its center. Leather restraints dangled from the slab's sides, and patches of dried blood encrusted its surface. Scalpels, scissors, clamps, pruning shears, and a claw hammer lay upon a nearby table, all scabbed with the same brown stain.

A fly crawled along a scalpel blade and zipped over to the slab. It sampled the crust and looped around to the shelves stocked with boxes labeled "Propofol," "Hydromorphone," "Succinylcholine." It skittered on those boxes and buzzed over to the IV stands lined up by the wall, each holding a bag and drip tube. It perched on a bag but left it for the rim of a washbasin, where it greedily rubbed its forelegs together.

Grady slowly stepped past portable lights, wheeled monitors, a table stacked with bedpans, edging around the slab and to the basin. Catheters and syringes floated in its filthy liquid. The fly took off, circled Grady's head once and again, and re-settled on the slab.

He wasn't afraid so much as baffled. For the first time, it seemed possible that Waters really might be up to something heavy, though he still couldn't quite believe it. So it looked like somebody might've been worked over on that slab. What did that prove, and how did this room square with the blue and green rooms? How does one guy go from home arcade to dressing room to butcher's block and function as the head of a contracting company?

Grady returned to the floor and hesitated before the red curtain, no longer so gung-ho. "Burdock Downs police!" he said, drawing his Glock as he bulled through a gap in the velvet.

Waters was straight ahead, sitting on a stack of newspapers several feet high. Two others were sharing a sofa to the right, a balding brown man in a lab coat and another Waters. Or make that an Asian girl he'd mistaken for Waters on his stakeout. She still wore the red wig but had turned the baseball hat backward and hung the sunglasses on the neck of her t-shirt. The man and girl regarded Grady with smirks. Clearly they'd been expecting him.

"Freeze, Chief," a man said behind him, and Grady felt metal against the base of his neck. "Stay cool now. We don't want an accident any more than you do."

Grady couldn't have moved if he'd tried. The man came around, steadying a pair of sawed-off barrels inches from Grady's face. Grady recognized him as the contractor from the demolition ceremony, the fat one who set up the detonator and left the scene with Waters. Pretty damn stealthy for a guy that size, Grady thought, or just fucking stupid of me to be here without backup. What the fuck was I thinking?

"Offer it up on your palm, Chief," the contractor said.

Grady complied. The contractor took the Glock and backed off a step.

"Well, it's about damn time," Waters said "We thought you'd never leave your nest over at Drax. So, you find what you were looking for? Go on, take a look. See anything interesting?"

Off to Grady's left stood a large object covered with a sheet, poking against the cloth at odd angles. Past the object was a chaotic workshop: rods upon rods of rebar on the floor; more rebar curled into hoops and piled by a bender-cutter machine; rolls of chicken wire; lumber and scraps, platforms of nailed-together planks; paint cans, buckets, and trays giving off the sour odor of sealant.

Grady didn't know what to say and said nothing.

"Relax, Chief. Scott's not gonna blow your head off. You think we'd want to clean up that shit?" Waters hopped off the newspaper stack and approached Grady. "Put it away, Scott. We're all friends here."

Scott pocketed the Glock and lowered the sawed-off shotgun. Waters roped an arm around Grady's back and walked him deeper into the room. Grady tottered ahead, willing himself to stay composed.

"Don't be shy," Waters said. "Let's meet the people. You remember Scott, don't you? He's the foreman, runs the construction project. And over there on the sofa, that's Dr. Ishwan, the greatest medical mind the Saudis ever deported. And Manami, the makeup sorceress and occasional stunt double. Together we are Team Freak!"

"Team Freak! Team Freak! Team Freak!" Ishwan, Manami, and Scott chanted as Waters went to the covered object.

"And there's someone else you need to see. Not a teammate, but a result of our efforts."

Waters pulled away the sheet to unveil a sculpture of a sea creature leaping up from the water. The creature measured about six feet, though only its top half was visible above the splash. Bits of brown glass covered its skin like scales. Two fins fanned out from its sides, a dorsal fin from its spine. Gills puffed out from its neck. Its eyes were lidless and as large as

167

Grady's open hand. Its mouth gaped, filled with knife blades for teeth. A tube trailed out of that mouth and hooked up to an IV bag hanging from a stand. Another tube ran through a groove in the splash and down to a bedpan on the floor.

"You don't recognize him after all those years of friendship? Maybe this will help." Waters reached into his back pocket, took out a small digital recorder, and hit the play button.

Vic's voice cried, "Please! Please stop! Please!" It broke into high-pitched girlish shrieks until it recovered enough to say, "No! No! Oh, God, no! Oh, God, please stop! Make it stop!" Then more shrieks until it broke down into sobs.

Grady averted his eyes from the sculpture, unable to look at it for another second. His head twitched from side to side, shaking no, his voice too faint to sound the word. Team Freak seized upon his weakness and laughed, hooted, and whistled, baiting him as Vic's shrieks resumed.

Waters turned off the recorder. "What's the matter, Chief? You look flustered. You flustered, Chief?"

"What is this?" Grady whispered. "What the fuck are you doing?"

"You'll find out. But first there's one last freak you should meet."

She popped up from behind the sofa as if on cue, towering over Ishwan and Manami. Grady tried to take in the sight of her strong jaw and broad shoulders, blue eyes and cropped black-cherry hair, leather boots and pants and long coat and pit-bull collar. She looked like a woman, but the very idea of a woman who could physically dominate Grady was inconceivable to him.

There she was nevertheless, taking off her coat to show chiseled muscles that stretched her white tank top. She clenched her fists, knuckles cracking and shifting, and locked her gaze onto his.

"Chief Grady Kagan, this is Mirzeta, who only speaks with her hands. And she would like to have a word with you."

Grady glanced at Scott and the lowered gun. The curtain gap was also visible in his periphery. He calculated how fast he could bolt versus the sawed-off's range, knowing Scott wasn't ready to shoot. It wasn't much of a chance, but it was all he had.

He broke for the gap. Out through the red curtains, out onto the floor, no shotgun blast. He ran past the yellow, past the green, no blast. Were they following? Hell if he'd look back. Past the blue, no blast. Grady saw the doorway to the loading dock, saw daylight, and ran harder.

Regina cut through the Flats as she had before, taking Sixth Street toward the river. She paid less attention to her surroundings this time, still thinking about Mason. From Garfield to Grant to Lincoln, she walked and saw nobody outside. No religious boombox guy, no kids harassing a sick woman. From gutted homes to warehouses, she closed in on the McKinley intersection, the Happ's ketchup mural growing bigger and redder.

Up on the loading dock, an open door led right into the plant. No need to knock. She climbed the steps to the platform and paused before the door. It wasn't just open but broken, its jamb cracked and hinges busted loose.

What happened next happened fast.

Regina heard footsteps within Happ's stampeding toward the door. She jumped clear just as a huge man came barreling through. He stumbled down the steps and fell to the asphalt. Another person shot through the doorway, leapt off the platform, and landed by the man.

As the man clambered to his feet, Regina recognized him as Chief Kagan. The other person was a leather-clad woman as muscular as a superhero. Regina gasped as the woman punched the chief in the mouth. He staggered back; she kicked him in the gut. He wrenched forward; she kicked his face. The chief dropped to his knees, nose bloodied.

Regina scurried for the nearest cover, which happened to be three rusty drums clustered on the platform. She squeezed into the crevice of space between them and the wall, able to peek over them while staying hidden.

The woman settled into a stance, fists raised, and waited for the chief to stand. Once he did, she attacked with a left hook. It caught his jaw with a click, snapped his head around. A tooth and a gob of spit flew from his mouth. The chief looked defenseless for all his bulk. Too slow to deflect her blows, too heavy and winded to counter. He took one swing, a right that missed by a foot. She came back with an uppercut that jacked his chin skyward, an elbow to his throat that crushed his Adam's apple. He collapsed and rolled over onto his back.

The woman stood over the chief's head and lifted her boot. She aimed her heel at his eye, poised to stomp, but a whistle from the doorway stopped her. Both she and Regina looked over to see Waters walking onto the platform.

"You'll have time for that later. Bring him in before someone sees you," he said. "Scott, get out here and help her."

The woman scowled down at the chief but didn't speak. Another person hurried out the door and down the steps, and Regina remembered him from the last time she'd passed Happ's. The fat guy with the clipboard and hardhat who said, "Whatta ya lookin' at?" This time he took hold of the chief's legs while the woman took the arms. With grunts and strained muscles, they lifted Kagan enough to move him. Up the steps they trudged, the chief's head thunking off each plank, and back into Happ's.

Waters surveyed the lot, the street, and neighboring warehouses, but he never checked the platform on which he stood. If he'd done so, he might have noticed the horrified little girl hiding among the drums. Seeing no one, however, he retreated inside and pulled the door as closed as it would go.

Regina slipped out of her nook, jumped off the platform, and hauled some serious ass.

She lay in bed with Bullet asleep at her side. For hours she'd pictured and re-pictured the beating, nauseated and unable to think about anything else. She'd had good reason to hate Chief Kagan for how he'd

170

treated Dad and the boys at the Pharm-Rite. He was a bully who liked to fight, and she assumed he'd started this one, too. He had a knockout coming to him, but that didn't make it any less sickening to watch. All that blood on his face, his body limp like he was dead, his head scraping the steps. Even he didn't deserve that, she thought.

Dad's car door slammed outside. His footsteps thumped up to the second floor and into the kitchen. He called her, and she didn't answer. Knocked on her door, no answer.

"Reggie? It's five-thirty. Don't tell me you're asleep," Dad said as he came in. "Come on. We talked about this. The dog's not one of your dolls. He crawls in the dirt. He has fleas. He sheds, he farts, he eats cat shit. He doesn't need to be on your bed." Bullet squealed but didn't struggle as Dad picked him up and plopped him onto the floor. "So, what did you do all day?"

"Same as usual. Read. Watched TV. Took Bullet out."

"Gets boring after two weeks, doesn't it? Ready for school tomorrow?"

She didn't answer.

Dad sat on the edge of her bed, which tilted the mattress toward him. He took a breath, looked at Princess Mononoke, Sailor Moon, and Catwoman like they could tell him what to say. Another breath, and he reached over and patted Regina's foot.

"Look, we gotta talk. When you got suspended, your principal said I should think about taking you to therapy. That's where these people – doctors, I guess – talk to you and try to figure out what's going on in your head. Then they're supposed to help you work out whatever problems they find.

"I was torn about it, you know. I didn't want to put you through that unless you really needed it, and I didn't think you did. I figured you'd explain what you were doing on that roof soon enough, but one day becomes two days, two days becomes a week, a week becomes two...

"I know 'time flies' is no excuse, but it sure did, and I feel like I let you down. I waited for you to talk when I should've pushed harder or taken you to someone who'd know what to do. Because I don't know. I don't know what to do with you sometimes. And I hate to admit that, but it's true.

"So I guess what I'm saying is, you can tell me anything. Absolutely anything. I'm your dad. That's what I'm here for. Understand?"

Regina mumbled a yeah.

"Okay, good. Then tell me how you got to the roof. I promise I won't be mad."

That sounded like a deal to Regina. Of all the secrets she'd kept over the last two weeks, her grappling line seemed easy enough to give up. She slid off her bed, stepped around her airship, ant farm, and 50-in-1 kit to open her closet. Then she brought out her sleeping bag and unrolled it onto the floor, revealing the bunched-up rope stashed within it.

"Magic powers," she said, and surrendered her handiwork.

Dad counted four bungee cords, their hooks crimped to make one eight-foot line. He stretched the elastic, inspected the crimps, and looked equally mad and impressed.

"Let me guess. You found these at that garbage dump and used the vise in the basement to crimp the hooks. You stood under that chute and kept throwing up your rope till this hook caught the bottom rung. When it did, you pulled yourself up."

"And coiled it all up and stuffed it in my hood. I don't know how you and Principal Klemko missed it," Regina said.

"Right. Then tell me this, Einstein: if you were gonna climb down the same way you climbed up, how were you gonna get the hook off the bottom rung?"

"I don't know. I only cared about going up, not coming down. I could've left the line behind if I had to."

"But why? What was up there that you had to see so bad?"

"I just did it to see if I could. And once I did, I got scared and froze up," she said.

"No shit! You could've killed yourself, and you damn near gave me a heart attack. You realize that?"

"Yeah."

"Yeah, and what?"

"I'm sorry, and I won't do it again."

"Like you weren't supposed to go to that dump again? You *better* be sorry. And damn straight you'll never pull a stunt like that again. I mean, the goddamn police chief bitched me out, remember?"

Regina saw the chief's bloodied face, his head scraping the steps. She closed her eyes and tried to stop seeing it but saw it again anyway.

Dad watched her choke up and pulled her into a hug. "Oh, Reggie. I didn't mean to – you know I love you. That's why I'm so upset with you. Because I love you, and I want to help you, but I can't unless you tell the truth. See, doesn't it feel better to tell the truth?"

She said nothing, which felt like the only honest answer.

19. Back To School

Regina rushed to her home room early, avoiding the eyes in the hallways of MacAdder Elementary. Miss Lillian was already drawing a long-division problem on the chalkboard. She smiled when she saw Regina, a stark change from her usual haggard look.

"Well, hello! It's wonderful to see you again! How are you today?"

"I'm here," Regina said.

"If there's anything I can do, anything you want to tell me, don't be afraid. You can always come to me. I may be your teacher, but I'm also your friend. I hope you remember that, Regina," Miss Lillian said with a wink as the other kids filed in.

Toby and Craig sat on either side of Regina. Toby, who'd tricked Regina into poisoning her ant farm, had a black bowl cut and the beginnings of a mustache. "Welcome back, Wednesday! Where's the rest of the Addams Family?" he said.

"So, where'd you go for two weeks? They put you in Arkham Asylum with the Joker and the Riddler?" Craig added.

Kiley, who sat in front of Regina, turned around. "You guys are jerks. Don't listen to them, Regina. They're jerks."

"Why don't you say something, Wednesday? Think you're too good to talk to us?" Toby said.

"She's silently plotting her revenge," Craig said.

"Why should I talk to you?" Regina said. "You have nothing to say, and you say it stupidly."

"Ooooh! She sure told us!" Craig said with a giggle.

"Children, that's enough," said Miss Lillian from across the room.

"We're just saying hi," Craig said.

"That's enough!"

"Teacher's pet," Toby whispered as the bell rang.

Principal Klemko then began her morning announcements over the intercom. "Good morning, children. Please remember that your fundraiser order forms are due on Friday. That will be the *last* day you can turn them in, and it's *very* important that you do so..."

Regina scanned the room for changes since her suspension and noticed the Halloween decorations. A black cat arched on his claws over the chalkboard, his fur spiked and fangs bared. Grinning jack o' lanterns were thumbtacked to the door. A skeleton and scarecrow with crepe-paper limbs were taped to the windows. On the near wall was a poster showing a witch stirring a cauldron, green steam rising from the brew. She had wild yellow eyes, bulging warts on her chin and hooked nose, one tooth in her cackling mouth. Regina knew the poster was supposed to be cute, but it made her itch between her fingers where she'd been licked, on her neck where she'd been sniffed.

"...and lastly, I'd like to say one more thing. You may notice a familiar face here today. A special someone who's been away for a while. I won't name names, but I think it would be kind of you to let that person know how much you missed her... or him. Have a good day."

Regina slouched deeper in her seat, eyes down, sensing multiple glances as Toby and Craig snickered. The first-period bell rang. Some kids left Miss Lillian's room while others stayed or arrived, and so the school day began.

Miss Lillian pointed to the problem she'd drawn on the board: 435,728 divided by 172. "Okay, problem number six from your homework. I want someone to come up here and show us how it's done."

No one raised a hand. Regina sure didn't want to volunteer. It wasn't the problem's difficulty so much as her shyness before the likes of Toby and Craig. She waited for someone else to step up, namely Kiley or Abby or Cyril. Any one of them could've aced it, but instead they doodled or yawned or sat with arms folded, looking at Miss Lillian like she was a fool.

"Anybody?" Miss Lillian said to a silent room.

Regina fidgeted, feeling guilty for stiffing Miss Lillian. The silence stretched from awkward to embarrassing to excruciating until she couldn't take it anymore and raised her hand.

Miss Lillian brightened. "Oh! Well, then. Yes, come on up, Regina."

Regina took a stick of chalk from the tray and started with a 2. 172 × 2.

She calculated it out to 344 and wrote 344 beneath the 435 of the 435, 728.

Subtracting 344 from 435: $5 - 4 = 1$; borrow the 1 from the 4 to make 13; $13 - 4 = 9$; $3 - 3 = 0$; 091. $435 - 344 = 91$.

Drop down the 7 of the 435, 728, and you have 917. Start over: 917 divided by 172.

She figured the next number might be 5 and multiplied 172×5 for 860. As close as she'd get to 917. Regina set about subtracting 860 from 917 when she heard the phantom song.

It sounded from the intercom. The first chords stopped her hand and caused her to screech the chalk. Descending melody, chord, chord. She looked back to her classmates as it continued to play, and of course they didn't hear it. They just sat there staring at her while Toby crossed his eyes and twirled a finger by his temple and Craig tried to stifle his laughter.

Regina turned back to the board. She closed her eyes, and the song stopped. That's right, she thought. You never heard it because it never played. She took a breath, resolved to finish the problem, and opened her eyes.

The board had softened to a fleshy texture. The numbers she'd written were carved into it, each an open wound. Blood trailed down to the chalk tray and pooled in its grooves. The chalk in Regina's hand had become a piece of jagged brass also wet with blood. She dropped it with a gasp. Blinding light flashed behind her, and a boom rocked the room.

Regina turned around to see her classmates burning. Nineteen separate fires for nineteen kids, and none of them cared. They neither moved nor showed any signs of pain. They stayed at their desks like nothing was happening even as their skin blistered. Cyril's eyes melted into gray fluid behind his glasses. The bones of Abby's fingers showed, still holding her pencil. Kylie's hair singed off her scalp, which peeled off her skull. Toby and Craig's faces fell away in charred strips and bared their mocking skulls. Nobody's mouths moved, and yet Regina heard distant screams, girls' screams.

"Regina? What's wrong?" Miss Lillian said.

Regina couldn't blink or speak. Whiffs of air shot past her, grazing her face and hair. Invisible metal clinked and ricocheted around the room.

A gash opened across Miss Lillian's forehead as she approached Regina. The wound bled, but Miss Lillian didn't notice it. Another metallic ping, and a piece of Miss Lillian's cheek went flying off. She didn't notice that, either.

"It's okay. You can sit down now," she said, and reached for Regina's shoulder. Another whiff, and half of Miss Lillian's forearm was sliced away to expose the bone.

Regina jumped back, screaming, "No! Don't touch me! Don't touch me!" To her classmates, "You're burning! Don't you feel it?! You're burning! *You're all burning*!"

Miss Lillian again tried to reach Regina, who swung both fists to fend her off. "No! No! *No*! You're dying!"

All nineteen kids gawked at this, too shocked to react. No one laughed, not even Toby and Craig.

"Regina! Calm down! It's okay! Calm down!" Miss Lillian said, struggling to hold Regina to the wall.

Regina clawed, kicked, and couldn't stop screaming, "No! Get off me! You're burning! You're dying! You're burning! Why can't you feel it?! You're all dying!"

> Caller: Bill Hargreaves
> Location: Burdock Downs, PA 15201
> Subject: Construction
> Hostility Index: Moderate

"Great. A neighbor," Shelton grumbled, and hit the Enter key. "Concilicom. Shelton Gundy speaking. How can I help you?"

"Gundy, huh? I used to know a Jimmy Gundy. You're his kid, right?"

Shelton hesitated and admitted, "Yes, sir. I am."

"Good. Maybe you can help me, then. These Condor sons of bitches, they're tearin' down Broadway, and they dump rubble in my yard. Big slabs of concrete, they just drop 'em right on my wife's garden. You know how much money she spends on that garden? I go outside and say, 'Hey, whatta you think you're doin'?' And they laugh at me! They laugh! One of 'em says, 'What's it matter? You're gonna die soon anyway.' How you like that?! Is that how you'd talk to your old man?"

"No, sir."

"The other one says, 'Yeah, go and die already. Free up some Social Security.' What's this world coming to? I want you to do something about this. I want reprimands. I want apologies. I want their rubble outta my yard. You can do that, right?"

"I can't promise anything, sir. What I can do is file your complaint for the official record and forward it to Condor Development Corps, who should act upon it. I can't tell you when or how or if they will, but they should."

"What? What's that mean? Why can't you – I called their number, and it went to you, and now you're sayin' you can't *do* anything? What the hell kind of shell game is this?"

"It's a complicated process, sir. I'm just trying to facilitate it."

"I knew your old man. Your old man hung off scaffolding five stories high, layin' brick in subzero degrees, and you 'facilitate a process.' It's nothing but a loop. A scam! How do you sleep at night? How do you look in the mirror every morning? How do you call yourself a man?"

"Would you like me to file your complaint, sir?"

"You're gutless. Your old man would kick your ass from here to Clairton if he could see you now, and you know it."

"Sir, I have the right to terminate this call."

"Gutless!" Mr. Hargreaves spat, and hung up.

Shelton ripped off his headset and threw it at the cubicle wall. Management might have been watching, and he didn't care. Fuck them, fuck Hargreaves, and fuck him for being stuck in this shitty job. His performance board ding-donged to register caller 014. Then it buzzed, and its red 000 – his satisfied callers – blinked and remained 000.

He rubbed the back of his tense neck. Eyes closed, he reminded himself to breathe and breathe deeply. Minutes passed, but his heart refused to slow. Then the Service Hub's intercom sounded its two-note tone.

"Shelton Gundy, you have a call on 101," announced Myrt the receptionist. "Shelton Gundy, 101."

Here we go, he thought. Here comes management. Here comes a trip to the office and their faux concern wrapped around a threat. *Shelton, are you okay? We've noticed that your numbers are down, and you've seemed upset lately. A bit off your game. Is there something you'd like to discuss with HR?* He picked up the nearest phone, braced to hear his supervisor's voice.

"Mr. Gundy? It's Sadie Klemko. I *really* hate to bother you at work again, but I'm afraid we're having another problem."

By eight o'clock that night, Shelton and Regina were sitting in a restaurant booth, silent and avoiding eye contact. They'd barely spoken all day until he'd declared they were going out for dinner. Looking for a kid-friendly place where she might feel comfortable, he'd driven a few miles outside the Downs and had found this Tastee Yumz joint in a strip mall. They were its only customers.

Having devoured his burger and fries, Shelton spent the lull looking at the traffic outside. There was nothing enthralling out there, but he was determined to ignore the girl behind the counter, who kept shooting him go-home glances even though the place wasn't supposed to close for another hour. He also sought a distraction from Reggie's double fudge sundae, which was melting to waste.

She'd taken two spoonfuls and could stomach no more. She was humiliated and ashamed, and above all she was afraid. Afraid of how mad he was and whatever punishment this sundae was meant to cushion. Afraid of what the song would bring next time and how powerless she was to stop it.

For his part, Shelton wasn't angry. He'd spent years fearing that he might be a failed parent, and now he knew. He'd spent the last two weeks wondering if she had a real problem, and now he knew. This was the muck, and they'd sunk chin-deep in it, but he would find a way to pull them out. He knew that, too, and refused to allow any doubt. Things could only get better. They just had to.

"You know we can't keep doing this. You can't be having these problems in school. I can't be leaving work, getting reamed out by your principal. Reggie, this is your chance. I need you to tell me what's happening."

"Only if you promise me something. You won't get rid of me, send me off to live with someone else because you think I'm crazy," Regina said.

"Of course not. You know I'd never do that. You know you can trust me, whatever it is."

181

Regina thought it over. Keeping her secret seemed like the smartest move three weeks ago, but now everybody thought she was crazy anyway, including Dad no matter what he said. Why bother, then? Why not spill the whole mess on this table and let him figure it out?

"Okay," she said. "It started with a song."

She skipped her Lonnie Waters encounters, which would only cause extra trouble, and fudged Tom's video to a book she'd found on her own. Otherwise, she told Dad everything about the song and the Folly, about Evelyn, Maura, the Boom Girls, and the curse. At first she worried about how weird it would sound, but as she continued, she felt lighter, freer, and relieved. The main problem of the curse remained, but she didn't have to hide it anymore. Now, finally, someone else would understand.

Or so she thought until she finished and looked at Dad, whose face had aged ten years. His eyes were glazed and vacant, skin paled a shade, stubble grayed. He'd withered right there before her, and it was all her fault again.

She's crazy, he thought. My kid's crazy. Not just odd but deranged. Unhinged. Insane. Maybe she'd read too many comic books, watched too much anime, too many horror movies. That might explain her story but not her belief in it. And unless she was a budding Oscar-worthy actress, she really did believe it, and that was the heart of the problem. All right. Now he knew. But how to proceed?

"Reggie, honey, you have a wonderful imagination. It's a gift."

"I'm telling the truth."

"You hear a song nobody else can hear. You see things nobody else can see. Why is that, if you're not imagining it?"

"I told you. Because I'm cursed."

"Because you're a MacAdder."

"Yes. But I might have some Lakatos in me, too."

"Right. Because the sorceress looked like an old-woman version of you."

"Can you prove me wrong?"

"Maybe, if we investigated your genealogy, but that would take a lot of time and money. I have a simpler, better idea. How about if I go to MacAdder's Folly and see these ghosts for myself? I'll get them off your back."

"No! You can't do that. I told you. Evelyn said not to bring anybody who's not a tyrant."

"Maybe I am, for all she knows."

"No, Dad! They'll kill you! I know what I saw. They touched me. I felt them. It's real, I *know* it is! You *can't* go there!"

He'd never seen Reggie so upset, not once in all of her ten years. Even the counter girl paused her texting to looked from Reggie to Shelton to the clock on the wall. 8:37. Back to the texting with a sigh.

Regina leaned back from table, arms crossed, staring into him.

Shelton held his face in his hands, took a long and heavy breath. One part of her story did beg further questions: her seeing herself as a baby trapped within glass, tangled in a jungle of plastic plants. He'd never told her about the fish tank, he was damn sure of it. He did tell his ex, Amy, a few years ago, but she wouldn't have mentioned it to Reggie. So how and why would Reggie's mind go there? She couldn't have remembered it herself, could she, somewhere in her subconscious? Shelton was curious but decided the answers could wait. This wasn't the time to get sidetracked.

He laid his palms on the table and said, "Remember what I said yesterday, about going to therapy?"

"You *do* think I'm crazy."

"Absolutely not. I just think it might help."

"Whoever you take me to won't believe me, either, and then what?"

"You have to admit, it's not easy to believe."

"So? Everybody believes in God. Nobody can see God or touch God. Nobody can prove there is a God, but everybody believes it anyway. Everybody believes Jesus died, stayed dead for a few days, then woke up, walked out of his tomb, hung out with his friends, and got beamed up to Heaven. That's not crazy?"

"That's different. Millions of people believe that."

"So that makes it true?"

"No, that makes it acceptably crazy. Look, for all I know, you would've been a prophet two thousand years ago. Today, you're going to therapy. I can't tell you that's right or wrong, fair or unfair. I don't know if it'll help. I just know your principal won't let you come back without it. Her and Dr. Wohler think I should send you to another school, one for kids with behavioral problems. That's what we're talking about here. That's what we're looking at. And I'm not passing the buck to them. Even if they weren't pushing me, I'd still think we should try therapy."

"But we aren't; I am. Because you think I'm crazy."

"Regina Marie Gundy, I never said that."

"Your face did, Dad. When I told you what happened, your face did. But since I could see it, and you couldn't, I guess that didn't happen, either."

Shelton resisted a quick and pissy comeback. He glanced at the sundae and said, "You gonna finish that?"

Regina pushed the container toward him.

He dug into the puddle, impervious to her stare and the counter girl's latest sigh. Get in line, ladies, he thought. If there's one thing I'm good at, it's disappointing people. 000 satisfied and counting.

20. Penance

Dolores took her seat behind the Sacred Heart organ and played "Hail Holy Queen" to begin Friday morning Mass. There were sixteen congregants in the pews, all of whom rose to their feet and sang:

"Hail Holy Queen Enthroned Above, O Maria

Hail Mother of Mercy and of Love, O Maria

Triumph all ye cherubim

Sing with us, ye seraphim

Heaven and earth resound the hymn

Salve, Salve, Salve, Regina"

Andrew listened by the sacristy door, eyes closed, letting the music inspire him with grace. He exhaled and proceeded down the central aisle, admiring his church's beauty all the while. The green altar cloth looked so lush draped across the marble. A hand-carved Holy Mother stood to the left of the altar, resplendent in her blue mantle. The brass tabernacle gleamed with reflected candlelight off to the right. Morning sun slanted down through stained glass in rose-colored shafts. Who could see such a place and remain unmoved, Andrew wondered, basking in the majesty. He pitied such a soul if it did exist.

"Our life, our sweetness here below, O Maria

Our hope in sorrow and in woe, O Maria

Triumph all ye cherubim

Sing with us, ye seraphim

Heaven and earth resound the hymn

Salve, Salve, Salve, Regina"

The final notes trailed off as Andrew stepped up to the chancel. He took his place at the pulpit and directed the Sign of the Cross to his congregants. "In the name of the Father, Son, and Holy Spirit."

"Amen," they answered.

"The grace of our Lord Jesus Christ, and the love of God, and the fellowship of the Holy Spirit be with you all."

"And also with you."

Andrew surveyed the pews and saw the usual faces: the Goleski sisters squinting at their missals with the same concentration they brought to their bingo cards; Donna Isgro pinching her rosary beads and mentally reciting Hail Marys, attending the Mass but oblivious to it; Eddie Colindi still dazed by his wife's death six months ago; Midge Dishman, who lived to give the First Reading, sitting up close – except no, not today. Andrew only assumed the figure in the front row was Midge, but it was actually Lonnie Waters.

The surprise caused Andrew to miss his cue. After a pause, he blinked and said, "My brothers and sisters, to prepare ourselves to celebrate the sacred mysteries, let us call to mind our sins."

Everyone but Waters responded, "I confess to almighty God, and to you, my brothers and sisters, that I have sinned through my own fault, in my thoughts and in my words, in what I have done and in what I have failed to do. And I ask blessed Mary, ever virgin, all the angels and saints, and you, my brothers and sisters, to pray for me to the Lord our God."

"May almighty God have mercy on us, forgive us our sins, and bring us everlasting life," Andrew said.

"Amen."

"Lord have mercy," said Andrew.

"Lord have mercy," said all the congregants but Waters, who said, "No, He won't."

"Christ have mercy."

"Christ have mercy." "No, He won't."

Andrew heard the discord and tried to ignore it. "Lord have mercy."

"Lord have mercy." "Nope. Not a chance."

"Let us pray for our community this morning. Let us have hope for its renewal and faith in those who've promised to rebuild it. Amen."

"Amen," the congregation said, and seated themselves as Waters walked up to the pulpit.

"Excuse me?" Andrew said.

"You're excused," Waters said, and leaned in toward the pulpit microphone to nudge Andrew aside. "If you're expecting Midge, she's indisposed at the moment. I'll be doing the First Reading instead, and I'm glad it's from the Old Testament because I'm an Old Testament kind of guy. Today's reading is from the Book of – sit down, Father. Your chair's over there."

Andrew lingered, not sure what to do.

"Today's reading is – please, sit down," Waters said a little louder.

Andrew retreated to a nearby chair, his customary seat during the Reading. He tried to appear calm, as if this were all part of a normal Mass.

"Today's reading is from the Book of Judges. And juries. And executioners," Waters said. "A long time ago in a village not so far away, there once lived a maiden. She was a kind but scarred soul, orphaned as a child and left to the care of her elderly grandmother. She was also beautiful, if it matters.

"At the age of seventeen, she made the acquaintance of a handsome prince. The village revered him for his great valor in combat as well as his lineage, for he was the only son of the king. The maiden was smitten with the prince but also wary of him, having heard rumors that he was not so very gallant in private.

"The prince took a liking to the maiden, too, and invited her to attend his autumn banquet. She arrived at his secret court hidden in the woods outside the village. The prince and his two most trusted lords were there along with his feeble-willed squire. No one else was present as far as they knew. The wine flowed, and the hours passed, and the maiden had come to understand the prince's desire. He wished to seduce her and rend her hymen with the same bloodlust he showed in battle.

"Perhaps the maiden knew what the prince wanted and had arrived prepared to give it to him. We will never know her motives, but we do know what transpired next. When the prince groped the maiden before his lords, she denied his advance. The prince was not one to accept rejection, and so he persisted while maiden resisted. The lords assisted their prince, holding down the stubborn maiden for the penetration-consummation. Once the prince finished spurting his seed, his lords jizzed theirs into her as well. Meanwhile, the feeble squire did nothing but watch, unwilling to participate or interrupt."

"Word of the prince's conquest quickly spread throughout the village. The no-longer-maiden recognized her new standing in the community. She had become the whore: a plaything to the whims of men, an object of scorn to women, a creature judged unworthy of respect.

"Ever selfish and headstrong, the whore refused to accept her place. She drowned herself in the village river, so ungrateful was she for the passion the prince lavished upon her. As we know, the Lord God does not look kindly upon this mortal sin of suicide. Thus He banished the prideful whore to Purgatory, where she no doubt remains today.

"The prince matured to inherit his father's throne. His trusted lords became knights, the most loyal defenders of his realm. The observant squire turned to the Lord and found fulfillment as the village priest. This quartet prospered in the court for many years, secure in their power and blessed righteousness.

"This is the Word of the Lord," Waters said, and returned to his pew.

"Thanks be to God," some of the congregants answered by habit.

The rest said nothing, baffled by what they'd heard. They looked from Waters to Andrew, who rose and approached the pulpit with the chalky complexion of a man about to faint.

"I'm sorry. I'm not feeling well. I... I can't continue. I'm – bless you. Bless all of you," the priest said, and hurried down the aisle.

Ten minutes later, Waters remained seated in the front row. He'd waited through the confused murmurs and abrupt closing hymn. He'd ignored the congregants' glares and whispers as they'd filed out. He'd listened to the bustle coming from within the sacristy and was not surprised when Andrew returned. Glasses absent and hair disheveled, the priest stood before Waters after everyone else had left.

"Who is that... that *woman* in the sacristy?" Andrew said, and waved a paper in his hand. "And what is this?"

"Self-explanatory, isn't it? You're going on sabbatical effective immediately. You can sign off on it and post it or not. Either way, you're leaving with me. We're going for a drive, you and I, during which I'll be happy to answer all of your questions."

"And if I refuse?"

"Did you not hear the Reading? Consent doesn't count for much on this planet. I don't need to explain that to you of all people."

"Who are you? *Who are you*?!"

Mirzeta appeared at the rear of the nave, her blue stare locked on Andrew. He couldn't meet it and shifted his eyes to the Mary statue. His holy virgin-mother, his hope in sorrow and woe, had never looked so wooden. The priest felt himself wilting and gripped the edge of the pew for support.

"We are the words in the wax, Father. Your ways are not hidden from us, nor is your sin concealed. Will you walk with us, or do you choose to refuse us?"

Drumbeats hammered the jeep's speakers, and guitars crashed in to blare lumbering heavy metal. "Living After Midnight." Andrew hadn't heard the song since high school, when it was a hit among the burnouts.

Waters lowered the volume and looked over to him. "What's the matter? You don't dig the Judas Priest?"

Andrew gave a forced smile and a head-shake no. Otherwise, he kept facing away from Waters, watching the passing scenery of Pike Street. Waters thrived on baiting and humiliating. That much was clear. Even so, Andrew suspected that Waters was sensible and this spiteful man-child persona was a ruse he used to unsettle people to his advantage. In response Andrew played the calm adult, neither rude nor rattled even as his ears rang with damage. He was practicing passive resistance, trying to regain the nerve he'd lost in his church.

"Suit yourself," Waters said, and spun the volume back up.

He slowed and cut a right onto a side street called Cherry Way. Past a Little League field and into the woods, Cherry's pavement gave way to rutted dirt. The trees darkened the path with a canopy of fall reds and golds. Andrew couldn't resist turning toward Waters' side when they passed a garbage dump painted with garish colors. He twisted around to see the dump recede behind them. This secluded route was new to him for all the years he'd lived in the Downs.

Waters drove onward into more woods and finally turned off the music. They arrived at the end of the path, and the jeep bumped to a stop. Waters stepped out and beckoned Andrew to follow. The priest obeyed, minding his steps on the riverbank's muddy slope down to the brown Mon. Getting his bearings, he saw the Works' stacks about a mile off to his left, the Flats a mile to his right. Gnat-sized cars zipped along the highway across the river. He also noticed red bricks lodged in the ground close to where he stood. The bricks had been arranged to resemble a Christian cross. Waters toed a brick and loosened it, clicking it against the others.

"Here's where they found her, you know. They said she put bricks in a sack and lugged it from Sheridan Street down to the Flats. Which isn't a quick walk, but it's the most direct route to the river. Tied that sack to her belt, waded in. The sack ripped, lost every brick but one, and the current dragged her here. That's the coroner's story.

"You're a man who contemplates mysteries, Father. Why would a girl like her – smart, charming, beautiful, college bound – why would a girl like her do such a thing? How could such a girl throw herself into those dark and toxic waters?"

"Mr. Waters..." Andrew said, and paused on the repetition. That had to be a coincidence, right? This person hadn't intentionally named himself "Waters" because... Andrew looked at that other person, who prodded him on with a stare.

"We've all seen or done regrettable things in our lives. We've all failed to be our best selves, sometimes with disastrous consequences. Obviously you've learned of an incident in my past in which I've done just that, failed to be my best self. I know it's –"

"You don't know a goddamn thing, Father. You don't even know who I am, do you? Here's a hint. We met that night, too, you and I. In the middle of a space invasion."

Andrew understood, and the shock walloped him. He could neither move nor speak. He stood paralyzed before a face radiating the same hatred now as twenty-five years ago, a voice still carrying the same venom.

"When I did the Reading, I left out an important part. The maiden had a little brother who lived with her and her grandmother. He was a weird kid, kind of a wimp. You might even call him a runt. He wasn't nearly as strong as his big sis, and he did cling to her. He looked up to her for braving their mother's death and adapting so well to their new life. He envied her, too, for how popular she was, how easily she made new friends. And he needed her. If a kid ever needed an older sister, that kid needed her.

"So when the maiden let slip that she was going to the autumn banquet, you might understand why her brother might follow without her knowing it. Which he did. Yes, he followed and hid in the woods surrounding the prince's secret court. He saw everything, Father. He saw the maiden try to push the prince away, heard the word 'stop.' He saw the prince and lords persuade her to change her mind. He saw what they did, and what the squire didn't do. He didn't know what to make of it, didn't know what he was seeing, but it scared him. He fled, he did. Ran all the way back to his grandmother's house, left his sister to the revelry of the banquet. He couldn't sleep that night and hasn't slept much since.

"How about you, Father? Lose any sleep over the years?"

Andrew still couldn't speak, couldn't even muster a rasp.

"And you're still here with them, still their bitch, which leads to another mystery. What *does* Colton Hauser have on you?" Waters said, and paced a circle around the priest. "You have a crush on him when you were kids? Can't fault you for that; he *was* hot. And he let you hang out with him, made you feel like you weren't a loser. And, to be fair, he did pay your dad's hospital bills. That was big of him.

"But how do you reconcile your weakness for him with your guilt? You *do* feel guilt, don't you, Father? I assume you do, with your trips to Suncrest, your plans to use your cut of the money for a women's shelter. A women's shelter! Imagine, *you* coming to the aid of a threatened woman!"

"Listen to me," Andrew said, voice quivering, "Listen to me. If what you say is true, then we both witnessed the same thing, and we both failed to act. Can't you see, we're not so far apart, and we're both still –"

"I'm not like you. You were seventeen. I was ten."

"But she was your sister. If you felt she was in danger, why didn't you intervene? You admit you fled. Many other boys would've rushed in to fight or called out for help. I can see this has wounded you very deeply, and I'm here to say it's okay. We share this wound, both of us, and the Lord –"

"You're trying to forgive me?" Waters said. "This ain't your church, and there's no wound. She's dead, motherfucker! Dead! And she's never coming back! There's no forgiveness here. No forgiving, no forgetting, no healing. No turning the other cheek. You know what there is?"

He swung and punched Andrew's crotch. Pain ripped through the priest, who lurched over with a groan and collapsed to the mud. He'd lost his wind and couldn't catch it. Eyes bulging and tearing, he saw Waters kneel to remove the loosened brick. Saw him rise and approach with it.

"That's all there is," Waters said. "And all there ever will be, now and forever."

Andrew closed his eyes, and the brick delivered an amen.

21. Unleashed

On that same Friday morning, Bullet parked himself beside Regina's bed and squealed to go out. She bunched her pillows to her ears to muffle his pleas, but it was no use. Soon he would start barking, and after that his bladder would become accident prone.

"Okay, okay," she said, which incited him to squeal louder and pad around in a frantic loop.

Regina lifted Bullet onto the wagon and hitched the rope to its handle. She donned her gloves and pushed the wagon toward the steps with her foot. The wheels set in the gutter-rails, and the wagon would have rolled down the sharp drop if she hadn't been holding the rope taut. Carefully, then, she fed the rope to the creaky bicycle-wheel pulley fixed to the floor. The pulley turned with the weight of Bullet and the wagon, lowering both until the wagon clunked onto the bottom landing. She plodded down the steps after it, as bored as Bullet was thrilled.

The downstairs neighbors had partied last night and littered the porch with new cans for the wheels to crunch. Their stereo was still playing some generic angry rock, the sound pounding their window draped with a Steelers banner. Regina lifted Bullet off the wagon, walked him around the duplex and down the hill to Cherry Way. Soon they reached the Little League field, where she unleashed him for his daily waddle.

A squirrel was perched upon the outfield fence, unnoticed by Bullet. It waited until he finished taking his dump and flicked its tail to provoke him. Bullet yelped and chugged after his tormentor, which darted off to the woods. After blobbing through a gap in the fence to give chase, Bullet stopped and looked back to Regina. His dark eyes sparkled, and his panting, smiley mouth seemed to say, "Come on! Aren't you coming?"

"Go, go! I'll catch up later," Regina said.

Bullet resumed his pursuit, dipping into the dirt road's furrows on his way to the woods. Regina watched him dwindle to a brown and white speck and knew he would track the squirrel to his favorite tree. He would circle and bark, and the squirrel would tease him for a while and escape. Checkmate, good game, and they would play again tomorrow and the next day. She saw no reason to hurry after him.

Regina wandered to the fence, leash and poop-bag in hand. The woods and Smash Heap awaited, and it was a perfectly lovely day to be outside, but she only wanted to return to her room. The song had played there, too, but had never brought one of those horrible visions with it. At least not yet. Out here in the open, though, she felt like a constant target.

She hooked her fingers around the fence links and squeezed the metal, thankful for something real and solid against her skin. Maybe Dad was right, and she just needed someone to scan her brain and debug it like a computer. But if her problem wasn't mental and couldn't be fixed, why live like this? If the movie Evelyn had shown her was an accurate predictor of her fate, why wait for it? Maybe it was Evelyn, not Dad, who was ultimately right, and "the more merciful option" was still open to her.

Regina closed her eyes and prayed. She wasn't sure if she was doing it right or even believed in God, but it had to be worth a try. Several minutes later, she heard a distant hum. It kicked up in pitch as it drew nearer and grew louder. She opened her eyes to glimpse slivers of a vehicle moving through the woods, speeding along the dirt road. It emerged and swerved past the fence where she stood, revealing itself as Lonnie Waters' jeep by its unmistakable space-alien sticker.

The jeep continued on Cherry and turned left onto Pike, revving in a great rush to get somewhere. Regina guessed that Waters hadn't seen her, but she didn't want to chance it after her last trip to Happ's. It was time go home anyway.

She whistled, clapped, and called Bullet's name. Seconds passed, and he didn't appear. She called him again. Another minute and still nothing.

Regina left the field for the dirt road and proceeded into the woods. She saw the brown and white speck far up ahead and knew something was wrong. The speck was on the road, but it didn't move.

She jogged toward it, broke into a sprint. The speck took the shape of her dog as she closed in. He lay on his side, facing away from her, slung over the hump between the furrows.

Regina stopped a foot short of him. Bullet wasn't breathing. Roughed-up fur and a dent in his flank marked where he'd been struck. The same eyes that had sparkled were now lifeless; the same mouth that had smiled now trickled blood. His right front paw was twitching to scratch the air.

For a moment she stood there and could do nothing else. *You caused this. You let him off the leash. You should've been with him. This wouldn't have happened if you were with him.* No, she told herself, no. Over and over, no. No, no, no!

She dragged him to the roadside by his legs and fell down onto him. Hugging him, burrowing her face into his fur, Regina screamed. And screamed again, scorching her throat until she broke down crying.

Around eleven that night, Shelton fixed the wrench onto a bolt and pushed. The wrench slipped free and clanged off the bottom step. He cursed it, picked it up, and tried again. The damn bolt wouldn't budge, and why would it? It had been that kind of day, starting with Myrt on the intercom. "Shelton Gundy, you have a call on 101."

"He's dead," Reggie said when he picked up, barely eking out the words.

His manager, always a peach. "This is the *third* time you've left early in three weeks, Shelton. Twice this week alone. Of course you can leave if it's a family emergency. Family comes first, no question. But you've been having a *lot* of family emergencies lately."

A round of glares from the Service Hub as if he were ditching work for something fun.

Reggie on the kitchen floor, looking sicker than she'd ever looked with the flu or strep, hugging Bullet wrapped in a blanket. Drops of blood on the yellow cloth.

The vet asking if Shelton wanted a common cremation. Shelton dumbly nodding, wondering what an uncommon cremation involved. The weird, wrong feeling of leaving the vet's with Bullet's collar, a receipt, and no Bullet. Choking up on the drive home, not caring if Reggie or anyone else noticed.

Not a peep from her in the car, the vet's, or the apartment. She went to her room when they returned and slammed the door. "Leave me alone" in so many words and nothing about how it happened. Shelton figured Bullet wasn't on the leash, but he didn't ask. It seemed cruel to press so soon after the fact, so he didn't. If he could dismantle the Bullevator now so she wouldn't have to see it tomorrow, that might limit the cruelty, too.

The bolt grudgingly loosened. He unscrewed the others on the bottom landing and realized there were dozens more. This wouldn't be so quick or easy, and he was already sweating, his back and neck already stiff. He told himself that he really needed to lose some weight, really for real this time.

Shelton started up the steps, thirsty for water, but the sight of Regina stopped him. She stood on the top landing, hands in her corduroy pockets, staring down at him. Who knows how long she'd been there? If she'd made any sound, he hadn't heard it through the action-movie explosions and machine-gun fire of the neighbors' TV.

For once she spoke first. "You couldn't wait till tomorrow?"

"I'm not trying to erase him. I'm trying to... make things easier."

Shelton passed her on his way to the kitchen and turned on the tap. After splashing his face, he poured a glass and guzzled. Then he slid down to the floor and sat with his back to the cabinets, regaining his breath.

"Are you having a heart attack?" Reggie said.

"No. Just fat and tired. And it's been one extremely shitty day, hasn't it?"

Regina walked over and sat down beside him. Dad roped an arm around her. She rested her head rest against him and noticed the relatively clean spot on the linoleum floor where he'd wiped up Bullet's blood. If only he could've believed how much more she'd seen lately: the movie at the library, the chief at Happ's, Miss Lillian at school.

"What are you thinking, Reggie? It's okay to say it."

She said nothing, still thinking of blood. How Bullet's left his body, how her own was the source of the curse. How today's violence was her fault, and there was no way to make it right except by more violence, by giving the Girls their tyrant "who has spilled blood for personal gain." Blood for blood for blood, and where would all this bloodshed end?

"You may not believe this, but I loved him, too. And I miss him, too. But you know what? I think Bullet's happier now. I think he's in a better place, running around like he used to."

"You really think that?" she said.

"Yeah, sure. Why not?"

"I don't know. Sounds acceptably crazy, I guess."

"I'm afraid to ask where you think he is," Dad said.

"I don't know. But if he's in a better place, I wish I were there with him. I hate it here, Dad. Everywhere I go, I see people getting hurt or hurting each other, threatening to hurt each other, enjoying hurting each other. It's brutal and sick, and I'm too weak for it. I want out, Dad. Not just out of the Downs. I mean I want *out*."

"Jesus, Reggie, you're too young to think like that. I know this is a really hard time, but you'll get through it. And as you grow up, you'll get through even harder times than this. Life is hard more often than not, but you'd be surprised how strong you are. A lot stronger and braver than you think.

"You're a special girl, Reggie Gundy. You have a good heart and a brilliant mind. Don't give up on this place. If it's ever gonna get better, it'll need you and a lot more like you."

Dad kissed Regina on the crown of her head, between her ponytails. She didn't react, didn't even blink. Regina knew only one person who might understand how she felt. Unfortunately, that person had been dead for twenty-four years, fourteen before Regina was born.

22. Recurring Dream

Regina slept very little over the weekend. When she did, she dreamt of Bullet on the edge of the woods, looking back to her with his dog-smile, his dark and sparkling eyes. When she lay awake, she continually came back to the idea that occurred to her in the kitchen with Dad. His words were kind, and it was nice of him to try, but he couldn't know what Regina meant about wanting out. Maura did know, though, and she'd had the guts to act on it. Why shouldn't Regina talk to her if she could?

Because going back to the Folly is the stupidest thing you could do, she thought. But Evelyn and the Girls can't force you to stay there, or they would've done so last time. But why give them a chance? Why not? If they can mess with you anytime, anywhere, anyway, what'll you lose by facing them? Back and forth her mind went on such questions, through two days of brooding.

At the same time, Regina tried to hide this struggle from Dad. She watched TV with him, played *Sorry!*, *Scrabble*, and *Monopoly* with him, went grocery shopping with him, talked and stayed active enough to keep him calm. She loved Dad but also recognized him as an obstacle. All he could do was monitor and restrict her in the name of helping her. And, she had to admit, it still stung that he didn't believe her about the Folly and dismissed her like anybody else would.

By Sunday, Regina was counting down the hours until Dad returned to work. Minutes after he left for Gladbury Parke on Monday morning, she stepped out onto Pike and headed for Broadway. So be it if she missed his check-in call. Between her guilt for failing Bullet and the endless tug-of-war in her head, no other punishment could matter.

This time she took Eighth Street through the Flats to avoid Sixth and Happ's. The new route's rundown homes and warehouses weren't different enough to distract her on her way. She reached the tracks all the same and followed their spur off the main line, soon arriving upon the rust-colored peninsula.

There was no mist on the river, but the temperature dropped, and the wind blew cold again, freezing her breath as she closed in on the cube. She went right to the lion face and thrust her hand into his mouth, knowing his trick but not yet trusting it, grasping for the lever.

That's right, she thought as the clicks sounded behind the wall, I am going through with this. The door mechanism groaned, and the ground shook. Vapor jets hissed from the metal and outlined the door panels, which slid apart on their own.

She entered the opening and didn't flinch when the panels slammed shut behind her. *Pfoom! Pfoom! Pfoom!* The light-spine extended overhead, and the silvery tunnel reflected its gleam. Regina proceeded, braced for the bubble and déjà vu that hindered her before. Her path was clear, however, leaving her to wonder if the déjà vu had been the Folly's way of introducing itself.

The main floor looked much like it had before. The Girls lay sleeping in the same clothes ingrained with workplace dirt, the violinist among them. Evelyn and Mother were seated at the table, both asleep as well. The manhole was still there, too, but nothing was lurking within it as far as she could see.

Regina sensed movement and glimpsed a figure in the dark gap of the nearest corner. Maura emerged from those shadows, again wearing her blue satin jacket. She did not look happy to see Regina, who crept around the Girls to approach her.

"You gave up," Maura said.

"No, not yet."

"Then why are you here?"

"Because I know you gave up. I went to the library and found a newspaper article about it. And if you gave up, why shouldn't I?"

Maura considered this for a moment and said, "Fine. Come with me, and I'll show you." She took Regina by the hand and led her back toward the darkness. "Close your eyes and don't open them till I say.

"Dreaming is one thing we can do here. That's why you see the Girls laying around, holding each other. They're not really sleeping, but they are dreaming. And sometimes when their energy overlaps, they can share the same dream."

They continued to walk until Maura stopped, and Regina spent the next minute waiting in blind silence. Just as she was about to speak, the darkness lifted. She had never opened her eyes but still saw Maura beside her, holding her hand. Somehow they'd come to an outdoor place where the sky lightened with dawn. Mountains materialized along a distant horizon, their peaks sharp against the powder blue. A flat field sprawled around Regina and Maura all directions, its turf gray with frost. Far off, about a hundred yards away, a little boy was pacing around the wreckage of a demolished house. He saw Regina and Maura and waved his arms to signal them. He also cupped his hands around his mouth to call them, but an unseen barrier muted the sound of his voice.

"Keep your eyes closed, like I said. And don't let go of me, either," Maura said.

"Where are we? Who is that?" Regina said.

"It's where I go when I dream. This or something like it, but usually this. That's my little brother, and my mom's behind us."

Regina turned around to see a woman as far away as the boy. She stood before an easel and dabbed it with paint, never noticing Regina or Maura. In fact, she didn't seem to be aware of anything beyond her canvas.

"Let's go to them," Regina said.

"We can't. This is the closest we get. If you try to get closer, things turn ugly really fast."

"So you just stand here and squint at them from a mile away?"

"Pretty much, yeah. That's the dream. I can't share the other Girls' dreams. I've tried, and it never works. But I hear theirs are happier. They talk to people they loved, go places they liked to go. Evelyn sees Raymond MacAdder all the time, if you can believe it. He left that table, chairs, and violin as a memorial to her. It ties back to some fling they had, and she's still reliving it. As much as she hates him, she sits there and dreams about him for hours."

"Here's what I don't get," Regina said. "I look like Mother, or Mother looks like me. I'm not the only one who sees that, right?"

"We all see the resemblance. It won't put you on Evelyn and Mother's good side. It might make them hate you more."

"Why?"

"Evelyn never had a child with MacAdder. But her sisters and cousins... The man got around, let's put it that way. And Evelyn and Mother will never get over it.

"They don't care if you kill yourself or go insane, and I doubt they want you to break the curse. They run this place like a couple of queen bees. They have power here, and they're not rushing to give it up. I bet they'd rather stay here for another hundred years than take a chance on whatever's next. Meanwhile, the Girls have been trapped here and dreaming so long, they're used to it. They've grown to accept it, maybe even like it.

"But this dream, this is all I have. Beautiful, isn't it? A constant reminder of a mistake, the worst I could make. After my mom died, I fell apart inside. I saw no point in anything, no purpose. I cared so little, I let three boys take advantage of me. Rape me, you could say. I got drunk with them, couldn't even remember everything they did. But they sure spread the word. Next thing I knew, half the football team was prowling around my grandmother's house, thinking I was easy. Which made me a bitch and a dick tease when they found out I wasn't. And to their girlfriends and most other girls at school, I was a slut, whore, fuck pig.

"I felt like I had nowhere to go, nobody to talk to. I knew I couldn't go to the police. Not against those boys in this town, not with how drunk I'd been that night. I had one more year, too. Just one more year to get through high school and get out of the Downs, and I couldn't do it. I was that weak, Regina.

"And I was never really alone. I always had Oscar to care for. He was a baby when our dad bailed on us and about your age when our mom died, like he is over there. He took everything twice as hard as I did, and kids were picking on him every day. I knew all that, I knew it, and I left him anyway. I left him to fend for himself when I knew he couldn't. What kind of person does that? What kind of person is so consumed by her own pain that she'd abandon her little brother?"

Regina watched the boy, who was still waving and calling, still muted. "Maybe he ended up okay," she said.

"I'll never know, but I doubt it. Evelyn and Mother know a little about the outside. When the curse hits a MacAdder, they can see the outside through his or her eyes for a few minutes at a time, enough to know how to torture that person. And when that MacAdder dies, each Girl can dream scenes from his or her life. It's like they take that person's memories as a trophy. I couldn't do that if I wanted to, though. I'm cut off. I don't even know what year it is out there. I lost track so long ago.'

"It's 2005," Regina said.

Maura repeated that year in a whisper and said nothing else.

Regina noticed the boy and demolished house drifting off to her left. She looked back and saw the woman, still painting and oblivious, also moving in the same direction. Together they appeared to be circling counterclockwise along the same orbit.

"It looks like they're floating," she said.

"This is what happens," Maura said. "This is how the end always begins. If you try to run to them, it only speeds it up."

The frost melted, and the grass withered away to ashen mud. Regina felt her feet sinking into it. Black water dribbled onto her shoes and wet her socks.

"Keep your eyes closed. You need to see this," Maura said.

"Come on! We can't stay here. We're sinking."

"Like quicksand," Maura said.

Regina strained to pull up either foot. When she freed one and tried to replant, it plunged inches deep into squishing mud. More black water seeped up in patches around her, expanding into each other to swamp the field. The boy and the woman continued to circle at a distance, bound to their own moving islands.

"Come *on*! Maura! We're gonna drown!"

"You think so?"

Soon Regina was stuck shin-deep, and the water rose to her knees. She squeezed and jerked Maura's hand, but Maura didn't try to help.

Something splashed behind them. Regina turned around and wished she hadn't. That something was still visible, swimming in the space between her and the islands, dozens of yards away but still too close. It looked as large as an orca but had no skin, for it was a moving skeleton, a prehistoric being held together with bluish sinew. Such a thing couldn't possibly live, let alone swim, and yet it did. Its tail and ribs sliced the water to create a wake. The four tusks jutting from its blocky mastodonic skull dipped under the surface as it submerged.

"What was *that*?!" Regina gasped.

"One of the nicer things that lives here. The things with tentacles are worse. Much worse."

Within seconds, Regina felt an icy touch on the small of her back. She recoiled, but it pressed on, sliding up between her shoulder blades.

206

Suction cups stuck to her skin, rolling the wet chill up to her nape. Another tentacle slithered around her waist while the first rounded her neck.

Regina grabbed at the strangling tentacle with her free hand and turned just enough to see the abomination off to her left. Its head was a bulbous lump of raw-pink muscle pulsating on the mud. Baseball-sized yellow eyes stared at her from either side of a star-shaped mouth that gargled porridge-thick mucous. It groped about with more tentacles all the while, lashing the air and thrashing the water.

Regina screamed as the creature pulled her toward its mouth, screamed with her last breath as the tentacle tightened around her throat. She panicked and opened her eyes to find herself returned to the Folly floor, still holding Maura's hand. She bear-hugged Maura, who whispered it's okays and it's all rights while Regina cried.

"Well, well, well," Evelyn said. "Our brave little acquaintance has returned."

She and the Boom Girls had gathered around Maura and Regina. Some Girls murmured, others whispered, and most just looked on with contempt. One shouted, "Kill the MacAdder! She's a coward, like all MacAdders!"

"Quiet," Evelyn said, and the Girls obeyed. "That's not entirely true. It takes a certain courage to accept one's fate. For that I commend you, Regina. As I said, submission was always the wisest course. Let's not prolong it, shall we?"

Evelyn offered her hand, but Regina held on to Maura.

"No. I'm not giving up. And I'm not going anywhere with you. Not after the library, Miriam."

Evelyn lowered her hand. "Do you fancy this your playground? Do you think we're your nursemaids?"

"No, but I'm not your punching bag, either. Not anymore. I'm ending the curse whether you like it not."

"Oh? So you've found a tyrant?" Evelyn said to scattered laughs.

"Yeah. I think I have. I do know somebody who likes to destroy people and places and doesn't care who he hurts. Somebody who's spilled blood, who needs to be stopped."

"I don't see this person. I only see you. If he does in fact exist, how do you propose to bring him here?"

"I'll think of something," Regina said, and wiped her eyes and nose. "That's my problem, not yours."

"Indeed, and stating your intentions won't save you. Don't trifle with us, child. Come here alone again, and we may decide to keep you. Then perhaps your friend Maura will finally have some company."

"And perhaps I'll meet Raymond MacAdder the next time you have lunch with him," Regina said. "Perhaps he can tell me why I look more like your mother than you do."

That drew a round of stunned sounds from the Girls. Evelyn cast a seething glare at Maura but maintained her poise and turned away without another word. The Girls followed her lead, retreating with glowers and mumbled disapproval.

Regina and Maura looked at each other, and Maura smiled for the first time in a lifetime.

Bolstered by her newfound spirit, Regina went straight to Happ's. She remembered the chief's beating vividly enough, and seeing the jeep parked on Sixth gave her pause. It couldn't deter her, though, not after Maura's dream. No way would she share Maura's fate, never and no how, not as long as she could walk and draw breath. If delivering Waters to the Girls is what it would take to escape, then too bad for him. That's what he gets for what he's done. Why should she suffer while he destroys Broadway, cripples the chief, kills Bullet?

Regina pounded on the steel double doors under the ketchup mural. No answer. She pounded again, numbing her fist until the locks clicked. One of the doors swept open, held by the fat guy she'd seen at Happ's twice before.

"Whatta ya want?" he said.

"I need to speak to Mr. Waters."

"You got the wrong place. Go away."

"No, I don't. That's his jeep right there. Tell him that I know what he did on Friday, and I'm not going anywhere till he answers for it. He'll know what that means."

The guy gave her a hard look, but she read surprise in it. He went back inside, and the door closed behind him.

It opened again a minute later, and this time Waters stepped out. He wore a black rubber apron over his t-shirt and jeans. A bandana covered most of his head, hiding his hair, and a respirator hung around his neck. He let the door close, and they stood alone on the sidewalk.

"Munchkin," he said, and stared her down with his dark-circled green eyes. "I did something on Friday, you say?"

"You killed my dog on the dirt road in the woods. I was at the Little League field. I saw you speeding through the woods. When I went to get Bullet, he was dead in the road."

"That's it? That's all you saw?"

"You killed my dog."

"Shit," he said, sounding relieved. "Oh, well, if that's it – that was your dog? Yeah, I guess it was. I thought I'd seen it before."

"You never stopped. You didn't even slow down."

"You're right. And I'm sorry. I am deeply sorry. I wish I could've stopped, but I was having an emergency that day. I had to go somewhere fast, really fast. One of my workers was injured on the job, see, and I had to get him to a hospital. It was critical.

"I'll tell you what. Have your mommy or daddy call Condor here, and we'll work something out. We'll see to it that you get a new puppy if that's what you want. There's plenty at the shelter just waiting to be rescued."

"No, thanks. I know what happens when anyone calls your company. They get redirected to another company called Concilicom, and nothing happens."

Waters couldn't help but smirk. "Okay. Fair enough. I've apologized. What else would you like me to do for you?"

"I want you to come with me to MacAdder's Folly on the river. I have something to show you there. I can't tell you what it is, but it's very important."

"Let's take a rain check on that. As you know, I'm a very busy man. What's today, the twenty-fourth? I have a big deadline coming up soon. I can't be taking field trips right now."

"It's not far. Only a few blocks away," Regina said.

"Tell me, by the way, how did you find me here?" Waters said.

"Just walking around, I noticed the jeep."

"You're moseying around this part of town on a school day. You hang out at that trash heap on a school day. You let your dog out in the woods on another school day. Are you ever *in* school? Do your parents know half of what you're up to?"

Regina didn't answer.

"You know what I think? You're too bright for bullshit." Waters reached around to his back pocket and pulled out a roll of bills. He counted off a few and held them out to her. "I run a cash business here. This will cover what it cost to bury your dog plus enough to adopt a new one. That's fair, don't you think?"

"I don't want money. I want you to come with me."

"Final offer. Take it or leave it. And I do mean 'final.' This settles it. If I hear from your parents about this, I'll tell them what we both know: you should've been with your dog, and he should've been on a leash. It's not my fault he wasn't."

Regina closed her eyes with those words, absorbed their sting.

"But I really am sorry," Waters added gently.

No, you're not, she thought. You just want to get rid of me, and you think it'll be easy. You think your cash will make me happy like it made Mason happy. You say you're sorry now, but you'll know what "sorry" means when I do to you what you've done to me.

Regina took the money and pocketed it without counting it.

"I like you. You're a good kid. But you really shouldn't come around here. This is no place for kids. Bad things happen when kids snoop around places they shouldn't go and see things they shouldn't see. Trust me, I know," Waters said, and started back inside.

"Wait. One last question. If your sculptures aren't stone or metal, what are they made of?"

Waters wondered why she would ask, and he didn't want to answer. She saw it in his face, heard it in his hesitation. "Still fixated on that, huh?"

"I liked your art, and I'm curious."

"Promise you won't tell anyone?" he said, lowering his voice like he had a top secret just for her.

Regina said nothing, blinked.

"Papier-mâché. Coated with sealant to protect it from the weather. That's it and that's all, swear to God. So simple you could do it yourself at home. Now, if you'll excuse me."

The door shut behind him, and its locks clicked.

23. Gaming

On the following morning, Skunk was skating around the Pharm-Rite lot. Jamal was sitting by the front door, MP3 player in hand, buds in his ears, trying to listen to Animal Collective's *Feels* for the third time.

The lyrics made no sense and annoyed him. ("The words cut open your poor intestines"? "Give me rabies, bring your babies in the hospital"? "Pretty little femur sitting in my cherry dreamboat"? "Can I tell you that you are the purple in me"?) The music tinkled and droned and lacked beats. The fourth track, seven minutes long, sounded like a collision between a barbershop quartet and a ring-around-the-rosie. The singer had a high-pitched creepy-ass voice, and on the fifth track he kept saying, "The bees, the bees," then distorted gibberish over aimless string-strumming. "The bees, the bees," at least fifteen times. That was Jamal's breaking point.

"Can't do it," he said, and popped out the earbuds. "Cannot do it. Shit's way too weird."

Skunk scraped to a stop and said, "It's brilliant. You just don't get it. And you're closed-minded."

"Get the fuck out. You listen to that Kanye I told you about? Jeezy? Common? No, you didn't 'cause you fear hip-hop. You fear it so much you listen to this shit and tell yourself it's brilliant."

"I don't fear hip-hop. Most of it just ain't that good."

"I'm *telling* you what's good. But whatever, yo. Keep waiting for rock to regrow some balls. Creed. Nickelback. Green Day. Coldplay. Yeah, dude. Rock on."

"That's low, man. You know I don't listen to that shit."

"But this shit's worse! Animal Collective? Nobody is partyin' to Animal Collective. Nobody is fuckin' to Animal Collective. Nobody's..."

A jeep pulled into the lot and drifted toward the boys. They froze and braced for something unpleasant, still bruised from their last run-in with the police. The driver parked and stepped out. He had long reddish-brown hair down to his shoulders and wore a navy blue t-shirt that read "CONDOR" across his scrawny chest. Jamal knew he'd seen the guy before but couldn't remember where.

The guy pulled a lighter and pipe from one pocket of his jeans, a baggie full of pot from another. He opened the bag, loaded the bowl, and fired up a hit. Lungs full of smoke, he offered the pipe to the boys, and neither moved.

"No?" the guy said, and exhaled. "Suit yourself. More for me."

"How stupid do you think we are? The cops would love to catch us doing that. If you're not one yourself," Skunk said.

"You don't have to worry about them anymore. The laws have changed."

"This is the Downs. Nothing changes here, especially the cops," Jamal said.

"I'm Lonnie Waters, founder and CEO of Condor Development Corps, and you are simultaneously right and wrong, my friend. Yes, this is the Downs, and yes, its cops are good ol' boys. But change has come nonetheless. Look at what my company's done for Broadway."

"That's where I saw you. You're the guy who spoke when all that shit got blown up that wasn't supposed to get blown up," Jamal said.

"Yep," Waters said with a giggle. "Wasn't that awesome?"

Jamal and Skunk looked at each other and tried not to smile.

"Anyway, I'm here for a reason. I hear there's a TV in the break room of that Pharm-Rite behind you, where a couple of boys like to play games. One's bragging that he's never lost at *Street Slaughter* while his buddy claims to have mastered *Carjacker*." Waters lit up, took another hit, and blew smoke at them. "You wouldn't know those posers, would you? I'm here to spank 'em back to school."

"I don't know *you*, crazy man," Jamal said. "I don't know what you heard or how you heard it. But you are smoking crack if you think you can touch me in *Slaughter*."

"So you say, son. I'll bet this jeep you don't win a single round and that your friend here can't beat *Carjacker*. I'm not even asking for a stake. You have nothing to lose but your dignity. Such as it is."

Jamal and Skunk looked at each other again. Neither spoke, but nothing needed to be said. They rose to their feet in unison as men.

Kim leaned against a wall in the cramped break room, having smoked away her reservations about Waters' visit. Skunk, also stoned, sat on the kitchen counter and feasted on a bag of corn chips. Jamal had abstained from the pot to keep his reflexes sharp. He sat close to the TV, eyes wide and fingers racing on his controller. Waters stood nearby, eyes glazed and fingers moving with methodical precision.

Jamal's character, a red and yellow beast with reptilian skin, kept trying to choke Waters' female space alien. The lithe, silvery alien slipped the beast's grip and whirled around to kick him upside the head. The beast staggered back and lunged forward. She leapt over him, landed behind him. Tentacles sprouted from her breasts and coiled around his neck. The beast's head turned purple and expanded as the tentacles choked him. Jamal furiously hit every button but couldn't stop the beast's head from expanding further and finally bursting with gore. The beast's corpse dropped. Blood spurted from its stump. The alien's tentacles retracted back into her breasts, and she took a bow.

"God *damn!*" Jamal slammed down his controller while Skunk and Kim laughed. "Six times! Nobody ever beat me twice in a day, and never with the alien. Everybody knows she's a weak bitch."

"Chill out, Jamal. There's always somebody better," Kim said.

"I never seen that move you just did," Jamal said to Waters. "Where you learn that? You gotta tell me."

"I knew someone who knew the guy who designed the game," Waters said.

"You knew somebody who knew Oscar Dougal?"

"I met Dougal himself once or twice when he was working on this stuff in New York, yeah."

"I don't believe you. No way."

"What are you talking about?" Kim said.

"Oscar Dougal designed *Slaughter*, *Carjacker*, *Medevil*," Jamal said. "Designed all the characters and everything. He was a fuckin' genius, like Rockstar Games before Rockstar Games. He was gonna be the next Miyamoto."

"Miya-who?"

"Miyamoto. The Nintendo guy who came up with *Super Mario* and *Zelda*. Dougal was like the up-and-coming successor, but then he sold his company and disappeared, and nobody knows why. He got all weird and did the recluse thing, hasn't shown his face in six, seven years. There's all kinds of rumors online. People say he went crazy, had a breakdown, got plastic surgery, maybe a sex change. I heard he quit games and took up pottery or some shit. Then I read he's laying low and working on the ultimate game.

"What do you think?" Jamal said to Waters. "You say you met him, knew somebody who knew him."

"I don't know what happened to him, and I don't really care. My only link to him was a girl who's no longer with us. It wasn't a happy story," Waters said.

The room fell silent for a moment.

"Well, fellas, all this gamer talk's a little too geeky for me. Have fun playing with yourselves," Kim said, and left the break room.

"Whatever. Ready to lose your jeep?" Skunk said to Waters. He took Jamal's controller and loaded the *Carjacker* disc in the game console. "I can beat this in my sleep. I'll beat it in twenty minutes without getting killed once."

The game's title screen appeared on the TV, showing a car crashing through a police barricade. *Carjacker* takes place in a nameless metropolis. Its premise dictates that you, the player, are a recently released ex-con named Rip. You're trying to go straight by working as a janitor when an old prison buddy imposes on you. Your buddy has been shot and will soon die, but first he gives you a mysterious package and says you must deliver it to Jose Del Mar, an underworld warlord. You don't know why or what's in the package, but you do know that many shady characters are willing to kill for it and are already closing in on you. As a man of limited means with only your buddy's gun for protection, you have no choice but to run and shoot your way toward Del Mar's lair. Naturally complications will arise, and the police will join the chase.

Jamal noticed that Waters was tapping the buttons on his controller as the game loaded. He thought that was odd since *Carjacker* was a one-player game and Skunk was the only player. Waters kept tapping, though, in a one-two, one-two-three rhythm, over and over, and set down his controller just as the title screen faded out.

The nighttime world of the game faded in as seen through Rip's eyes. Skunk hurried him along a city street, toward a Cadillac stopped at a traffic light. The street was otherwise deserted. Rip opened the driver's door, startling an old man at the wheel.

"Move, bitch!" Skunk said with a laugh as Rip grabbed the old man by the collar and yanked him from the car. The old man fell to the asphalt with a grunt. Rip kicked his head, dislodging his hearing aid.

"Back over him. That's the best part," Jamal said.

"No time. Not worth it," Skunk said, and seated Rip behind the wheel.

The car revved and charged ahead. Oncoming drivers swerved to avoid it. Headlights and city lights blurred past, painting the night with ghostly streams. A pedestrian wandered partway across the street, saw Rip speeding toward him, and dove back to the sidewalk for his life. Sirens whooped in the distance; red and blue dots glowed in the rearview.

The Cadillac took a screeching turn and then another.

"Whoa! What up? I didn't do that," Skunk said. "I didn't take those turns. I never take those turns."

Rip drove through a tunnel and arrived in a more upscale part of town. He parked on the corner of a bustling drag, close to a restaurant crowded with well-tailored patrons. Alongside the restaurant was a wine bar, and next to that was a cafe with candlelit sidewalk tables and kissing couples.

"What's wrong?" Jamal said.

"I'm telling you, I can't move," Skunk said, and tap-tapped the buttons for emphasis.

"Welcome to God Mode, a hidden feature Mr. Dougal once showed me. I keyed it in while the game was loading," Waters said.

"God Mode? All I'm doing's sitting here waiting to get killed."

"No, you're observing. Nobody will notice you here."

College kids walked the drag in small groups, their voices too muffled to overhear. Two bicyclists coasted past a teenage girl lugging a laundry sack. A muscle car with pounding bass crept along the street, followed by a minivan with kids in the rear seats, followed by a port authority bus with a drunk slumped against the window.

"You've never done this?" Waters said. "You've never gone to a lively corner at night, a bus stop at rush hour, and just watched the people?"

An old couple tottered across the street, arm in arm, the woman limping and the man stooped. A pizza deliverer, mom and little daughter, and pack of junior-high kids passed them from ahead and behind. The couple hadn't finished crossing by the time their walk signal had changed, and a driver laid on his horn to shame them.

"You've never wondered about the strangers around you? You're not curious about how they live, if they're satisfied or disappointed with what they've become? What they do when they go home, if they snuggle up with someone or sleep alone? When you see a couple like that, you never wonder how long they've been together or what's kept them together? If they had kids, and if so, what became of those kids?

"Personally, when I've placed myself somewhere like this, observing but unobserved, I've realized that I am apart from these creatures we call 'people.' Disconnected. I don't belong in their world, and I never will. I'm surrounded by them, but I have nothing in common with them. I see them, I'm aware of them, but I can never know them. Nor can they know me, for I am alone, and I don't feel I have a choice in the matter."

Digital figures continued to pass. Couples entered and exited the restaurant. A woman in a track suit jogged around a homeless man sitting on the sidewalk and shaking his cup of change. Another woman walked her golden retriever to the nearby hydrant and paused to let him mark it.

"Um, okay, man," Skunk said. "But this is a game. You gotta *do* something. Something's gotta *happen*. It's boring to just sit here."

"Oh, don't you worry. You'll get your show. It's all about the show, isn't it? The action, the spectacle, the big wow kapow. God forbid we shouldn't get that. Rest assured, there she is."

A teenage girl appeared on the corner, her back to Rip. She wore jeans, a navy blue jacket, and red sneakers. The streetlight shone off her long dark hair while she waited for her walk signal. She crossed the main drag when prompted and proceeded onto a side street.

Rip left the car to follow, though Skunk still wasn't controlling him. She walked along a residential block of parked cars and sleepy-dim houses, the lights and noise of the main drag fading with every step. Rip stalked her, staying close to the houses' yards for cover. When she first paused, he hid behind a tree. When she paused again, he crouched behind shrubs.

The girl reached a corner where two other figures were already standing. They were men much larger than her, wearing football jerseys numbered 7 and 80. 7 grabbed the girl in a headlock and covered her mouth before she could scream. He quickly forced her around the corner while 80 scanned the scene for witnesses. Not seeing Rip or anyone else, 80 also disappeared around the corner.

Rip stepped up his pursuit, turning the corner to enter an alley behind the houses. The figures' shadows flickered in and out of sight. Rip persisted, trailing them from the paved and Dumpster-lined alley to a dirt path overgrown with weeds. The path led to an open cinder-block garage far removed from the rest of *Carjacker*'s city world. A work light hung from the garage ceiling, dangling over a broken-down car and two more men. One was dressed in black and wore glasses. The other had a horseshoe mustache, maroon baseball cap, and roll of duct tape.

Rip hid behind a tree, his view partially obscured as 7 and 80 dragged the girl to the garage. 7 threw her against the car. 80 grabbed her as she tried to run, slammed her onto the hood. Horseshoe wound tape around her mouth and eyes and wrists as 80 held her in place. The one with glasses backed away from the garage. He didn't touch the girl but watched his friends from a slight distance while Rip watched all of them from a bit more.

"Holy shit. What's all this?" Skunk said.

"Yo, do something. You got a gun, don't you? Smoke those bitches," Jamal said.

"I said I can't move," Skunk said, showing that he was hitting the buttons.

With the girl bent over the hood, 7 pulled down her jeans and penetrated her from behind. He thrust and thrust while 80 held her down. When 7 finished and stepped away, 80 stepped in, and Horseshoe took over holding her. The girl had gone limp, all resistance gone, and 80 kept penetrating her anyway.

Jamal picked up the second controller. Hitting its buttons did nothing to stop the rape, didn't even make Rip move. "What is this shit? What's the point?" he said to Waters.

"That there is none. If you believe in God, you believe he makes these people and allows them to do things like this. And they often get away with it, never facing anything close to justice. He makes people who watch this happen, who don't stop it, who can't stop it. People who see it in their head every hour of every day and can't stop it. What does that tell you about your God? That he's sadistic, indifferent, a sick joke? What does it tell you about these creatures he made, that some would do this while others would watch?

"I don't know, but I bet you'll never see *Carjacker* the same way again, now that you know what it meant to Oscar Dougal. This doesn't end, by the way. It goes on and on, each rapist taking and retaking his turn. You could spend hours watching this. Days. Months. Years. You could spend decades."

Skunk and Jamal watched 80 pull out, Horseshoe unzip. He stepped up behind the girl, who was bleeding, and penetrated her. Jamal leaned forward from his chair and turned off the TV.

"Sorry. Not feeling it. And if that was real, I would've stopped it. Even if all four of those dickheads kicked my ass, I would've stopped it. I know I would've," he said.

"Good," Waters said. "I'm glad you know your brave self so well."

Kim knocked on the door and stepped in to say, "Hate to interrupt, but I think somebody's waiting for you outside. Somebody in a van with 'Condor' on it, parked next to your jeep, just sitting there."

"Right on," Waters said, and looked to the boys. "Thanks for hanging out. I had fun. Did you have fun? I know you didn't, but thanks anyway. I'm keeping my jeep, but the pot's all yours."

He walked out with Kim, and another silence befell the break room.

"What the fuck was that?" Skunk said.

"Nothing," Jamal said. "And don't ever mention it again."

Scott was behind the wheel of the Condor van, and one of his underlings occupied the passenger seat. Both men wore sunglasses and blue coveralls, but only Scott was scarfing down a chocolate pudding pie. He chewed with an open mouth, every lip-smack audible as Waters approached his window.

"Mission accomplished, boss."

"No witnesses?" Waters said.

"Went like clockwork. All that casin' we did paid off. Secretary goes to lunch at eleven like always, leaves him alone for an hour. We walk right in, say you need to see him. He's scared but more scared to say no. We walk him downstairs and out the back doors, and he's shakin'. Sees the van, don't wanna get in.

"I play it subtle, boss. Calmly tell him he knows what you're capable of, and if he don't shut up and get in the van, there's gonna be trouble. He gets in, the Russski does the rest. Clockwork."

"And you're sure nobody saw this?"

"No, boss, no way. It was the back alley, nobody around. No guards. No cameras. Nothin'. Even if somebody *did* see us, which they didn't, it didn't look so bad. Just a guy gettin' in a van."

"You left the memo for the secretary?"

"Come on, boss. We're professionals here."

Waters knocked on the back doors, which unlocked from within. He opened them just enough to see an unconscious Colton belly-down on the floor, blinded and gagged with duct tape, wrists and ankles shackled with handcuffs. Mirzeta straddled Colton's back. She grinned upon seeing Waters despite having a black eye, scabbed lip, and flecks of blood on her tank top.

"You're a miracle," he said.

She narrowed her eyes, giving him a flirty not-buying-it look.

Waters had been sincere, though, and truly did admire her work. Here was the rapist pummeled half to death, ripe for payback. Could there be a more beautiful sight? He reached in and patted Colton's battered head, hoping to find out soon enough.

24. Workstation

"But I have to go, Dad. Remember all that homework you picked up from school? I need to use a computer for a lot of it," Regina said into the phone.

Dad sighed and stretched out the pause, which was encouraging. His noes generally came quickly and decisively; the yeses involved some fussing, enough to let you know he disliked an idea but could accept it just this once.

"Fine," he said. "But you'd better be home before me. And you'll show me the work you've done."

She climbed Elsinore Avenue and approached the library's front entrance. A sign taped to the door stopped her hand on the handle. "CLOSED – EFFECTIVE NOVEMBER 20 Due to budget cuts from the federal library fund, Commonwealth of Pennsylvania, and Burdock Downs municipal authority, MacAdder Library will cease to operate on November 20, 2005. The MacAdder Foundation truly regrets this decision and wishes the wonderful borough of Burdock Downs all the best going forward."

Regina reread the sign in disbelief, thinking she must have misunderstood. She entered the main floor, however, and saw about twenty people crowding the long tables stacked with books. A poster board was taped to a nearby column, and its hand-painted text read "FREE BOOKS! HELP YOURSELF!"

Tom was watching the people and scowling from his desk. She chose to avoid him and go to the computers, but he noticed her and came over anyway.

"Look at these vultures, just look at them," he said. "I've never seen a single one of them here before. Where were they when the library needed them? Where was their support? But you put up a sign saying 'last chance for something free,' and they sure turn out for that. That's the Machine for you, the greedy mentality it creates. Screw the community. It's all about me, me, *me*. Look at them, picking away at the bones. That's it, suck out the marrow while you're at it. Suck it!"

A few people heard him well enough to glance his way.

"Worse yet, my dear, the printed word is dying before our eyes, and nobody cares. Nobody reads books anymore. Here we have this vast wealth of knowledge and wisdom and human experience that spans the centuries, and we're throwing it away. Just throwing it away!"

Regina felt sorry for him, but he was embarrassing her, and she had stuff to do. She would console him fast with the tools at hand and the first comparison that came to mind. "Hold on, Tom," she said, and pulled up a search engine. She entered the term "dinosaur" and scanned the top result.

"It says dinosaurs ruled the world for 135 million years, and that we 'modern humans' have only been around for 200,000. We know how dinosaurs ended up. Chances are we won't last as long as they did, not even close. But if we last just one million years, I doubt we'll still be using books. We're gonna phase them out sometime, so why not now? You look at it that way, it's not so bad," Regina said.

Tom's eyes went from hers to the screen to the floor. He gulped and shuffled off, a walking husk of his usual self.

Regina returned her attention to the screen and typed "ivoryeagle" in the browser's address bar. The faces of McVeigh, Kaczynski, and Rudolph appeared to the tune of "American Bad-Ass" once again. She scrolled down past the eagle logo and text ("Are YOU oppressed by the government and its so-called laws? FIGHT BACK!...), down to the list of links. Pipe; Mail; Nail; Truck; Dirty; Molotov.

This time nothing interrupted her. There was no phone call from Gladys in Harrisburg, no song, no Miriam or Tom. She studied the site's Molotov recipe and watched its demonstration video, memorizing every detail.

Regina took Elsinore back down to Broadway and proceeded to Ribbitski's. She didn't see anyone else on the block, most of which remained demolished, and tried the keys Mason had given her. After finding the key that worked, she entered a dark room that had only one glass-block window. Her sight adjusted enough to guide her to the bar. She climbed up onto it, hopped down behind it, and felt around until she located the light switches.

Overhead bulbs illuminated a pool table and stools, poker machine and jukebox, photos of military men, the Stars and Stripes tacked up by the ceiling, a hardhat and picture of the Twin Towers. So here's where the grown-ups hang out, Regina thought, and took a whiff of cigarette stink. She saw nothing fun or appealing about Ribbitski's besides its being off-limits to her. If Dad banned her from the Smash Heap, how mad would this trip make him? Best not to dwell on it.

Regina concentrated on her latest project instead, taking two random bottles from the many behind the bar. She went to the back room, turned on its light, and froze as a rat scuttled across the floor. Mangy and as big as a kitten, it squeezed through a chewed-up gap in the basement door.

Otherwise, the back room showed no signs of life or surprises. Double sink, rag-filled laundry basket, shelves, stacked boxes, step stool, and a calendar on the wall showing a huge-boobed woman costumed as a vampire for October. Above the calendar was another glass-block window with a crank that could open a vent.

As Regina emptied both bottles into the sink, she heard a loud engine outside followed by the warning beeps of a truck backing up. The engine and beeps cut out. Doors opened and slammed shut. All of these sounds came from the lot next to Ribbitski's, the vacated place that used to be MacAdder Plaza.

She set the stool under the window and stepped up to reach the crank. On her tiptoes she could peek through the parted vent well enough to make out two men in blue coveralls. One stood near the center of the lot and shook a can of spray paint. He then crouched and marked the concrete with big white X's as the other guy directed him.

"When we droppin' 'em off again?" the painter said.

"Sunday night," said the director.

"He gonna be done by then? I heard he ain't finished yet."

"That's his business."

"What are these things anyway? I been hearin' statues, sculptures, some modern art shit. You been in Happ's? You seen 'em yet?"

"You ask too many questions. That's why you got no clearance. You ain't gettin' paid to know anything. You're gettin' paid to put the fuckin' X right there. No, *there*!"

Regina slunk away from the vent, down to the floor. She listened to their voices while her thoughts jostled back (You're not really doing this, are you? You can't do this. You don't have it in you) and forth (You have to do this. What choice do you have? None. Admit it, you have none), back and forth. She watched the gap the rat had gnawed through the basement door and wondered if the curse hadn't done the same to her brain.

25. Reincarnation

Colton awoke in a daze. He'd partied enough in his youth to know he'd been drugged but didn't know where he was, the time of day, or the day of the week. He was standing upright but couldn't move. Nor could he speak, for tape or some other adhesive sealed his mouth. He sensed others around him but couldn't see their faces, his blurry vision slow to clear.

The nearest figure came into focus as a balding mouth-breather in a bloodstained lab coat. A foreigner, Colton thought, maybe Indian or Pakistani. The man leaned in close and shone a pen-light in Colton's eyes, causing him to squint.

"Congratulations, Mr. Mayor," he said with an accent Colton couldn't place. "You've been Gitmoed."

Somebody laughed. Somebody else chanted, "U.S.A.! U.S.A.!"

Colton saw Scott, the construction foreman, standing off to left and began to remember. Scott and another Condor contractor had come to his office, led him outside to a van... A muscled hulk stood off to the right, arms folded across its chest, and oh, God, did he remember. It (he couldn't call it a "she") had beaten him down, hitting him harder than he'd ever been hit on the field. Directly ahead, between Scott and the hulk, was a dressing screen like the one Lorna had in their bedroom.

He craned his neck to look down. Someone had mummified him with plastic wrap layered inches thick from his shoulders to his shins. His feet were buried in cement contained in a terra cotta planter fit for a tree. He felt a metal post against his backside and head, and his hands were bound behind it.

Panic seized Colton's breath and sped his heart. He darted his eyes from face to face to every corner of his surroundings, questions overloading his brain. Who are these people? What do they want? Where am I? Is this Happ's? Why the dressing screen, why the curtains blue green yellow red?

A figure walked around from behind him. At first he thought it was Waters, but on a closer, longer look, he saw it was a young woman wearing sunglasses, a baseball hat, and Condor t-shirt. Her hair was long and reddish brown like Waters' and might have been a wig. She carried a tripod mounted with a camera and set it down about ten feet from him.

"Hold yourself together, Mr. Mayor," she said, and adjusted the camera. A red LED glowed by the lens and kept glowing as she approached him. "We have a message for you, and it's important that you understand it. But first let me introduce us. You'd met Scott before yesterday. And I can see you've met Mirzeta. Our medical expert over there is Dr. Ishwan, and I'm Manami. Together we are Team Freak!"

"Team Freak! Team Freak! Team Freak!" Scott and Ishwan chanted.

"You're expecting someone else?" Manami continued. "Someone named Lonnie Waters? There is no Lonnie Waters, Mr. Mayor, and there is no Condor Development Corps. There never was. Those FBI agents who came to you, Poole and Martinez? They were dinner-theater actors desperate for a paycheck, and you were stupid enough to fall for it. Stupid enough to hand Burdock Downs to *us*.

"The person you called 'Lonnie Waters' had been here for years, observing you and your town and how it works. He stood before you and your friends, stared you in the face, and you never noticed him. Or you pretended you didn't because he was beneath you. He was the scum. He was the bum pushing a shopping cart full of garbage around the Pharm-Rite lot. The drunk slumped over the bar at Ribbitski's. The palsied old man playing bingo, hands shaking too much to keep up.

"How does it feel, Mr. Mayor, to know those little people weren't so little after all? To know they saw right through you and your local-hero bullshit, right to your corrupt core? How does it feel to know your karma's finally come to collect?"

Her words only stoked Colton's panic. He strained his limbs and found them hopelessly immobilized. He tried to scream and shredded his throat, which already burned with thirst. All the while his mind still failed to comprehend how this could happen. What was wrong with these people, and what had he done to them?

Manami gave him a moment and resumed with a softer tone. "Yes, embrace the fear but know we're your captors, not your torturers. We do not torture." She looked to her teammates. "Do we torture?"

"*Nooo*, not us!" Scott said, drawing a chuckle from Ishwan.

She pulled a water bottle from her back pocket, took a swig, and licked the excess from her lips.

"Mmmm. And to think you've gone almost a whole day without this. Maybe I'd share some if I knew I could trust you. If I knew you'd be a man and not a bitch – no screaming and crying, no questions, no hysterics – maybe I'd consider it."

Thursday morning and time was running tight. Tomorrow afternoon through Sunday night was lost; Regina would never be able to get away from Dad or do anything unsupervised. Which leaves today, she thought, rolling her wagon along Broadway. Have to make the Molotovs today so they're ready by Sunday when the guys deliver the sculptures. I can do this. If my great-great-great-great-grandpa could wrangle lions, I can do this.

She passed the demolished blocks and Ribbitski's, BDH the closed-down hospital, and the Pharm-Rite, not stopping until she came to the Dollar Mart. She'd been there enough times with Dad to know the aisles and find what she wanted within five minutes.

The cashier, a woman past sixty, watched Regina wheel her wagon to the checkout. With rote boredom she rang up the two 2.5-gallon plastic gasoline cans, PowerSoaker water gun, and funnel. Regina handed her one of Waters' hundred-dollar bills.

"You kidding?" the cashier said.

"I was hoping to get change."

The cashier shook her head, making a show of her disapproval, but did her job nonetheless. "Shame on your parents for letting you walk around with that much money. On a school day, too," she said, counting out the change. "You can tell them I said that."

"I will. Thanks."

Regina towed her load for another block and arrived at the Stop-N-Go gas station-convenience store. Morning traffic crowded the pumps and compelled her to wait by the air compressor for a while. Once a pump opened, she parked the wagon against it and went inside.

Six other people were standing in line before her, all headed to the same cashier. She noted his ponytail, beard, pirate earrings, and skull finger-rings and thought he might belong to a biker gang. He seemed to be friendly enough, though, when she reached the counter with her money ready.

"How can I help you, sweetie?"

"Five gallons of gas," she said.

The cashier looked outside. "Which pump? The one with the wagon?"

"Yeah."

"You got an adult with you?"

"No."

"Sorry, I can't do that. You gotta be old enough to drive."

"But it's for my dad. He has a landscaping business. He sent me to fill those for his mowers. I'll be in trouble if I don't."

"Sorry. The law's the law. Your old man's gonna have to come here himself."

Regina walked out stumped but undeterred. This was not going to stop her. She would think of something.

Water dribbled down Colton's chin. He tilted his head back and licked whatever moisture he could, savoring every droplet. He'd downed a liter and still felt parched.

"To the future," Manami said, and raised the bottle for a toast. "To knowing what's coming. We're still bringing our sculpture garden to Burdock Downs. We never lied to you or your town about that. It's happening but not how you thought.

"Has it occurred to you that you will be a sculpture in that garden? We've already processed your friends, the priest and policemen. They're back there behind that red curtain. You'll never see them again, but they're there. I know what you're thinking, and no, we didn't kill them," she said, and looked to Ishwan. "They are still alive, yes?"

"Technically, yes," he said.

"And soon you will join them, encased in your own sarcophagus and set upon a pedestal for all your people to see. Of course they'll only see a sculpture. They'll never know you're inside, suffocating and starving, unable to speak or move. Think of it, Mr. Mayor. You'll die slowly in your own town square, hidden yet exposed, decaying on display, entombed in a living death.

"Here's the true beauty of it: we made the sculptures to break down. Rebar, chicken wire, papier-mâché, and sealant are all we used. The sculptures will last a month outdoors at the most. Then, when they fall apart, your town will find you. Or what's left of you after the rats and maggots have eaten their share.

"Right now your family and colleagues believe you've resigned and fled to pursue 'a matter of the heart.' Imagine what Gus Bixler will say when he becomes mayor by default. You think Lorna and little Taylor and Jayden are hurt now? Imagine their faces when they see your stripped corpse propped up like a scarecrow. Then they'll see what you really look like, Daddy. Then everyone will see you for what you are, Football Star. How handsome and charming you are! What a man you are!"

"What do you want?!" Colton blurted. "Why are you doing this?! Why?! *Why*?!"

"That is the question, isn't it? Only one person is fully qualified to answer it, and I'm not her. She is here, though, here in this room. Right behind that screen. Would you like to see her? I know she'd like to see you again. It's only been twenty-five years."

Jamal and Skunk were sitting by the Pharm-Rite entrance on lawn chairs borrowed from the store. Regina heard them arguing from a distance and over her wagon's rattle. Apparently Skunk thought *Scream* was the best horror movie ever while Jamal was partial to *Saw*. They quieted when they noticed Regina approaching, and by the time she reached them, they could agree that she was worth a laugh.

"Pastyface! You shopping again?" Skunk said.

"What's with the wagon?" Jamal said. "You running away from home?"

"I need a favor," Regina said. "Do either of you have a car? I have to fill these, but they won't let me pump gas at the Stop-N-Go. If you have a car, you could do it for me."

"Whatcha need gas for?" Skunk said.

"I'm doing chores for my granddad. He lives up on the Slopes, on one of those dead ends in the woods. He'd old, and he can't get around too good, and he needs gas for his generator. He's like a hermit."

"He sent you all the way down the Slopes with that wagon and expects you to haul it all the way back up?" Jamal said.

"He says it'll build character."

"Old man sounds like a hard-ass," Skunk said with a laugh.

"Or the Unabomber," Jamal said.

"Guys, I'm asking nicely. Please."

Skunk and Jamal looked at each other. Regina stared at the space between them, determined not to beg.

"I guess a little chivalry wouldn't hurt," Skunk said.

"Don't look at me. You're the one who drove today," Jamal said.

Ten minutes later, Skunk carried one full can from the trunk of his banged-up Civic to the wagon. Jamal unloaded the other.

"Thanks, guys. It means a lot," she said, and offered them another twenty dollars after the twenty she'd paid to cover the gas. Neither moved to take it, so Regina pocketed it.

"Sure you don't want a lift up to the Slopes?" Skunk said.

"Thanks again, but no. I'll be fine."

Jamal and Skunk watched Regina take up the wagon handle and pull away, moving noticeably slower than before.

"You know what's fucked up?" Skunk said.

"No, but I'm sure you'll tell me," Jamal said.

"That's *not* the weirdest thing that's happened here lately."

"Yo. Do I need to say it again? Don't mention it. Don't. Mention. It. God *damn*."

Upon further reflection, Skunk said, "You know, maybe I shouldn't have done that. With that kid."

"Shouldn't've done what? Buy her gas?"

"No. Turn down that twenty bucks. It's not like my time ain't worth something."

Manami walked away from Colton and stood alongside Mirzeta to the right. Scott and Ishwan stayed off to the left, keeping open the space between Colton and the screen. He heard someone moving behind it, but after a full minute no one emerged.

"Is it money? Is that what you want?" Colton said to no response, to the camera lens, to the red LED. "I'll give you money. I'll give you..."

A girl strolled around the edge of the screen and stopped Colton's words in his throat. She had long dark hair and dark eyes, wore a blue satin jacket with a rainbow over the hip and a long-extinct brand of red sneakers. Second by second he recognized her. Even if her face didn't look exactly like he remembered, Colton still knew who she was. Neither the plastic wrap nor the cement gripped him half as much as the shock of seeing Maura Dougal again.

But it can't be, he thought. She's dead, has been dead, will always be dead. That's a lookalike, they hired a lookalike.

As she drew nearer, however, the lookalike looked a little less like Maura Dougal and a little more like someone else. She came up close to him, within a few feet, and stood with her hands in her jacket pockets. Colton met her gaze, and another shock dropped his jaw. She was Waters, or the person he'd known as Waters, made up to resemble the girl. Black wig, brown contact lenses, foundation to darken his complexion, lipstick, and eyeshadow. It was a complete and detailed disguise, and only someone who'd known the girl could have created it.

"What's the matter, champ? Don't wanna fuck me when I'm sober?" she said in a voice forced above its natural pitch.

Colton closed his eyes and began to cry. "Oh, God," he whimpered. "God! Please! Stop!"

"But you're gonna like it. It's gonna feel good. It's gonna feel *good*. You're gonna like it."

Colton wept and whispered more pleas until she slapped him hard across the face.

"Calm down! You'll like it! It's gonna be fun!" she said, and struck him with a backhand. "You wanna scream? Go ahead and scream. Nobody can save you now. Nobody!"

Colton couldn't scream. He could only cry while the lookalike pulled a box cutter and roll of duct tape from her jacket pocket. She peeled off a length, cut it, and pressed it to his mouth. Colton sucked in a breath through his running nose, wheezed it out, sucked and wheezed.

The lookalike peeled off another length. "Look at me, Colton. I am her spirit made flesh, the last sight you'll ever see. I destroyed your family, your town, your name, your legacy. This time I fucked you, Colton Hauser. I fucked you hard, I fucked you deep, I fucked you down to a bloody puddle of nothing. Think about that. Spend your dying hours thinking about that."

She pressed the tape upon his blue eyes and thumbed it down to prod a muffled scream.

26. Shadow Menagerie

Regina watched the red digits of her clock-radio on Sunday night. 9:36. She looked at her Sailor Moon and Princess Mononoke posters and her Catwoman action figure and wondered if she had a smidgen of her heroes' courage. She'd never snuck out at night, never would've considered it before the curse and losing Bullet. She saw no way out of this nightmare except to fulfill its terms, but did she have the nerve? It was one thing to make a Molotov cocktail; to use it was something else altogether.

The floorboards creaked outside her door, and a knock followed. Dad came in and sat on the corner of her bed, squeaking the mattress springs. She couldn't help glancing at the clock-radio again. 9:42.

"So. Last time I'll ask. You sure you don't want to go out tomorrow? It's not like you. You always loved Halloween. We can still whip up a decent costume with a little imagination."

"No, thanks, Dad. Not into it this year."

"Reggie, there's only so many times in your life when it's okay to go door-to-door asking for candy. Maybe you shouldn't waste one."

"I never liked candy."

"Of course not," Dad said, and spent a minute avoiding her stare, winding up to change the topic. "There's something else, too. Remember our talk at the ice-cream place about going to a therapist? I found one. Her name's Susan. She seems like a... like a real knowledgeable lady. We're starting Tuesday after I get home from work, and you're going back to school on Thursday. It's gonna be a big week for you."

"Yay for me."

"Do you have any non-smart-ass questions?"

"Do you want dumb-ass questions?"

Dad opened his mouth to answer, exhaled instead. "Good night," he grunted, and left without a kiss. He closed the door behind him, 9:49, and that was a break. She didn't like to be so short with him, but the sooner he went to bed, the better.

By 10:34 she heard him snoring.

At 11:23 Regina eased off her bed as quietly as she could. She zipped up her kelly green jacket, picked up her backpack, and listened. The train horn sounded, distant and faint, and left no more time for debate. She would never have another chance like this. As the coal cars rumbled along Pike and rattled the glasses and dishes in the kitchen cabinets, she crept from her room to the steps. And down, and out into the night. Dad never would've heard her leave even if he were awake.

Regina walked briskly beside Pike while the train thundered along. She passed the houses and stayed close to the woods, ready to hide at the first sign of a car. Only after the train dwindled off did she notice that Pike had become as tranquil as she'd ever seen it. The streetlights cast a cold glow on the asphalt. Frost dulled the double yellow lines. Blue-black clouds drifted over a sliver of moon. Tree branches wavered with the breeze and let loose their silver leaves. The horn sounded again, distant and faint again, and somewhere a dog howled in response.

She kept walking, gut-sick with dread, breath freezing even as she itched with sweat.

Regina avoided Broadway for a parallel alley and passed the ruined stretch from behind. The wreckage had remained unmoved since the demolition, but darkness had transformed it to an alien landscape. I-beam trees populated rolling hills of loose bricks. Pools of broken glass twinkled

240

around cinder-block ridges. Vines of rebar overgrew meadows of crumbled drywall. It was a place that never should have existed, a disastrous mistake like the one she was making that very minute.

Then go back, she thought. It's not too late. Turn around, go home.

No, you're in this now. You don't care if it's wrong. You know you can do it and not get caught. And you won't get caught if you're careful.

She finally saw other people when the plaza came into view. Only two men still a block away, but she couldn't risk them spotting her. She left the alley for the rubble of Murdoch's Pawn Shop and the better cover it gave her. Peeking around an I-beam, she waited while the men prepared to leave. One climbed into the cab of a flatbed truck idling on Broadway. His coworker backed a forklift onto the lowered bed, which rose with a loud hum. The second man joined the first in the cab, and off and away they drove.

They'd delivered four objects, each mounted upon a platform and shrouded with black cloth. One occupied the center of the plaza, and three more formed a triangle around it. More people may have been coming, but for the moment she had an opening. She dashed for the back door of Ribbitski's, keys in hand.

Regina found her wagon in the back room and rolled it out to the alley. Liquor bottles clinked with every bump. Gasoline sloshed in those bottles, in the tank of the PowerSoaker gun, in red plastic cans. She steered the load to the plaza and stopped in the shadow of Ribbitski's wall.

All four platforms were made of black-painted wood and stood chest-high to her. Bricks held the shrouds to the platforms. Leave the shrouds on or pull them off? She decided to pull them off, figuring they would best serve as fuel on the ground.

But quickly now. You haven't much time.

Regina went to the nearest platform and dropped the bricks. She gathered up the cloth and jerked it free to unveil the sculpture beneath.

The sea creature splashed over her, the same sculpture Team Freak had shown Grady at Happ's. It didn't horrify Regina so much as captivate

241

her. It looked like a cross between a fish and sabertooth tiger, having gills, fins, and scaly skin but also a snout with a mouth full of sharp and shiny points. Looking closer, she saw that its scales were beer-bottle glass and its teeth were knife blades.

She touched the water, which felt rough and tacky, and doubted it was really papier-mâché because she doubted everything Waters said. Besides, why would anybody make such a large and complex piece with such temporary material? Whatever he'd used, though, she was sure it wasn't stone or metal.

Are you going to stand there petting it or do what you came to do?

At the next platform, she yanked down the shroud to reveal a big crippled insect. Its body was dome-shaped like a ladybug but partially squashed with a massive dent. Six mannequin arms stuck out of its trunk, posing as legs and spiked with countless nails. Its spherical head glared with a metallic sheen, and mirror balls comprised its eyes. Copper-tipped bullets lined its gaping mouth, filling in for teeth.

Regina felt inclined to pity it as a suffering thing left for dead. Between its teeth and condition, it also reminded her of her dog.

No, it's different. Stop distracting yourself. Are you trying to get caught? Is that what you want? Come on! Get on with it!

Across the plaza and to the next platform she went. The cloth fell away to uncover a chimpanzee wearing miter and robe like a joke on the pope. An upside-down cross of gold sequins decorated the miter; dollar signs glittered on the breasts of the robe. It knelt on the platform, knees spread and robe opened, fondling its crotch with both hands. Four more overly long and elastic arms sprouted from its back. With its extra hands, the chimp simultaneously plugged fingers in its ears, shielded its eyes, shushed its mouth.

She heard a vehicle approaching on Broadway and crouched behind the platform. A car passed, and another followed, and another went the opposite direction. None stopped or slowed, for all the traffic lights were blinking yellow.

You don't have to do this, she thought. They're not cute or pretty, but they are unique and lifelike, and it must have taken a ton of work to make them. *Who cares?* You can still change your mind. Just take the wagon back inside, dump the gas down the drain, and go home. *How could you come this far and chicken out? Because you're a coward. Just like those kids at the Little League field said, just like Evelyn and the Girls said. You're so weak, you deserve whatever you get.* But see the last one before you leave. You can do that much, at least.

All clear on Broadway. Regina hurried to the platform in the center of the plaza and took down the shroud. At first she thought the sculpture resembled an ostrich. Yet the more she looked at it, the more it looked like something else, something closer to a mutated rooster.

It stood upright and tall like a person, but its arms were outstretched like wings. Each arm was draped with a green and white banner. "Burdock Downs Spartans – Regional Champions 1979" read the banner on the left arm, "Burdock Downs Spartans – Regional Champions 1980" on the right. It also wore a football helmet, kneepads, tube socks, and varsity jacket with the sleeves cut off. Spartans pennants stuck out of its backside to evoke tail feathers.

Its helmet lacked a facemask and was crested with real green and white feathers. Crushed beer cans doubled as its eyes. Half of a football jutted from its face where its mouth should have been, the ball's point forming a beak. A wattle drooped under that football-beak, and it took Regina a moment to see the wattle for the human tongue it was. Then she understood. This thing had a human mouth, but its jaw had been wrenched apart, the football rammed halfway down its throat. Its lower jawbone was discarded, its tongue left to hang.

Regina froze before the sculpture, taken aback by its mutilation, and that was when she heard the phantom song. Chord, chord, it played, notes flowing downward, chord, chord, echoing about the plaza.

"No," she whispered, holding her ears and hearing it anyway. "No. Not here, not now. No! Stop it!" Before she could utter another word, the chords warped into a voice.

"Little girl!" it hissed. "Little girl, save us! We're alive! You can save us!"

It was a male voice, and it sounded like it was coming from the rooster sculpture.

Another male voice joined it, hissing, "Help us! There's still time! We're alive! *We're alive!*"

"Stop it! Stop talking!" Regina said, but a third male voice hissed, "Don't burn us! Help us! We're stuck here, but we're alive!" "No you're not!" she said, and a fourth male voice answered, "We are! We're alive! Don't kill us!"

That's it, she thought. I'm finished. I've had enough. This must stop.

Regina brought the wagon into a gap between the center sculpture and the others. As the voices kept pleading, she pumped the PowerSoaker gun and aimed it at the rooster. A stream of gasoline shot forth to spatter the sculpture. Its voice screamed as if she'd thrown acid upon living flesh. The force of that pained cry burst its football-beak apart at the seams. It shook its head no no no, ruined beak flapping about its neck, and still its voice screamed.

The gasoline stream petered out to a trickle. Regina pumped the gun again while the bird-screams tore at her nerves. She turned to the bug and sprayed it with a jet. It flexed its legs when the liquid hit it, lifting itself a fraction of an inch. A greenish sludge leaked from its ruptured gut and dripped off the platform's edge. The bug didn't scream but let out a croak.

She pumped the gun with shaking hands and lined up the sea creature.

It clacked its knife-blade teeth and exhaled a dead-fish odor even stronger than the gasoline. "Don't kill us!" begged its disembodied voice.

"You're killing yourself, too! Can't you see that? Kill us, and you kill yourself!"

"Shut up!" she cried, and doused the creature. Its voice shrieked to further punish her as she pumped the gun again.

The chimp moved the hand that hid its eyes, splaying its fingers. It peered down at her with a single eyeball, and its voice said, "Why are you doing this? Why are you hurting us? Please, for the love of God, we implore you –"

Regina blasted it with gasoline, drenching its limbs and robe. Its voice screamed like the others. The eyeball swelled and dislodged itself from its socket, swelled and pushed through the fingers, swelled to the size of a grapefruit. Dangling by a nerve cord, the eyeball lowered toward her while the chimp's voice continued to scream.

She tossed the emptied PowerSoaker aside and slipped one Molotov and one empty liquor bottle into her backpack. Leaving the wagon and gas cans behind, she carried her backpack and four Molotovs to the alley. With the screams still hounding her, she rubbed and smelled her hands to check for spillage. Detecting none, she opened a Ribbitski's matchbook and lit the rag-wicks.

The sight of fire spurred her on. She lobbed the Molotovs toward the plaza, one after the other after the other after the other. They landed with pops and flares, and she didn't wait to see how well they worked. She bolted, running down the alley as hard as her legs and lungs would allow.

Regina looked back just once, from two blocks away. Flames engulfed the plaza but also Ribbitski's. Smoke billowed up over Broadway in a cloud darker than the night sky, choking out the streetlights. There were no sirens or any other signs of anyone knowing what she'd done. She ran again but slower, weighed down with a sudden guilt that made her want to cry.

But she didn't hear the screams anymore. And that was all she needed to confirm she'd done the right thing whether it felt right or not.

27. Reunion

Waters dozed on the air mattress in the blue room of Happ's, his shaved head bared and face cleared of makeup. The wall-mounted TVs played at low volume, their recorded eyeballs and games flashing in the darkness until Mirzeta whipped open the curtain. She nudged him once and again, impatient for him to wake, and tugged his arm hard enough to signal trouble. The smell of something burning further roused him as she led him out to the loading dock.

The van was smoldering in the lot. Masked with respirators, Ishwan and Scott sprayed the blackened roof with extinguishers. They'd contained the fire before it reached the gas tank, at least, but Waters was hardly relieved. Whos, hows, and whys aside, all that smoke threatened to attract attention to Happ's.

Manami was also watching from the dock, holding a damp cloth to her mouth and avoiding eye contact with Waters. Ishwan and Scott noticed his arrival, unmasked, and sulked their way toward him. Nobody was eager to speak.

"Somebody tell me something," Waters said.

"I was callin' it a night, boss. I come outside, the roof's on fire. I run back in, grab Ishie, and we snuff it. I didn't see nobody else out here, nobody. You ask me, I think it's some kids fuckin' around. It's Devil's

Night, y'know, and we're in the ghetto. They ain't throwin' toilet paper on trees out here," Scott said.

Waters had parked his jeep on Sixth Avenue. The streetlight glinted off objects someone had left on its hood, and a sheet of paper was tucked under its windshield wiper. He walked to the vehicle and saw that the objects were sunglasses and a liquor bottle. The bottle was empty except for a strip of cloth trailing out of its neck. The sunglasses were his own, misplaced or lost for some time. He lifted the paper from the wiper and read a note written in cursive.

"Go see what I did to your sculptures. If you don't like it, come tell me so at MacAdder's Folly. I'll be waiting. – Regina (not "munchkin")"

Waters looked to Broadway, where more smoke arose in the distance. He tracked its source to the plaza and glimpsed a white light speckled with red glimmers. Listening closely, he heard sirens.

His (What the fuck?) shock collided with (This can't be happening) denial with (I'll kill her. I will fucking kill her. I'll rip her head off by those ponytails) rage, all of which negated each other. He tried to rationalize (They were practically dead anyway. All she did was cremate them.) (But what if they survive now, thanks to her?) (Impossible.) (But it's the insult that matters. The lack of respect...), which settled nothing. His mind pivoted to what it could grasp: business, prioritizing, doing right by his people and saving face. He deliberately folded and pocketed the note and rejoined Team Freak in the lot.

"Game over, friends. Time to scatter. I know it's a day early, but you'll find your fees banked plus bonuses. It was a pleasure and honor to work with you."

"We win, boss?" Scott said.

"Yes, thank you."

"But the... ?" Scott gestured to the van.

"You were right. It was kids acting up on Devil's Night. That's all. Just know that a small army of badges will be swarming this place by dawn. Exit accordingly and thanks again."

Ishwan, Scott, and Manami traded glances and retreated into Happ's. Mirzeta stayed behind, waiting to be alone with Waters. She offered her hand and knew he was shaken when he clasped it in his own.

"I have one more thing to take care of, and I have to do it alone. I'll meet you where we planned in an hour. If I don't show, leave without me. I'll find you," Waters said, and kissed her hand.

Mirzeta watched him climb into his jeep, rev it, and swerve around toward Broadway. The sunglasses and bottle flew off the hood and shattered upon the curb.

Regina paced before the Folly, trying to stay warm. She, too, could see the small persistent glow on Broadway if she chose to look for it. The red pinpoints, the smoke, none of it going away. Worse yet, the glow only brightened and widened with each passing minute. She chose to face the river instead.

Pacing and shivering, she knew what she'd done; shivering and pacing, she clung to the notion that she hadn't hurt anyone. She'd destroyed property away from people's homes and among blocks already demolished, and she'd done it for good reason. She knew, she knew, and yet none of it felt right. And where was that part of her that urged her on, that called her a coward? Why was it so silent now?

The sound of an engine jolted her back around. Headlights sped along the riverside and toward the peninsula, and Regina knew it was him. She didn't need to see the jeep itself as he braked to seek an entrance, nor did she need any other reason to pull the lever.

The jeep lurched and bounced onto the peninsula. The Folly awoke with its clicks and earth-shaking groan, and for once Regina wanted it to hurry up. "Come on," she said as vapor jets hissed from the metal. "*Come on!*" as the panels roared apart.

The headlights closed in, and the jeep skidded to a stop about twenty feet away. Waters threw open the door and jumped out, and for a second his appearance confused her. He must've shaved his head since she'd last seen him.

"Come here. Don't make me chase you," he said.

Regina ran into the Folly. Waters ran after her.

He would have caught her anywhere else, but she had the crucial advantage of having been there before. She knew the Folly's layout and its tricks. When the doors slammed shut behind them, Waters stopped, surprised and blinded; Regina expected the darkness and kept running. When the light spine activated overhead, *pfoom! pfoom! pfoom!*, Waters again stopped, stunned by his gleaming surroundings; Regina pushed herself to run even harder. When Waters regrouped and ran again, he met the same invisible membrane that had enveloped Regina on her first visit; meanwhile, Regina didn't dare let up or look back.

I'm coming, Maura, she thought with the stone chamber in sight. I'm coming, Evelyn, and all the rest of you Girls. I'm coming, and you'd better be ready.

The membrane stretched around Waters, and like Regina before him, he didn't know what to make of it. He followed the same process of touching it, testing it, and finally charging it. It broke for him as it had for her, with a flash that forced him to close his eyes. When he squinted them open, he found himself in a different but familiar place.

He stood in the doorway of a studio in San Jose, a room he hadn't seen in four years. A clay dragon sprawled upon the nearest worktable, talons hooked into the wood. Scales textured its skin, and plates jutted up along its spine from nape to tail-tip as it sized up all comers with a shrewd crocodilian face. Three robot busts occupied the neighboring table. They had smooth globular heads with bug-like eyes on the sides, cartoonish underbites, and slender necks that resembled the stems of adjustable lamps. A full-scale werewolf crouched on its haunches by the far wall. Ears back, teeth bared, eyes crazed, it was set to pounce and feast.

Is this déjà vu, Waters wondered. He hadn't just seen that room before, he'd lived that very moment before. He was conscious of the repetition and yet detached, an observer unable to do or say anything differently than before. He knew he wasn't supposed to be there, couldn't possibly be there, but then he saw Estrella washing her hands at the utility tub and knocked on the door. Just like before.

She turned around, and her brown eyes sent an instant pang of regret through Waters. He already missed her even though she looked more startled than happy to see him. She approached, stepping around the buckets, armatures, and forty-five-pound boxes of clay that cluttered the floor.

"Whoa, what is *this*?" She touched his shaved head. "You didn't join some weird separatist group, did you?"

"No," he said, trying to sound playful. Lacking the tact to soften his message, he simply added, "I'm leaving, Essie. I won't be around anymore."

"Why? What's wrong?"

"Nothing I can explain. I have to go away."

"And this is goodbye?" she said with a bit of bewildered hurt.

Say something, Waters thought, something comforting. Better yet, change your mind. Say "never mind" and see what happens. Instead, he said nothing again and looked to the floor again. Too weak to face her disappointment then, too weak to face it now, too determined to return to Burdock Downs.

Estrella walked to the worktable where she'd left her coffee. She took a sip and regarded him from the slight distance. "I always knew you'd go back to your games. It's okay. I don't fault you. Why waste your time here when there's another *Carjacker* to be made?"

"I'm not going back to games. That world's passed me by. I'm a dinosaur there now."

"Then what is it? Why leave?"

"I can't explain. I would if I could."

"Typical you. It's fucked up how I'm gonna miss you when I never knew you. It's been what, two, three years? You walked in here, threw yourself into it, and now you're gone. You show a lot of promise. You know I believe that. But there was always something holding you back, too. I wanted to know what that was, wanted you to break through it while you were here. I guess that won't happen. C'est la vie, right?"

"I have a favor to ask. Would you do a head cast before I go?"

"Of who? You? Tonight? You've gone insane. I really think you've gone insane."

"You're the best, Essie. Why shouldn't I want the best?"

"What the hell are you gonna do with a cast of your own damn head?"

"Prosthetics. Masks. I'm sick of this face, and I want to try another one. Let's call it a parting gift?"

"And that's why you shaved yourself bald. Wouldn't you look silly if I said no? Sit down, for God's sake. Stop looking at me like that and sit down. Like I have nothing else to do."

Waters seated himself upon a stool by the tub. Estrella filled one bucket with steaming water and dumped a powder alginate called Maxi-Mold into another. She poured the water onto the powder and hand-stirred the mixture.

"You really won't tell me what you're up to?" she said.

"I can tell you that it's a top-secret project. You'll hear about it when it's done, one way or another. I'll be dead or in hiding by then."

"Uh-huh," she said, unamused. "Take off your shirt."

Estrella looked over his exposed skin and into his eyes. He knew she cared about him, felt affection for him. Beyond that, he'd never known what might have grown between them because he'd never taken a chance to find out. For more than two years, he'd told himself she was too pretty for him, too upbeat, too normal, too good. But there were those times, those glances and silences when she'd seemed to be waiting for him to make a move.

This was one of those times, and it would be the last. In this hindsight, she clearly wanted more – a kiss, maybe, or a caress, or just an honest emotion – and he failed to respond. Now he could do nothing to change that failure; he could only relive it.

Estrella looked back to the mixture and stirred it for another minute. She stood away from the bucket, hand caked with blue glop, and said, "Well, whatever you do, I think the joke's on you. Travel where your money will take you. Hop from art to craft to science. Wear all the masks you can make. But in the end, you'll always be Oscar Dougal. It's not up to you to change that."

He closed his eyes as she slapped the glop on his head and slimed it down his face. In the darkness, he soon heard a phone ring. And ring and ring again.

Waters opened his eyes to a dim room, his New York apartment from seven years ago. Heavy curtains blocked out the sun, leaving flickering screens to provide the only light. An infomercial for a spandex girdle played on his TV, and an animated electric eel swam in circles on his computer monitor. He was lying on the sofa, unwilling to move as the phone kept ringing.

How he'd arrived there from Estrella's studio, he had no idea, but the sense of déjà vu continued. He'd lived this day before, too, and recalled it falling somewhere in a shut-in funk when he'd squandered untold hours doing nothing but drinking, sleeping, and watching women binding their flab.

The answering machine beeped.

"Dougal, it's Jordy. I know you're there and won't pick up. Crashed out on your couch like a lazy sack of shit, aren't you?

"Not that you care, but I just got back from the meeting, and they are *pissed*. I can't hold these guys off. They want *Carjacker 2*, and they want it yesterday. If you don't give it to them, they're gonna take it. And don't think they won't. It's in the contract when they bought us, and it's one clause they're happy to quote. You should've seen how much yellow ink they used to highlight it. They are not fucking around, bro, not this time they're not.

"I tried to defend you, I really did. I told them how hard the last one was, how it wiped you out. They didn't care. Gerhardt asked if you're on drugs. Kruck asked if you realize you're making video games, not building Gothic cathedrals. Morris told me to remind you that *Carjacker* was two years ago, which might as well be two decades ago.

"Look, I get it. You take yourself seriously as an artist, and you're a perfectionist. That's great. That's noble. But they do have a point. I'm not saying I *totally* agree with them, but you gotta produce, like, ASAP, or everybody's gonna think you're done. And you know how it is. Perception is reality. I don't mean to be a dick. Just being honest. I'm trying to help you here.

"So, where *are* we on this? You gonna get off your ass and deliver this thing or what? What do I say to these guys?"

Click. Dial tone. Beep.

Waters noticed the computer monitor brightening. Jordy had followed up with an e-mail, setting off an inbox alert that cleared the electric-eel screensaver. The desktop reappeared as Waters had left it the prior night, with a browser open to the *Pittsburgh Press* regional Election Day roundup, November 3, 1998.

"Hauser Wins, Succeeds Father" read the headline over a photo of Colton and his wife laughing onstage at campaign headquarters. Balloons, signs, and crepe streamers filled the background. Grady Kagan stood off to the side, beer and cigar in hand. Old white men crowded around the boy-king, angling for a chance to slap his back.

Waters sat up, rose from the sofa. He went to the computer and scrolled the browser down to show the text beneath the photo. He'd read it several times before and couldn't stop himself from reading it again.

"Colton Hauser won the Burdock Downs mayoral election on Tuesday night, trouncing the incumbent Althea Walsh in a landslide. Walsh entered the race with two terms and thirty years of political experience. Hauser served a single term on the borough council but enjoyed local name recognition. His father, Garrison Hauser, served as mayor from 1976 to

1984. Hauser also led the Burdock Downs Spartans football team to consecutive regional titles in 1979 and 1980.

"'I know you're looking down from Heaven, Dad. This one's for you,' Hauser said during his victory speech. 'As good as those back-to-back championships were, this is the sweetest win of my life.'

"Walsh had argued that a new Hauser administration would be 'a leap backwards to the bad old days,' but her electorate disagreed.

"'I trust the Hausers. They're good people,' said tavern owner Frank Ribbitski. 'Colt's old man was a stand-up guy, and I always liked Colt when he was a kid, running around, cutting up. Great quarterback, a real winner. That's the kind of mayor we need.'

"'He's so handsome and young, a real fresh breath of air,' said Dolores Jickler, organist at Sacred Heart parish. 'I know he'll turn things around for us. When he talks to you, he looks you in the eye. You can really feel his grace and values.'"

"Hauser faces severe economic challenges. The MacAdder Works steel mill, Burdock Downs' leading employer, closed in 1982. The town lost half its population in the following decade while the violent crime rate has risen.

"Hauser has promised to restore jobs and reduce crime throughout the campaign. He is expected to appoint a new police chief, Grady Kagan, after inauguration. Kagan's father, Charles, also served as the Burdock Downs police chief during the elder Hauser's terms.

"'Call it a dynasty. Call it whatever you want,' said Hauser. 'This is our town. The Hausers and the Kagans, we know the people here. We relate to them. We take care of them. We're going to clean up Burdock Downs, you watch.'"

Seeing those words again, Waters remembered his anger even after seven years. If he didn't feel it the same way, he still understood it and knew he couldn't prevent it. Resigned to repeating this eruption, he hoisted up the monitor and threw it at the nearest wall. It didn't break like he wanted, so he picked it up and bashed it against the desk until its screen cracked. He ripped out the wires from keyboard to tower, tower to monitor. Picked up the tower and heaved it at the TV. The girdled women disappeared with a flash and electric pop. He kicked the mess of plastic and glass, stomped the circuitry screaming, "Fuckin' runt! Pussy! Cocksuckin' piece of shit cunt! I'll kill you! I'll fuckin' kill you!"

Hoarse and dazed, he staggered toward the door and listened. His neighbors were gathering in the hallway, hesitant to check on him. He had to leave. Had to get the hell out of there, go anywhere, didn't matter where. He barged through the doorway, expecting a corridor full of awkward concern.

Waters stepped outdoors instead, into the nighttime. He stopped, turned around, and found himself on his grandmother's front porch. I'm ten again, he thought, seeing that his body had shrunken. He wore black sweats like he'd meant to sneak out, which he'd done only once, on one particular night. Sheridan Street lay empty and still before him, except for a lone figure heading uphill a block away.

He crept off the porch to follow her just as he had twenty-five years ago. You can't let this happen again, he thought, even as he repeated every step. He used parked cars and trees for their shadowy cover, stalking her from a safe distance. Say something, he thought. Make a noise. Do something different! *You can't let this happen again*! But however loud his thoughts, they remained unspoken and detached.

She stopped for the train that cut across Sheridan, and he hung back behind someone's shrubs, thinking, Sis! Look at me! I'm here, sis! She did look back, too, like she'd heard him. Looked back toward Broadway for a few endless minutes while the coal cars rumbled past. Back then he'd ducked and hoped she hadn't seen him; now he wanted nothing more but couldn't make himself visible.

She continued uphill after the train had passed, and he continued after her. This has to be a nightmare, he thought. This can't be happening. You cannot let her get to Suncrest. At a certain point on Foster Street, she stopped again and turned around like she'd heard him.

256

She looked toward him but never saw him, for he'd slipped behind an oak on the edge of Foster's woods.

Maura! he screamed inside. MAURA!

She started away but then spun around once more to catch any follower off-guard.

He didn't hide this time. With all the will he possessed, Waters stayed put to let her see him. She froze with shock, his sister in her blue jacket with the rainbow over the hip, hands in her pockets. He ran to her, calling, "Maura! It's me, Maura!"

Waters grabbed her by the arms and pulled her hard against him. He said her name again and again and kissed her. She pushed him off like he was a stranger, not her brother.

Their surroundings changed in a blink. They were no longer on Foster Street but in a cavernous indoor space with stone walls and floor. This space had no doors or windows, no exit but the steps and tunnel behind him. Light intensified overhead from a source he couldn't see, and figures appeared as the nighttime darkness lifted.

There were dozens of them, all girls, from grade-schoolers to teens. Waters met their stares and noted their factory work clothes from a hundred years ago. A woman in a suit observed him from farther away. She was seated at a table with a cloaked, hooded figure and a girl in a pearl dress who held a violin. A large iron-rimmed manhole gaped in the floor between him and that table.

Waters looked down over himself, regrown and aged to thirty-five.

He looked back to Maura, and Regina was with her. The girl clutched Maura's hand, her eyes wide with fear. He remembered what she'd done, his chasing her, wanting to wring her neck. For all that, he could ignore her. She wasn't important at that moment, not with this sister there.

"Sis, don't you know me? It's Oscar, your brother," he said.

Maura couldn't speak, unnerved by this crazed, emaciated man. She recognized her father's eyes and nose, her mother's cheekbones and mouth, but she couldn't believe it. She knew how old her little brother would've been by then, but to physically encounter him as an adult older than herself was unfathomable to her.

"Where are we? Who are these people?" he said. "Is this a dream? This has to be a dream. But you look the same, just like you did before."

You don't, Maura thought, if you are who you say you are.

He pulled her into another hug and said, "I can feel you, sis! This can't be a dream! I can feel you!"

Regina backed away from them with a sickening feeling churning in her gut. "No!" she said. "You don't know each other. He's not your brother. His name's Lonnie Waters."

"My real name is Oscar Dougal," Waters said to her and everyone else. "Sis, it really is me. If this is a dream, don't let me wake up."

Evelyn left the table and passed through the crowd of Girls to join Waters, Maura, and Regina. "Well, now, you appear to have quite the dilemma, Maura. You spared the girl once, citing the blood trade, and this is who she brought. Assuming he satisfies the trade, it's only right that you decide who stays. Of course we'll accommodate both if you can't choose."

"Oh, fuck you," Maura said.

Evelyn smiled. "Ah, yes. The eternal retort of the outclassed."

Maura took a breath and faced her brother. "You need to tell me something. What are you doing out there in the Downs?"

"He's a killer, Maura! I swear, he's a killer!" Regina said.

Waters looked at Regina. "I apologized about your dog. Did I not apologize? I hate to be the one to teach you this, but a dog's a *dog*."

"What about the police chief? What did you do to him?" Regina said.

"What needed to be done! What do you know about it anyway?" Waters said, and looked back to Maura. "You know who the police chief was? Take a guess. Grady Kagan. Vic Valducci was a cop, too. Andy Dorovich was the pastor of Sacred Heart parish. How do you like that? Dorovich preaching and forgiving sins! And take a wild guess who the mayor of this fucking dump was. Colton Hauser. The big man! The hero! Mr. Marching Spartan with his brass bands and ticker-tape parades!

"I knew what they did to you because I followed you out of Gram's house that night, all the way to Suncrest. I hid in the woods and spied on you because I wanted to see what the big kids did for fun. So, yeah, I saw everything, and you know what I did? I ran. Instead of helping you, I ran all the way back to Gram's like a coward, like a little pussy. I got home before Dorovich brought you there. I was too ashamed to ever tell you about it, and then you were gone.

"But I never forgot what you told me before you snuck out that night. You said I needed to stand up for myself more, fight back. It took a long time, sis, but I finally did it. I finally got the balls to fight back, and *bam*! I let 'em have it!"

"You killed them?" Maura said.

"Almost. She beat me to it," Waters said, and looked at Regina. "That's right! They were in those sculptures, still alive when you burned them. Which makes you a killer, too, doesn't it? How does it feel to be a killer?"

"No!" Regina cried. "No! I didn't know! They were sculptures, just sculptures!"

"You didn't know? That was your police chief you torched, munchkin. And your mayor and a priest and another cop. And that's all on you. Does that hurt? Does that make you cry? *Too bad*! That's what you get. Good luck living with it!"

"Oh, God, Oscar," Maura said.

"They didn't deserve it?! Okay, so this little brat fucked things up. I can get over that but not what they did. Never what they did, never! You're gonna tell me I was wrong, you of all people?"

Waters paced, glaring at Evelyn, Mother Saraya, his audience of Girls.

"Am I on trial here? Is that what this is? That's why the brat led me here? Then I'll make it easy for you, kids. I am guilty. Guilty of waiting too

259

damn long to kill those fuckers. I should've done it that night, when I was ten. I should've broke their bottles and cut their dicks to ribbons! And don't think I haven't spent every minute of my life regretting that I didn't. And now that they're dead, I don't think they suffered enough."

He stopped before Maura and said, "If it weren't for them, you'd still be out there instead of here. I owed it to you. I couldn't let them go through life pretending you never existed. I could *not* let them win. I did it for you, all for you."

"Oh, God, no. No, Oscar," she said, her voice breaking. "I never wanted that for you. Never wanted you to... to turn out like this."

He searched her eyes and lowered his own. "But you weren't around to stop me, were you?"

Those words hit their mark as only a sibling's words could. Maura flinched with a pain as harsh as any she'd felt, a pain fraught with truth. It told her what she had to do and dared her to summon her courage. She looked from her brother to Evelyn to Mother Saraya to each and every Boom Girl. No help there, nothing but expectant silence. She looked to Regina, into the girl's teary eyes, and said the words before she could stop herself. "Get out of here."

Regina blinked, tried to speak.

"Get out of here! Go!" Maura shouted.

Regina didn't need another word. She ran from the group, up the steps, into the tunnel. Gone without a pause, Waters and the Girls watching her flee.

Maura turned to Evelyn with a look that said, "There. Now it's on you to follow through." Evelyn understood and conceded with a nod. They both looked to the table, where Mother straightened up from her slump and rasped in a language only Evelyn knew.

"Very well," Evelyn said with a tinge of unease. "Brace yourselves, girls. We're moving on." They answered with gasps and murmurs and wails, which Evelyn quelled by saying, "We all knew this day would come, and we've all had more than enough time to prepare for it.

Let's face it with dignity, shall we? Repeat after me: Servant of our Lord, we call upon you to restore the balance!"

The Girls followed her lead, sounding more confused than confident.

"Again!" Evelyn said, and the Girls repeated the words with more volume, more conviction. "Once again!"

Having finished the incantation, the Girls turned their backs to Waters.

"Let's get out of here," he said, and moved to take Maura's hand. He struck an invisible barrier instead. It curved to enclose him like the membrane in the tunnel but thicker with no give. It funneled the space around him in one direction, toward the manhole. "Sis? Sis, what's happening?!"

Maura was too devastated to speak. Evelyn approached her and said, "Turn around and don't look. It's the only way."

One by one, the girls faded from Waters' view as the overhead light dimmed. Darkness also overtook the cloaked figure at the table, the girl in the pearl dress, and the woman in the suit. Only Maura stayed in sight, but she turned her back to him, too, shunning him.

"Sis! Don't leave me, sis! Don't leave me again!" Waters beat his fists against the barrier and threw his body against it, but it didn't budge. Then even Maura disappeared, and he was trapped alone though not for long.

He smelled a foul blend of smoke and rot, heard liquid sloshing in the hole behind him. A moan followed, echoing up from the depths. Slowly he turned and was paralyzed by what he saw.

A slug-like thing oozed up out of the manhole, gaining mass and girth. Its grayish flesh became more transparent as it expanded, showing liquid turbid with human scrap: limbs with burned skin, eyeballs and tongues, lungs and kidneys, intestines and bones. Dripping with river water, the thing continued to emerge onto the floor, growing to a child's height with no end to its length.

One of its eyeballs spotted Waters. Others swam to it and clustered to form a bunch, which pushed against the flesh. The thing's skin stretched and parted, and the eyeball-cluster protruded. Jawbones and teeth coalesced as well and gashed open an orifice beside the eyes. From this gouged-out mouth the thing unleashed a deafening bellow. An acrid smoke-rot odor and a whiff of gunpowder gusted forth on its breath. Motes of ash clouded the constricted space.

Waters didn't move to protect himself, didn't move at all. He gazed at the thing before him, awed by the impossibility and obscenity of it. Backed against the barrier, he knew this was his end, and the thought made him laugh. That he would see and touch such a monstrosity but never have a chance to sculpt it or paint it or draw it or photograph it also made him laugh. As the thing inched closer, Waters laughed so hard he cried, submitting to the obliteration of his mind.

The thing spewed a bluish tentacle, which slithered around Waters' feet, coiled up around his shins, and retracted. Yanked forward, Waters fell backward. His skull cracked upon the stone floor. The tentacle dragged his limp body toward the orifice.

Maura closed her eyes and trembled with his dying screams. When they stopped, she heard slurping and panting and orgasmic grunting. "Don't look, Maura," she heard Evelyn say. "Don't look." But she had to look.

Blood and pieces of her brother had splattered the invisible barrier. He was gone except for one hand, the one that had touched her just minutes ago. It twitched along the floor on its way to the mouth, where a dozen charred tongues lapped it up.

Maura fell to her knees with a shriek. Hiding her face, she cried and begged forgiveness of anyone or anything that might listen. The ground quaked in response. She heard Evelyn and the Girls praying and saying their goodbyes, but the seismic shift soon drowned out their voices. The stone walls shook, their metal shell creaked, and Maura never uncovered her face to see the collapse. Down came her prison, finally granting the peace she once sought in the river.

Regina reached the edge of the Flats when she felt a tremor. She looked back to the now-distant peninsula, discerned the cube in the darkness. Its top face dropped straight down, and the others fell away from it. Slab after slab landed with resounding crashes. Water burst up from the wreckage and washed over the site. Within a minute, the river had buried the ruins of MacAdder's Folly.

The spectacle brought her no joy, no reason to celebrate. Not after what happened there, not after what she learned about the sculptures. Not when the fire – her fire – still glowed on Broadway, still filled the valley with smoke, still threatened the people charged with stopping it.

Regina had hatched a hazardous plan and carried it out. She'd found bravery she never believed she had. She'd gambled her very life and won. And yet her guilt still weighed upon her, more so with every homeward step.

28. Parting

On Tuesday after work, Shelton washed the dishes in a rare fit of anticipation, for he and Reggie were set to begin her therapy within the hour. It had taken time for him to come around to the idea, to figure out what his insurance would cover, to find someone who seemed respectable, but he'd done it. He dared to believe this Susan Hirschberg could help or at least identify Reggie's problem. Yes, he was anxious about what she might think and recommend, but he was also hopeful. If nothing else, he had to try. It felt right to try.

"You better be getting ready. We're leaving soon," he called, scouring a pan with a steel wool pad.

Reggie mumbled something inaudible through her closed door. She'd barely left her room all day yesterday and today. She wasn't feverish and said she wasn't sick. Just another one of her stay-in-bed downturns, and even that was okay with him. It was one more quirk he could serve up to Hirschberg. Surely she'd seen this behavior in other kids and would know what to do.

Shelton pulled up the stopper, let the dirty water swirl down the drain. Things were bound to get better, he could sense it. October had been a nightmare, but he'd handled it without panic or histrionics. Through it all he'd maintained a certain level of composure, he liked to think. As he rinsed the dishes, he even allowed himself a bit of pride in the job he'd done.

Someone pounded on a downstairs door. He assumed the neighbors had a visitor and continued rinsing. The pounding resumed, maybe on his door after all. It was always hard to tell, and how many times had the landlord promised to fix that broken doorbell?

Shelton lumbered downstairs toweling his hands and opened the door to a pair of men. One looked to be in his fifties with blue eyes, wrinkles, and a nose that had taken a punch or two over the years. The other was younger, broader-shouldered, and standing so ramrod straight Shelton expected him to salute. They both wore suits, and their shiny shoes were jarring among the beer-can clutter. Their black SUV was parked on Pike and twice the size of his Cavalier.

The older man showed a badge and said, "Mr. Gundy? I'm Agent Pruitt, and this is Agent Velasquez, FBI. We'd like to speak with you and your daughter for a moment. Is this a good time?"

It occurred to Shelton to try a joke. Something about them being a day late for Halloween, too old for trick-or-treating, ha ha, but he realized they weren't kidding. "I, uh, I guess. What's this about?"

"You're aware that a fire wiped out three blocks of Broadway two nights ago?"

"No. Not really. I mean, I heard there was a fire, but I missed the news yesterday. What's this have to do with us?"

"Can we come in? We don't expect this to take long. We're just clearing up a few minor details," Pruitt said.

Shelton led them up to the kitchen. To his surprise, Reggie was already waiting there. She stood against the counter, arms crossed, dark rings of sleeplessness around her eyes. She looked up at him and the men, looked to the floor.

"This is my daughter, Regina," Shelton said. "Reggie, this is Agent Pruitt and Agent Velasquez. They want to talk to us for some reason. If they ask you something, you be honest with them, okay? No funny business."

Velasquez stayed near the stairway door while Pruitt approached Reggie. He squatted down to meet her at eye level and said, "Hello, there,

266

Regina. We won't take up much of your time. We just have to ask you about your trips to the library. You have been there recently?"

"Yes," she said.

"And did you use the computer there to look at some websites?"

"I did."

"Okay. Now, did you happen to check out any websites that weren't written in English? Any that showed things blowing up, maybe?"

Reggie kept staring at the floor. After a long pause, she said, "Why are you asking when you already know?"

"Reggie..." Shelton said with a note of warning.

"I guess I didn't think of anyone spying on the library computers. You connected the websites to the fire, didn't you?"

Pruitt looked at Velasquez. Both agents looked at Shelton, cold looks he didn't like.

"Sounds like one of you watched the news," Velasquez said.

Pruitt turned back to Reggie. "We did make a connection, yes. You could understand why. A big suspicious fire happens, and we investigate. We find that someone around here was looking at websites about explosives and Molotov cocktails, and naturally we'd want to talk to that person. Silly as it may seem, we do have to be thorough. So, anything else you'd care to tell us?"

"Yeah," Reggie said, and raised her eyes to meet his. "I didn't mean to kill anyone. I just meant to burn the sculptures."

"Reggie, don't be a smart-aleck," Shelton said.

"Don't blame my dad. He doesn't know anything. I did it all while he was at work or asleep."

"Did what, exactly?" Pruitt said.

"Went to the library, looked at the websites. Figured out how to make the cocktails. Bought the stuff to make them and made them. It wasn't that hard."

"How did you have the time and money to do that?" Pruitt said.

"I've been suspended from school all month. I got the money from the guy who killed my dog, Bullet. He gave it to me like a pity donation. But I killed him, too, in a way. I didn't want to; I had to."

"God *damn* it, Reggie! Stop lying!" Shelton said.

Both agents looked at him again.

"She has been suspended, that's true. But she's making up the rest, obviously."

"No, I'm not, Dad. The guy who killed Bullet called himself Lonnie Waters, but his real name was Oscar Dougal. He ran that company Condor that was doing construction all over town. He made the sculptures for MacAdder Plaza and put the mayor, police chief, and two other guys in them. I didn't know they were in the sculptures when I burned them. Maybe I should've since the sculptures screamed. But that was the curse tricking me, making them scream like that."

The agents looked at each other. Velasquez raised his eyebrows. Pruitt lowered his head and took a breath like a man whose workload had just tripled. He rose to his feet, knees crackling, and faced Shelton. "Could we have a word alone?"

"To your room," Shelton said to Reggie with a glare. Once she closed her door, he followed Pruitt to the living room. Velasquez stayed in the kitchen.

"I apologize for all this," Shelton said. "Reggie's a special-needs kid. She claims to see and hear things that no one else can. We're actually starting therapy tonight. We were just about to leave when you showed up."

"You'd better cancel that appointment, Mr. Gundy. This is going to take a while."

"What?"

"We haven't disclosed the victims' identities to anyone, but your daughter was correct. The mayor, police chief, and two other men died in that fire. And they appear to have been abducted and confined to that site against their will. Would you care to tell me how she knows what she knows?"

Shelton stared at Pruitt and through Pruitt, dumbfounded for a solid minute. He shook his head, couldn't utter a syllable. He tried again, saying, "You don't... you don't *believe* her, do you? It doesn't make sense. Doesn't make sense!"

"The press knows there were four victims. They don't know the victims were an elected official, law enforcement, and clergy. Nor do they know about the apparent abductions and restraints. When the full story breaks, and it will break imminently, can you begin to imagine the reaction? We're going to make this make sense, Mr. Gundy, as soon as possible.

"I'm not presuming anything, but I think you should know the stakes. We'd been tracking suspicious activity at that library for some time, namely threats against heads of state. So this thing happens two nights ago, we run a check on the library's computer usage, and here we are.

"Right now we have reason to believe your daughter was involved in some way. If she's as involved as she says, she'll be charged with second-degree murder, not manslaughter, because of the arson. She'll also be charged with creating weapons of mass destruction, causing a catastrophe, and criminal mischief, and those are all felonies. Since she's older than ten, and considering the homicides, she'll be tried as an adult in this state. If she's convicted of murder-two, she'll get life without parole.

"So, once again, would you care to tell me how she knows what she knows?"

"Reggie, come out here!" Shelton said, returning to the kitchen.

She stepped out to meet him. He crouched before her, held her by her arms. Pruitt stood where he could see her face. Velasquez stayed by the stairway door.

"We're gonna try this again," Shelton said. "It's very important that you tell the truth. No jokes, no games. This is serious, okay? Did you really have anything to do with that fire?"

"Yes. I caused it."

"Reggie —"

"I'm serious!"

"Oh, yeah? Why would you do something like that?"

"To make Lonnie Waters mad enough to chase me to MacAdder's Folly. I wanted the ghosts to take him instead of me to break the curse, to get them to leave me alone. I know you don't believe me, but that's what happened."

"Regina Marie Gundy, this is the absolute last time I'm going to ask you. And I don't want to hear any more nonsense about ghosts, curses, monsters, witches, talking lions, flying monkeys, or any other bullshit that doesn't exist. This is real now."

"I did it, Dad. I can show you how, and I'm trying to tell you why. I'm not lying."

Reggie looked at each agent and back to Shelton. With tears in her gray eyes, she smiled a beaming grin he'd never seen before. His weirdly beautiful little girl was lost even as he held her in his hands, lost without hope.

"I haven't heard the song since Sunday, Dad. Haven't seen anything unreal since then, either. I think it worked. I think we're free now, me and the Boom Girls and Maura and all the other MacAdders. I'm sane, Dad. I had to do bad things to stay sane, but what else could I do?"

State troopers arrived within minutes. Shelton and Reggie had hugged, cried, and kissed, and were too exhausted to resist when a trooper said it was time. They all went downstairs and outside together, though Shelton stayed on the porch while the troopers walked her to their car. Pruitt and Velasquez had a few more questions for him.

In the seconds it took for Reggie to reach the car, thoughts knifed through Shelton's mind, too vicious and quick to censor. Maybe he'd been wrong about her all along. Wrong to underestimate her sickness, wrong to believe the world needed her. Because it didn't, and it never wanted her. Her own parents hadn't even wanted her. But he found her on this porch ten years ago and rescued her, and maybe that was the fatal mistake. Maybe they both would've been better off if he'd never noticed her in that fish tank, crawling in plastic seaweed. Dying then or life now and forever locked in a cell, what's the difference?

One trooper opened the driver's door and sat behind the wheel. The other opened a rear door and guided Reggie to her seat. She looked out the back window and to Shelton once more. As the car pulled away, she raised a hand and wiggled her fingers at him. Magic powers and goodbye, Dad, leaving him hollowed and alone in his hometown of Burdock Downs.

THE END